CL

1/09

W9-DFW-871

SAVAGE QUEST

SAVAGE QUEST

CASSIE EDWARDS

WHEELER
CHIVERS

This Large Print edition is published by Wheeler Publishing, Waterville, Maine, USA, and by BBC Audiobooks Ltd, Bath, England.

Wheeler Publishing is an imprint of The Gale Group.

Wheeler is a trademark and used herein under license.

Copyright © 2007 by Cassie Edwards.

Savage Series.

The moral right of the author has been asserted.

LIBRARY OF CONGRESS CATALOGING-IN-PUBLICATION DATA

Edwards, Cassie.
  Savage quest / by Cassie Edwards.
    p. cm. — (Savage series) (Wheeler Publishing large print romance)
  ISBN-13: 978-1-59722-638-7 (alk. paper)
  ISBN-10: 1-59722-638-6 (alk. paper)
  1. Siksika Indians — Fiction. 2. Large type books. I. Title.
PS3555.D875S29 2007
813'.54—dc22   2007029057

BRITISH LIBRARY CATALOGUING-IN-PUBLICATION DATA AVAILABLE

Published in 2007 in the U.S. by arrangement with Leisure Books,
a division of Dorchester Publishing Co., Inc.
Published in 2008 in the U.K. by arrangement with
Dorchester Publishing Co., Inc.

U.K. Hardcover: 978 1 405 64310 8 (Chivers Large Print)
U.K. Softcover: 978 1 405 64311 5 (Camden Large Print)

Printed in the United States of America on permanent paper
10 9 8 7 6 5 4 3 2 1

With much love and pride I dedicate
Savage Quest
to my wonderful grandson,
David Scott Edwards,
and his adorable new bride, Nicole!
Love,
Grandma Edwards

The rolling hills,
the open plains,
the tall, green trees,
and the wet, cool rain.
The flowing rivers,
the chirping birds,
the deer on the horizon,
and the buffalo herds.
The glow of the fire,
the horses running free,
the children playing,
and the buzzing of the bees.
These are the things
the native people loved,
from Mother Earth,
to the stars above.

— by Crystal M. Carpenter,
Poet, fan, and friend.

BLACKFOOT

PROLOGUE

Illinois, 1872

Annamae Jacobsen, a petite and pretty child of twelve, shuddered again as she swept cobwebs away from her round face and took the last step into her family's fruit cellar. She always dreaded having to come down here, since there were not only spiders in the underground cellar, but also snakes and mice.

She lifted the lantern higher as she took a slow step from the stairs onto the earthen floor, her brown eyes searching for a jar of canned green beans. Many canned items lined the shelves, thanks to her mother's busy days of canning vegetables from the family garden and fruit from the orchard near their cabin.

She shuddered again when she caught movement at the far side of the dark, dank room, and let out a gasp when she saw a mouse rush behind a shelf.

Wanting to complete her task as quickly as possible, and hoping the mouse stayed hidden until she was gone, Annamae stepped over to the shelf that held several jars of green beans.

Just as she reached for one of them, she went cold inside when she heard horrible war cries coming from outside the cellar.

"Indians!" She gasped, turning pale at the thought of what might be happening outside. "Mama . . . Papa."

She sobbed as she thought of her tiny baby brother, Charlie, yet could not even imagine Indians killing him. He was only eight months old. He was so innocent. So sweet!

Then her heart skipped a beat when she realized that at any moment the Indians might find and kill her. She looked up at the door overhead, which she had left propped open.

Her heart pounded as she set the lantern down on a step and hurried to close it.

Oh, how she wanted to rush outside, to see if she could help her beloved family. But she knew there was no way she could. She was only a child. She had just recently been taught how to shoot a rifle, but she didn't have one with her.

No. She was helpless, maybe even the next

one to die.

Die!

How could she bear to think that those she loved had been killed by savages?

But surely they had.

She knew that even if she got the cellar door closed, the Indians could find her and . . . and . . . would surely scalp her before actually killing her.

Her pulse racing, she closed the door and rushed back down the steps.

She lifted the lantern and held it up so that it lit the interior, where it would frighten away hidden snakes and spiders.

But they were now the least of her worries.

She listened and heard nothing outside.

The war cries had stopped.

It was totally silent.

She was so deep in the earth, she didn't think she would hear the horses overhead. She couldn't be sure whether the savages were still there.

She prayed that she would be spared, and knew there was a good chance that she would be. Her father had dug this fruit cellar far from the house, in the forest that surrounded their cabin. He had decided that was the best way to protect their stores of food from thieves. Most fruit cellars were built close to the house, and sometimes even beneath it, but her papa had felt this was the safest way to safeguard the family's hard work. Her mother was a devoted housewife, and her father an industrious farmer.

Annamae had hoped to follow in her mama's footsteps, for Annamae loved to cook, and even clean house. She was already skilled at doing household chores in order to take some of the heavy load from her mama's shoulders.

But now, surely everything had changed.

Her papa had warned the family that he had heard tell of renegade Shawnee Indians who were leaving a bloody trail across Illinois. She just knew those were the Indians who had come today, their war cries hideous and frightening.

"But why are they so quiet now?" she whispered to herself, still trembling as she stared at the earthen ceiling.

Had the Indians been fooled into believing there were no survivors?

Or . . . or . . . would they come into the grove of tall maple trees any moment now and find the door that led down to where she was hiding?

Tears streamed down her hot cheeks as she imagined what she would find once she left this dark hole in the ground. Feeling empty and sad, she waited and waited.

When she believed that she had been spared and the Indians must have left, she crept up the stairs, opened the door, then stepped outside, where she was met by the stench of black, roiling smoke.

"Oh, no," she sobbed out. "They burned our cabin. They . . . surely did . . . kill my family."

Afraid to actually see what she knew would be a massacre, yet hoping that perhaps the savages had left someone alive, she dropped the lantern to the ground, lifted up the hem of her skirt, and set off toward the cabin. With knots of fear in her belly she ran through the smoke, choking and gagging on it until she stepped free of the trees and could see the homestead.

The cabin was all aflame.

She swallowed back the urge to vomit when she saw three bodies spread on the ground, even her baby brother, lying only a few feet from his mama's arms.

Annamae could only stand there, looking at her family. Her feet seemed frozen to the ground, the blood from where their scalps had been streaming down across their faces.

The arrows protruding from their bodies were so ghastly a sight, Annamae couldn't help herself: she was spared further suffering by fainting.

She was still unconscious when several wagons carrying an assortment of animals and people stopped a few feet from where she lay. Soon an odd collection of men and women were circled around her.

"She's alive," a woman with a beard said as she looked over at a man who advertised himself as the snake man.

"Step aside," Howard Becker said as he brushed through those who belonged to his carnival show. He fell to his knees beside Annamae. He gently touched her brow. "She must be the daughter. Poor thing. She lost her whole family in one swoop, thanks to these damn savages."

His wife, Ellie, a stout yet pretty woman, knelt down beside him. "Howard, we can't leave the child here," she murmured, reaching out and touching Annamae's long, wavy black hair. "She's so pretty. Let's take her with us. She'll be the daughter we never had."

"She can be more than that," Howard said, giving his wife a sly grin. "She's so pretty, she'll eventually be drawing men from every town we stop at. Yep. She'll be of good use to us, Ellie. I'll figure something out for her that will bring many a fellow into her tent at every town where we stop."

"What about . . . her . . . family?" Ellie asked, swallowing hard as she gave the bodies a quick glance over her shoulder, then covered her mouth with a hand to hold back a gag.

"We'll give them a proper burial, that's what," Howard said. He looked over his shoulder, then back at Annamae. "But we've got to make haste. Who can say where those Injuns are now? I don't want to tempt fate. So far no redskins have bothered us. I imagine it's because we don't stay in any one place long."

He stood up and gave everyone instructions as to what each would do to help. "Get these people buried, and don't be slow about doin' it!" he shouted. "I'm not anxious to add my scalp to the scalp poles that are now holding this family's hair on display."

Annamae was still unconscious when she was carried to a wagon and covered with a warm blanket.

"Poor, poor child," Ellie murmured as she stroked Annamae's soft cheek. "But you're safe now. I'll see to it, sweet thing."

CHAPTER ONE

Montana, 1879
June, In Moon of Flowers

The Indian village of one hundred tepees sat in the shadow of Mount Hope, and near the great Yellowstone River, where dark, fertile soil discolored the moccasins of these Indians, which was why they called themselves Siksikawa, Black Moccasins, or Blackfoot.

Beyond this wide river and the shadow of the great mountain, magnificent bear grass grew to the height of five feet, and a great number of wildflowers were in full bloom. There were dense caps of white flowers, floating above narrow, stiff leaves. Pink flowers adorned vines of shiny dark green leaves climbing the trunks of flowering dogwood and birch trees. An assortment of towering trees cast their shadows over other flowers, such as bishop's caps and light yellow adder's-tongue.

A fire burned low, and there was the aroma of baked venison in the largest tepee of the Blackfoot village, where Chief Cougar of the Turtle Clan sat with his sister, Morning Flower.

Morning Flower, a widow who was still young and beautiful, with black hair hanging in one long braid down her back, pushed her empty wooden platter aside, as did Chief Cougar. They had just finished the early afternoon meal.

The snows of two winters had passed since the death of Morning Flower's husband at the hands of Ute renegades, and now her chieftain brother was her caretaker, as well as the provider for her son, Gray Stone.

Yes, Morning Flower's son was like a son to Cougar, but she knew that was not enough for her brother. She knew that he longed to have a child of his own, yet he had not chosen a woman to bring into his lodge and bed. He had fallen in love in his teen years, but many moons ago the girl's people, of the Owl Clan of Blackfoot, had moved far away, so far it had been impossible for Cougar to court her when he reached the age for marrying.

Morning Flower knew that her handsome brother's memories of this maiden were now beginning to fade. He had said that he no longer pined for her and knew it was time to let go of the past and look forward to a future that would include a wife and children.

She knew that among the neighboring Blackfoot clans, many a maiden's eyes followed her brother's every movement when they came to join the celebrations of the Turtle Clan. And why not? Her brother, a man of noble countenance, was twenty-six winters of age and handsome beyond description, with broad shoulders and great muscles.

He stood tall and straight over his brethren Blackfoot, his face sculpted, his hair most times worn long and loose down his back.

Today he was dressed in a fringed shirt, beaded buckskin leggings, and moccasins. One lone eagle feather was secured in a loop of his hair at the right side. His eyes, as black as midnight, spoke as he spoke, yet when he did not want to reveal his feelings to someone, he knew the art of keeping his emotions hidden.

"My sister, as usual the meal was good," Cougar said, then chuckled. "But I do not know of a time when it was not. Thank you for keeping your brother's stomach warm with food."

"My brother, I am certain soon I will not be the one bringing food into your lodge," Morning Flower replied, stacking his empty plate onto hers. "You will take a wife soon, will you not?"

He smiled with quiet amusement at his sister. "Yes, surely soon," he said. "But I see in your eyes that you do not wish to talk about your brother and his plans for a wife. My sister, you are again troubling yourself with useless worry. I say to you once more that your son, my beloved nephew, will be safe as he undergoes his vision quest. All our youths go to the mountain to pray for a vision to come to them so that they may become warriors of much standing. Like those who have gone before him, Gray Stone will receive what he seeks, then return to us a proud man."

"But my brother, there are many wild creatures roaming Mount Hope that can harm my son," Morning Flower said in a whining tone that she knew irritated her brother. But when she was disturbed, she could speak no other way. "There are animals who hunger for warm flesh, and . . . and . . . we can never forget Ute renegades who often roam near our village . . . and our mountain."

"My sister, shame be upon you," Cougar

said, his smile waning as he gazed intently into her dark eyes. "You are a woman of too little faith. Must I remind you again and again that from the beginning of time, all male Blackfoot youths have left their homes for their vision quests? A rare few have not returned to their village. Gray Stone will be one who will come home. He will become a man we both will be proud of."

"But, brother, I am already proud of my son," Morning Flower said. "He is as no other child I have known, except for you when you were but a mere boy wanting already to walk in the moccasins of a man. Even then, if you will recall, I dreaded your going to the mountain for your vision quest. You have no idea how relieved and happy I was when you returned home safely."

"Then you must recall, as well, the pride I brought into our mother's and father's hearts," Cougar said, reaching over and resting a hand on his older sister's shoulder. "Although they are gone from this world, I can even now see the pride in their eyes, as though they are sitting with us beside this fire, discussing along with us their grandson and his vision quest."

"Yes, I recall their pride. But it was such a relief to your older sister that you were home, safe and unharmed, I cried," Morning Flower said as Cougar slowly removed his hand from her shoulder. In his eyes was the same irritated disappointment she always saw when she could not stop worrying aloud about something.

But this was not just "something." This was her son she was concerned about. If anything happened to him, she would not be able to continue to live. She would take away what breath was left in her lungs and join her son, her husband, and her mother and father in the Sand Hills, finally at peace with herself and the many things that worried her.

"Morning Flower," Cougar said, leaning closer to her and gazing directly into her eyes. "My sister, listen to what I say and know the seriousness of it. I want no one else to see your doubts about your son's vision quest. That could cause doubts in other mothers' hearts when it comes time for their sons to pursue their own visions. I do not want any of those mothers to see your doubts . . . your concerns. I understand, because I understand you and know that you were born to worry more than others about things. But you know that no one else understands."

"Must I remind you again, chieftain brother, that I have only my son now,"

Morning Flower said tightly. "I lost my husband at the hands of the renegades. To lose my son would be to lose my soul."

"Morning Flower, you not only have a son, you have this proud brother as well as the people of our village to love you," Cougar said, growing tired of reassuring her.

But because he did love her so much, he tried hard to ignore this bad trait. He had seen this side of Morning Flower since she was a child, who even then worried constantly about things, and whose faith was not as strong as it should be.

Yet he knew that he had said all he could to help her today. Any more words would be wasted, and he would not squander time that could be used more profitably.

He took her hands and urged her to her feet. He drew her gently into his embrace. "Come outside with me," he said, then stepped away from her. "Let us look up at our mountain, where Gray Stone is at peace with himself as he prays and waits for his vision to come to him. You will see how peaceful our mountain is. You can then go on your way to begin your day's normal activities. You will see how quickly the time passes before Gray Stone is home again with you and his uncle. We will show him, together, how proud we are of him."

He went and lifted the door flap, then stepped aside for her to leave.

He followed her outside and turned with her to gaze up at the towering mountain that shadowed their village. "Do you see the many beautiful golden eagles soaring peacefully where your son surely sits and waits for his vision?" he said, gazing upward at the spot where he knew his nephew would be sitting on a bluff that overlooked the world below him. "Sister, those eagles are an omen. They are Gray Stone's guardians. He will see them in a vision. He will be home soon."

"I wish he were here with me now," Morning Flower said sullenly, then turned and walked away from Cougar, worry wrinkles creased deeply at the corners of her eyes.

Cougar watched her for a moment, then turned and looked around him at the men, women, and children who were outside their lodges doing the normal chores of his people. Some women were bent over their outdoor cookfires, slowly stirring large kettles that might contain a stew of service berries and tongues for their evening meals.

A few elderly men were sitting around the brightly burning communal fire that was always kept lit, night and day, in the center of the village. These men were gossiping as they shared the smoke from a large pipe of polished red stone, each of them passing it on to the next, stem first.

Elsewhere children were playing, the boys engaged in a game of tag, while some girls rocked dolls made from cornhusks.

It was good to see his people happy, but he knew there was one who might never know the true meaning of happiness: his sister. Oh, but he did wish he knew of a way to lift the burdens from her heart so that she could laugh and talk of ordinary things with the other women, not of how she constantly worried about this and that.

Needing to get away for a breath of air after his strained moments with his sister, Cougar went to the corral behind his tepee and readied his coal black stallion for riding.

Soon he was away from his village and riding slowly up the side of the mountain, where trails had been made and worn deep into the ground by generations of his people.

He would go far enough to be close to his nephew, but not near enough for Gray Stone to see him.

He did not go because he was concerned about his nephew; he just wanted to feel Gray Stone's presence, knowing his nephew's prayers would connect their souls.

He rode until he came to a bluff far below

the one where Gray Stone sat, and where his nephew could not see him.

He dismounted and secured his horse's reins to a rock, then went to the edge of the bluff and knelt to say prayers of his own. His prayers were mostly for his sister, who needed divine guidance more than anyone else he knew.

Once he felt peace inside his heart, Cougar stood and looked all around down below him. He was proud of the land where he made his home. The village was far from any white man's fort, although there was a small white community that had been established not far from the Blackfoot camp. Fortunately, no one in that community had interfered in the lives of Cougar's people.

Yes, this was still a wonderful place for his people to find happiness and peace. The mountain slopes still abounded with beaver, moose, and mountain sheep.

But before the arrival of the white man on this Montana land, immense herds of antelope and buffalo had roamed the plains, furnishing the Blackfoot with an abundance of meat for food, and skins for clothes and shelter.

The irresistible advance of the white race had been like the invasion of a hostile army in its effects upon this Indian paradise.

But some things had not changed. The air was sweet with the fragrance of wild rose thickets. The sky was the deepest blue, and the river wound past his village into the distance, passing through open glades and grassy meadows.

He looked farther still and grew tight inside when he spotted something strange and unfamiliar to him. From this vantage point he could see brightly hued tents with colorful flags at their peaks. He could even see huge animals with long trunks that he had never seen before.

He saw white people moving about, both men and women, and even children.

"What is that place?" he asked, his eyebrows lifting. "And what are those strange animals?"

Cougar was a leader who needed answers about everything; he was too inquisitive not to want to know all that he could know, especially about something as peculiar as this encampment on the tawny plains below him. Cougar hurried to his stallion, grabbed his reins, and mounted.

He took one last look overhead, where he knew his nephew was at peace with himself, and where the spirits of his father, grandfather, and grandmother watched over Gray Stone. Then he made his way slowly down the trail that had brought him to the cliff.

When he came finally to flat land, he sank his moccasined heels into the flanks of his steed and rode toward the peculiar place where tents seemed to grow from the ground, and where flags of all colors whipped in the wind, and strange animals puzzled his mind more than anything had for many winters.

Chapter Two

Annamae Jacobsen, now eighteen, sat in a dark tent, the only light a candle on a round, skirted table. As she sat at the table, awaiting a new customer, she could hear much laughter and music outside the tent.

That terrible day, when she was but a child, had never left her memory. But she felt fortunate that she had been rescued after losing her entire family.

She had been happy enough growing up with the carnival folk. But then, when she turned fifteen, her life had changed again. Howard Becker and Ellie, the couple who had rescued her that day and had taken her under their protection, had told her that it was time for her to earn her keep. They had told her that she would now be a part of their carnival acts.

She would never forget how she dreaded hearing what they would have her do. There was a woman with tattoos on display at the carnival, whose entire body was covered with hideous drawings, and there was a woman who had a beard that dragged the ground when she walked.

There were so many other strange men and women, all peculiar to look at, who attracted people at each town where the carnival stopped.

When she had been told that she would be an interpreter of dreams, a part of her had been relieved, because to do that she would not have to alter her appearance. Yet a part of her was afraid, because she knew nothing about dreams.

Howard had purchased a book about dreams. He told her to study it, then explained how to look as though she were interpreting the dreams herself as people came into her tent.

Over time, and with much study, she had become quite skilled at interpreting her customers' dreams.

With her long, flowing black hair, her dark brown eyes, fair skin, and cheerful disposition, she was someone everyone liked to be around. Her customers felt at ease telling her their dreams.

Each evening, after she returned to her own personal tent, she pored over her dream books in order to sound convincing the next day.

She had soon discovered that those who came to hear her interpretations were very troubled people.

She had begun to hate every minute of what she did. She didn't like pretending that she had some supernatural ability to see the truth through people's dreams. But because Howard and Ellie had so graciously taken her in, she felt obliged to give something back.

Yet the more she thought about it, the more she was certain they had not taken her in out of the goodness of their hearts. From the beginning, she sensed, they had planned to use her somehow in their carnival acts.

Now that she was grown-up enough to fend for herself, she planned to flee at her first opportunity.

Today had been a busy day, with people coming in one by one from the moment the carnival had opened. It was early afternoon now, and Annamae was tired.

Sometimes the people would go away afraid because of what she had told them. She hated that, but Howard felt it was important to add a little intrigue to her dream interpretations. But Annamae felt cheap. Every day things seemed to get worse for her as she sat at that table in the dark tent with only her customers for company.

Lost in thought about what she had just told a genteel-looking middle-aged lady, Annamae didn't hear someone slither into the tent. The newcomer stood silently in the dark shadows, staring quietly at her.

Annamae had just interpreted the woman's recurring dream of being chased by an unseen but terrifying presence. Annamae had told the woman that terrifying dreams such as hers indicated that aspects of the self were clamoring for integration into one's consciousness. The dreamer's fear would usually dissipate if he or she could turn and face the pursuer and gain clues as to what this symbol represented at the conscious level. The very act of facing fear in one's dreams could increase courage in the dreamer's waking life.

The woman had left with the hope of being able to turn and face her pursuer in her dream, so this time Annamae felt good about what she had achieved.

But that was rare. Usually the interpretations left those who heard them uneasy, and often people left almost in a panic.

Suddenly she was aware that someone was in the tent with her. When the intruder stepped out of the shadows, and the candle's glow revealed who it was, Annamae grimaced. She had become alarmed by how often this man came for her interpretations. No matter how far the carnival traveled, he was always there, waiting for her to interpret another dream.

She believed that the man with the pockmarked face was obsessed with her, not her interpretations, because of the way he stared at her as she talked. His pale gray eyes seemed to be looking through her even in the darkness of the tent, mentally undressing her.

She had begun to see a troubling pattern, and not only because he was now obviously following the carnival in order to see her. His dreams were becoming more macabre, with an increasingly sexual content.

Her expression grew angry as he eased down on the chair opposite her at the table. His eyes were twinkling with a mischief she had not seen before. She was afraid to hear the sort of dream he was going to tell her today, but had no choice except to listen, for when she had complained to Howard about this particular man, he'd just laughed off her concern. He had actually told her to encourage the man, saying that his money was as good as anyone else's, that it helped pay the bills . . . helped pay her keep!

When the man, whose name she now knew was Reuben Jones, slid several coins over toward Annamae, she hesitated to take them. But Howard's words kept coming into her mind, telling her to laugh at this man's foolishness and gladly take his money, so she reached out and took the coins, dropping them into her beaded coin purse. Then she readied herself to hear Reuben's latest dream, which she believed would not be a dream at all, but something he conjured up in order to pester her.

"All right, let's get this over with," Annamae said, sighing. "What dream have you had this time?"

"It's like this," Reuben said, wiping saliva from his mouth. This drooling was a habit that made him even more repulsive to Annamae. He leaned closer, his stench, something akin to old cigar smoke and dried urine, making her wince. "I keep dreaming about masks. I dream of wearing a mask but cain't get it off. It's a mask that some hidden force puts on me. No matter how hard I try, I cain't get it off."

"And when you wake up, how do you feel?" Annamae asked. "Do you feel threatened, or relieved?"

"Kinda threatened," Reuben said, running his thick fingers through his long, greasy red hair. His shirt was a faded red plaid, and wrinkled. His breeches had holes in the knees. She knew that he wore the same boots every time, scuffed and with mud dried on their soles.

"Masks represent the way we present ourselves to the outside world, and even to ourselves," Annamae explained, hoping that if she interpreted his dream, he would leave quickly. The longer she was with him, the more she felt threatened by him.

There was danger in his gaze. He looked at her with those pale gray eyes in such a way that she turned cold inside.

"If you, the dreamer, are unable to remove the mask, or are forced by others to wear one, this suggests that the real self is becoming increasingly obscured," she continued.

"Now, that makes no sense at all to me," Reuben grumbled, obviously irritated by her interpretation. Again he wiped at his mouth. "So since you're playing word games with me, instead of making a true interpretation that makes sense, let me tell you a dream I've had that you cain't help but understand."

"What are you talking about?" Annamae said, slowly scooting her chair back. She glanced quickly at the entrance flap, hoping someone else would step through it and stop this nonsense with Reuben. But no one was there. She was at his mercy for a while longer.

"I'll do the interpreting this time," Reuben said, laughing throatily. He squinted his eyes as he leaned even closer to Annamae. "I been dreaming of red velvet roses. Roses that I can pick and stroke. Did you know that in dreams, a red rose indicates female gentalia?"

Her gasp and sudden blush made him snicker. He continued before she had a chance to interrupt him. "Did you know that velvet, or moss, also represents female gentalia?" he said, then threw his head back in a fit of laughter.

"You get out of here," Annamae said between clenched teeth as she rose quickly to her feet. "And don't you ever come back or I'll have you arrested for your insults."

"Yeah, yeah," Reuben said, standing and backing toward the entrance flap. "So you see, pretty thing, I know how to study and find out interpretations, too. Want to know some more? Hats and gloves are often used by the dreaming mind to represent female gentalia because they enclose parts of the body."

Before Annamae could say anything else, Reuben fled from the tent, leaving his stench behind him.

"Lord, Lord," Annamae whispered, leaving through the back in order to avoid seeing Reuben again.

Being out in the fresh air and sunshine helped clear her mind. She was tempted to go and tell Howard of this latest confrontation with Reuben, but she knew it would be a waste of time. Howard measured things only by the amount of money he received. He didn't care how it was earned, or from whom.

Glad to be outside, Annamae took the time to walk through the carnival grounds. She enjoyed seeing people having fun at the carnival. She saw children even now who were gazing in wonder at the three elephants Howard and Ellie owned. To her right were two lions in separate cages, each growling ferociously at her as she passed by. Then there was a bear cub looking lonesome in a cage by itself. Howard had found the cub only yesterday, and loved showing it off to the local children.

But she felt it was wrong to cage such wild creatures, especially the cub. Surely its mother was wandering aimlessly around even now looking for it.

Annamae longed to turn it loose, but knew she'd have hell to pay if Howard ever found out that she had done it. So she went on her way and smiled at the very tall man who walked past her, a man advertised at the carnival as a giant.

She smiled at a woman who sat on a stage at her far right. The woman was so heavy she had to have help getting up from the chair or to walk. She was called the fattest woman in the world.

Annamae also smiled at the man called the snake man, because he was so skinny and seemed to resemble a snake, with two extra-long fanged teeth in the front of his mouth, and a tongue that was forked just like a snake's. She had often wondered if Howard had done that to the man's tongue to make him look more snakelike, or if he had been born that way.

She shrugged and went on, pushing her way through the crowd, enjoying the sun and soft breeze. Then she looked quickly and fearfully behind her, for she felt as though she were being followed. When she saw no one except carnivalgoers walking behind her and enjoying the sights, she continued onward.

A moment later, she stopped again. Now she felt as though someone might be watching her from the shadows of the forest at her far right.

She looked carefully there and still saw no one.

This could not go on. Too often she felt as though she were being stalked. She hated feeling so afraid of this man Reuben. She must leave this horrid place.

Sighing, wondering when she might be able to effect her escape, she returned to her tent, but just before entering she caught a glimpse of Reuben jumping behind another tent. She was truly frightened now, and knew what she must do, and soon. She had craved a normal life for a long time now. This was as good a time as any to leave.

She left her tent and went to Howard's. She found him sitting behind his desk, counting coins. He didn't look up from what he was doing, but seemed to know who was there.

"So why aren't you in your tent making money for me?" he asked, still without looking up at her.

"I've got to get out of here," she said, drawing Howard's quick attention. His blue eyes gazed intently into hers as he slowly rose from the chair and came around the desk to stand over her.

He placed a gentle hand on her cheek. "Sweet thing, do you think I'll let you leave just like that, because you have a strange notion you want to?" he said, thrusting his hands inside his front breeches pockets. "Get back to your tent. It's not closing time yet."

"Howard, I don't think you heard me," Annamae said, her voice strong, her hands now on her hips. "I'm leaving. I'm tired of this type of life. I'm tired of men like Reuben Jones. If you only knew what he said this time when he came into my tent, even you would throw him from the carnival grounds."

"I don't care what he said," Howard said, glaring down at her from his six-foot height. "But you'd better care about what I'm saying, and I'm saying you can't leave. You owe me. Do you understand? You're a main attraction of my carnival now. People flock to the carnival just to hear your interpretations." He laughed throatily. "But yes, a lot of the attention you are getting from the gents is because you're so pretty. No, sweet thing, you're not going anywhere."

He leaned his face down into hers, then stepped away and waved a fist in her face instead. "Get back to work," he growled. "Now."

Annamae swallowed hard. She was frightened of Howard and his temper. She had seen him explode, unleashing his anger on other people who had wanted to leave the carnival.

But she wasn't about to let that temper stand in the way of her freedom. No matter what Howard said or did, Annamae was leaving at her first opportunity.

"Where's your gratitude, woman?" Howard shouted at Annamae. "We're moving on tomorrow. You'd better be packed and ready, for by God, you are going to the next town with us, and the next, and the next."

Anger flaring in her eyes, Annamae ran from the tent, her heart pounding hard. She would not let this man bully her any longer. She would leave as soon as possible, fleeing into the night. She had saved money from the coins she earned each day that she didn't hand over to Howard.

She would find her way to Missouri, where she had been born. She would try to find some kinfolk there, and if she didn't, she would find a way to make her own way in the world somehow.

She hurried to her tent, ready to make more dream interpretations. When no one came for a few minutes, she stepped to the door of the tent. She gazed into the distance, toward Mount Hope. She knew that Indians made their homes near the mountain; perhaps some even lived on it. If she managed to get away, would she run into them?

A chill coursed through her veins as she recalled the day of the massacre of her parents and baby brother.

But she reminded herself that those who came that day and changed her life forever were Shawnee renegades. For the most part, the Indians in this area were the more peace-loving Blackfoot.

Cougar had managed to get close enough to the place of tents, music and laughter, and white people to see things that amazed him. While hiding in the shadows of the forest he had seen animals that he did not know existed, most of which were locked up in barred cages.

The largest of the strange-looking animals were outside the cages, held in place by ropes. He stared even now at the long noses hanging in front of the animals, and the large ears.

Then he looked toward one of the tents. He had seen a white woman leave that tent not long ago; she had come close enough to where he stood hidden amid the trees that he could see her full features. Although she had white skin, so different from his own,

44

she had dark hair. She was the most beautiful woman he had ever seen, quiet and graceful in her movements, with lovely breasts that pressed gently against the white fabric of her blouse.

Yes, her beauty almost drew his breath away, yet he had seen such sadness in her brown eyes, even an occasional tear as she seemed to be thinking troubled thoughts.

She seemed so fragile, like someone who needed strong arms to protect her.

He could not help wondering what man was her protector. It seemed whoever it was did not make her happy.

And then she disappeared from his sight into one of those strange-looking tents. He wished to know if that tent was her home, and who shared it with her.

Stunned by where his mind had taken him, and knowing that he must return to his own world, where he had his own business to tend to, Cougar ran stealthily back to where he had left his horse. Mounting in one leap, he rode farther and farther away from the woman he now longed for.

He must not give in to the temptation that ate away at his heart. He knew he must forget the woman, but doubted that he would ever be able to, even though he would never see her again except in his mind's eye, and in a heart that now carried her image within it.

CHAPTER THREE

As Gray Stone knelt high on the cliff, he combated his fear of being alone for so long. He did not want to return home until he had succeeded in his vision quest.

This fear was the very reason he and his chieftain uncle had chosen such a high and remote place. Here he would be safe from renegades or evil white men.

Thus far his prayers had not brought anything special to him that might be interpreted as a vision. But he hadn't been there for very long and knew that he had three more days and nights before making a decision about whether he should stay longer or go home to a worrying mother. Already, he was sure, his mother was afraid for him.

He sighed heavily as he gazed at the sun. It was already making its descent in the sky, which meant that soon he would be alone in the dark. As twilight deepened and settled over his village, it would also reach the bluff where Gray Stone must find the courage to spend another night alone in the dark.

Fortunately, at this moment, he did not feel all that alone. Several golden eagles had kept him company all day as they swept down from the sky, their large eyes on him.

He had seen two of the eagles go to a nest not far below him on the side of the cliff. More than once he had taken time from his prayers and meditating to watch their babies being fed.

But now the eagles had grown quiet as they settled in for the night.

He took a step closer to the edge of the cliff to gaze one more time at something very peculiar that he had seen earlier in the day.

Past the forest and the prairie of brilliant wild roses in various shades of color, where larks and savanna sparrows nested, he could see a collection of strange tents. They had been pitched in the opposite direction from where his people's homes were nestled peacefully together beside the river. He was almost certain none of his people knew that whites had come this close with their strange colorful tents and even stranger animals.

The tents were unlike any tepees he had ever seen before. Most were larger than the tepees of his village, colorful, and with flags flying at their peaks. He had seen many white people meandering around outside that small settlement of tents, and had heard music wafting through the breeze and up to him from that place of wonder, where he had also seen strange sorts of animals, some of them caged behind bars.

Always full of curiosity, with a driving need to have answers about things that seemed peculiar to him, Gray Stone was tempted to leave his place of prayers in order to inspect the strange tents and animals. He could then return and resume his vision quest with no one being the wiser.

He did not plan to stay long. He just wanted to get close enough to see as much as he could, especially those animals in cages. He loved animals and did not think any should be confined, especially behind bars in cages.

He knew that such a diversion went against all that he had been taught about vision quests. He might be terribly punished if anyone found out, but he could not help wanting to go and see all of those strange things up close. He would look, then return quickly to his vision quest. Only the eagles, who nested now with their offspring, would ever know what he had done!

His mother had made him tuck a knife amid his belongings, although he knew weapons should have been left behind. And although it was also not right, his mother even knew where he would be seeking his vision. She had begged him incessantly to tell her.

He grabbed the knife and secured the sheath at the right side of his waist, then began the descent, leaving his bag of belongings on the bluff. Young, alert, and fast, he made good time along the worn path that had led him to his place of prayers and meditations.

His uncle had introduced him to this very place more than once, to prepare him for the time when he would stay during his vision quest. There was water close by, as well as plants and berries aplenty. He was to eat no meat during his quest.

His heart pounding, anxious to see up close the oddities he had spied from a distance, he hurried down until he reached flat land.

Then he ran onward, first through a thick forest of trees, and then across the flat plain filled with brilliant flowers that he had seen from high above. As he entered another forest, his heart pounded eagerly with anticipation. He was about to witness something new and different in his life.

CHAPTER FOUR

Although he knew that it would be dangerous to make the trip back to the mountain
after it got dark, Gray Stone was willing to
take that chance in order to observe the
activity around the white people's tents
more closely. He knew that once night fell,
he would be able to blend into the darkness
and watch the strange happenings by the
light of the lamps now hung at the entrance
of each of the tents.

After he had arrived earlier, he had remained hidden in the shadows of the forest
close to the tents. His curiosity had doubled
when he had seen many strange-looking
people on platforms just outside the tents,
people who would disappear inside when
enough of a crowd had gathered.

He knew that something peculiar must be
going on in those tents, and he could not
return to his vision quest until he saw for
himself what it was. But to do so required

darkness. Surely no one would see him move stealthily from tent to tent, somehow finding a way to spy on what was happening. He had studied the tents and had decided to go to the back of each and lift a corner up and peer inside.

Now that night had come, he felt it was finally safe enough to put his plan into action. He had studied the tents from this vantage point, deciding which one he would sneak up to first.

His heart pounding at the knowledge that he should not be there, that his chieftain uncle would not approve, Gray Stone watched until no one was near.

When he saw that the area was clear enough of white people, he broke into a hard run and dashed behind the tent he had chosen to explore first.

Breathing hard, Gray Stone fell to his knees and ran a hand beneath the edge of the tent.

When he found a place that was loose enough, he slowly lifted it so that he could lean low and peer inside.

As he looked into the semidarkness of the tent, he first saw white people sitting on chairs, their eyes focused on something ahead of them.

Unable to see well enough what those

people's object of interest was, he scooted over some. What he saw then made his eyes widen. A tall, thin man, with the forked tongue of a snake, stood on a platform before the people, with a large snake wrapped around his neck.

At first, the snake hung on the man so quietly it seemed to be dead, but then it moved, wrapping itself more tightly around the man's body. The people who were watching gasped in fear.

Even Gray Stone's belly seemed filled with knots, for though he had no love for people with white skin, he would not enjoy watching that horrible-looking snake squeeze the breath out of the man.

Not waiting to see what would happen, Gray Stone moved quickly to the back of the next tent, and again found a loose place at the bottom. He carefully lifted it enough for him to look inside, and his eyes widened. He saw a man standing on a platform in front of a crowd of white people, displaying a body covered by painted figures, which he knew were called tattoos.

As the man flexed his muscles and so caused his belly muscles to ripple strangely, the figures drawn on his skin seemed to move and dance. Again, the audience of white people gasped, but this time in awe.

Now truly intrigued, wondering what might be in the next tent, Gray Stone went from one to the other without being seen, amazed at how white people treated their bodies and then put themselves on display for others to see.

Realizing that each time he spied on another act he was taking the chance of being caught, and knowing that he must return to the mountain while the moon was bright and full so that he could find the path, he decided to look into just one more tent. Then he would flee into the night with the strange memories that he would love to tell his friends about, but must keep to himself. He could never let his mother or his uncle know that he had deserted his vision quest in order to view the oddities of white people.

Moving stealthily behind the tents, he paused when he saw an animal with the strangest long nose hanging from its face. The creature was tied by a rope to a tall stump of wood, and as Gray Stone watched, it swayed its head with its huge ears back and forth.

Then he heard a growl not far from him, and recalled his uncle warning him of mountain lions. His spine stiffened and he looked slowly around, only to find a huge animal that seemed kin to mountain lions, yet with a much different coat. He was saddened to see it caged up, for he had been told that no man should place wild animals in cages.

When it bared its teeth at Gray Stone and knocked at the bars with one of its massive paws, Gray Stone inched his way back, only to catch sight of another cage. In it was a tiny bear cub.

The sight of the caged cub tore at Gray Stone's heart. He wondered if this cub had a mother somewhere longing for it, as he had longed for his father after he had been killed by renegades. This cub had surely been stolen away by whites, who gave no thought to the ones they were leaving behind. Worse yet, they might have killed the parents in order to have the cub.

Knowing that he could do nothing about the cub, since there was a lock on its cage, Gray Stone moved toward the last tent he would examine before returning to his vision quest.

When he got there, he again looked beneath the tent, but this time he saw something quite different from before. His eyes locked on a pretty white woman sitting at a table in the center of the space.

A man sitting across the table from her

listened intently as the woman told him an interpretation of a dream. The scene reminded Gray Stone of his people's shaman, who was their dream interpreter.

But this was a white woman!

Was she a shaman?

Suddenly large hands reached around Gray Stone's waist and yanked him to his feet. "Gotcha!"

Annamae had heard the commotion behind her, outside her tent, and she recognized Howard's voice.

"Pardon me," she said as she hurried to her feet, leaving the man sitting at the table. He grumbled behind her, saying he'd not gotten his money's worth.

She ignored the threat in his voice and arrived outside just in time to see Howard half dragging an Indian child away. He was perhaps around twelve years of age and was pleading in good English, saying that he hadn't meant any harm by watching what was happening inside the tent.

But even though the boy was only a child, it was enough that he was Indian. Annamae was momentarily thrown back in time when she had been forced to hide in that fruit cellar, listening to the hideous war cries as her parents and her brother were being slaughtered.

She shuddered, closed her eyes, then opened them again quickly when she heard the child begin to cry and beg for mercy.

Yes, this was a mere child, and Howard was mistreating him.

"Stop that," Annamae screamed as she ran toward them. "Howard, let the child go. Can't you see that you have scared him to death? Can't you see how he is trembling?"

Feeling that he had perhaps found an ally, even though she was a mere woman, Gray Stone gave Annamae a pleading look. He prayed that she would continue to speak on his behalf, for if she did not, he was alone in a world where Indians were despised, and sometimes heartlessly killed.

"Howard, release him," Annamae said as she ran up to Howard.

"Damned if I can understand why you're taking the side of an Injun," Howard grumbled as he stopped and glared into Annamae's eyes. "Since when did you become an Injun lover? Have you forgotten how your parents died? Now, you go back to what you do best. I believe you left someone waiting to get what he paid for. I have plans for this little savage. He will be put in a cage and called 'the Wild Boy from Borneo.' "

"What?" Annamae gasped. "That's horrible, Howard! How do you think you can get away with such a thing? The Indians will miss this child and search for him. They will not hesitate to make the one responsible for the child's misfortune pay for the crime. That person is you, Howard. Do you want me to explain how it's done? You saw my parents . . . and my baby brother, didn't you? Do you think you'd be shown any more mercy than they?"

"I don't have to worry about that," Howard said, keeping his hold around Gray Stone's waist. "We're heading out as soon as everyone can get ready. We'll take this child far from his home. The Indians will never know what happened to him."

"Howard, please," Annamae begged. "Oh, please don't do this."

He grabbed Gray Stone up into his arms and carried the boy away, laughing.

Shivers raced up and down Annamae's spine at the thought of where Howard's stupidity could end.

Surely in tragedy!

Chapter Five

Cougar's thoughts had strayed more than once this morning to the woman he had seen two sleeps ago, where the many tents had been erected by white people. He was still in awe of her loveliness, yet he knew it was not the thing to do . . . to think about a woman of white skin. Focusing his thoughts on the here and now, Cougar realized it was well past the usual time for his sister to bring him his morning meal. It was not like her to forget him, nor their time together in the mornings when they discussed the upcoming day's activities.

He stood and held his entrance flap aside. He peered at his sister's tepee. His eyes widened when he saw no smoke spiraling up from the smoke hole of her lodge. That had to mean she had not added wood to her fire in some time; perhaps she was not even there.

Was this strange behavior because she was

still too worried about her son to function normally?

Cougar could not help being disappointed in her, yet at the same time he was concerned. Too often since her husband's death, she had become a stranger to Cougar.

She distanced herself from the normal activities of his people. She even distanced herself from her own brother. Her state of mind had never been the same since she'd lost her husband.

And what concerned him most was that she was drawing negative attention to herself. He had actually heard her complain to the other women that she did not want her son to go alone on the mountain to seek his vision quest, that she feared for his safety.

Being the chief's sister, she should instead be setting a good example for other mothers who must let their own sons go to prove their manhood.

But today his concerns had escalated beyond what others might say or do as a result of his sister's complaints. There was no sign of a fire in his sister's lodge; that had to mean only one thing: she was gone. But where?

He stepped from his tepee and hurried to hers. He did not bother to speak her name because he knew she was not there. But he must check inside for whatever clues he could find as to where she might be.

As he stepped into the tepee, his concern deepened. The ashes were not glowing in her fire pit, which meant that there had not been a fire there for some time.

He knelt beside the pit and held his hands over the coals. There was no heat whatsoever. She had not prepared her fire this morning, nor cooked any food.

Something else had taken precedence over her normal morning activities.

He stood and gazed slowly around him in order to find some a hint of why she wasn't there, or where she might have gone.

"Is she praying in her private praying place?" he whispered to himself. Yes, that was the only thing that made sense. Being so afraid for her son, she had probably decided to devote her time to prayer.

With that hope in his heart, Cougar returned to his tepee. He did not want to disturb her prayers.

Although he was hungry, he ignored the hunger pangs. His sister should return soon. They would resume their usual day's activities by eating together and then going on to their separate chores. He would be meeting with his warriors in the early afternoon to discuss the timing of their next hunt. But until then he would busy his hands.

He went to the back of his tepee and gathered up the material that he used for making new quivers for his arrows. With the large piece of buckskin draped across his arm, he went back to his lodge fire and sat down beside it.

He pushed aside several mats that covered the earthen floor, then spread the buckskin flat on the ground. He took his knife from the sheath at his right side and started to cut the shape of the quiver, but something made him pause.

He just could not get his sister from his mind. It had never taken her this long to say her prayers, and she most definitely had never neglected her duties till this late in the morning. That had to mean she was doing something else, and there was only one other possibility.

"She's gone to check on her son," he whispered just loudly enough for himself to hear.

Filled with disappointment, ashamed of his sister's lack of strength, although he did admire her deep love for her son, he hurried from his lodge. He chose one warrior to confide in and told him that he would be gone for a while, but did not tell him where or why.

Dressed in only a breechclout and moccasins, his thick black hair hanging long down his back, he ran from the village. He knew that Gray Stone had shown his mother where he would be seeking his vision quest, although that was not the usual practice. But nothing was usual about Gray Stone's mother these days.

Yes, Cougar had found out that Morning Flower knew where her son was seeking his vision. He disapproved, but it was already done, and he had not forced his nephew to choose another location.

He was sure his sister had gone to check on her son, although it would be a dangerous trek for someone who was not accustomed to climbing to such a high place.

But Cougar now realized just how worried she was about her son — far more than he had ever imagined — and worry made a mother do things that she would not normally do.

Having reached the foot of the mountain, Cougar began making his way upward to where Gray Stone should be. But when he finally reached the bluff, only Morning Flower was there. She was on her knees, hugging her son's blanket and crying.

Realizing that Cougar was standing over her, Morning Flower looked pleadingly up at him through her tears. "Do not be angry, my brother," she sobbed out. "I had to come. Through the night I saw my son in my dreams, and he was not here. He . . . he . . . was far, far away from this place; I could not tell where. But . . . but . . . I knew that I must come and see if my dream was true, or just an expression of the fear in my heart."

Cougar knelt down before her. He placed a gentle hand on her cheek. "My sister, do not put so much stock in what you dream," he said, trying to reassure her, even though he felt a quiet panic inside his heart that Gray Stone was not where he should be.

"My brother, do you not see?" Morning Flower said, her voice rising in pitch as the panic increased inside her heart. "Something has happened to him. He is gone. Why? Where would he go unless . . . someone came and took him?"

She swallowed hard and lowered her eyes as she shuddered. "Perhaps a mountain lion . . . dragged him away," she said, her voice breaking.

"My sister, listen to yourself," Cougar said, placing a hand beneath her chin and lifting it so that they could look into each other's eyes. "You always make the worst of a situation before you even know what has happened. Surely my nephew is searching for berries for food. Perhaps he has gone to seek water. Do not get carried away thinking things are wrong when you do not know for sure that they are."

"He's been gone for too long," Morning Flower said, her voice breaking. "I have been here since daybreak. I found him gone then. He has not returned since. He . . . is . . . missing!"

"You stay here," Cougar said, rising. "I will search. I will find him and bring him to you. Then you must return home. This constant worrying about things is not good for you."

"My son is worth all of the worries in the world," Morning Flower gulped out. She reached a hand to her brother's face. "Go. Please bring him back to me. I will sit here and pray that you succeed."

Cougar left her there, his heart thumping hard within his chest, because he, too, felt something was very awry. Even in the time that he had been there, his nephew should have returned if he had merely gone to seek food or water.

But as it was, Cougar found no signs whatsoever of his nephew. Nor did Gray

Stone respond when Cougar called his name over and over again. The only response was an echo of his own voice drifting back to him.

Knowing now that something was definitely wrong, that Gray Stone was nowhere near where he should be, Cougar returned to his sister.

When she gazed into his eyes, she knew that what her brother was about to say was not good, that he, too, now believed something had happened to her son.

"Come with me," Cougar said thickly as he held a hand out for his sister. "We will return to our village and I will form a search party. Gray Stone will be found."

Trying to keep her composure when what she truly wanted was to scream and wail, Morning Flower moved shakily to her feet.

Clutching her son's blanket in one arm, and holding on to her brother's arm with her free hand, she followed him down the mountainside.

Morning Flower gazed over at her brother. Cougar had been wrong about her son. More than once, of late, she had not approved of her brother's decisions, and at times she had not been able to keep her doubts to herself.

She hated to be disloyal to her brother,

but as though something deep within her caused continual doubts, it was as though a demon were eating away at her heart!

CHAPTER SIX

The tent was dark except for meager light of the lone candle as Annamae awaited her first customer. She hoped that no one came tonight. She was too edgy and upset to pretend much of anything. She found it hard to concentrate on anything except the small Indian child.

It had been two days now since the carnival wagons had left the spot where the boy had been abducted. Howard was still too afraid that other Indians might see the child, so for now he was keeping him hidden when they stopped at other towns to set up their tents.

Annamae deplored the way the young Indian brave was being treated. He was in a barred cage beside the pen in which the tiny bear cub was being held captive.

But Howard had told Annamae this morning that he would start showing the child as one of his acts at the next town. It would be a private showing for those who paid extra to see "the Wild Boy from Borneo." Howard was hoping they would not see through his ploy and recognize that this child was, instead, a full-blood Indian who surely did not even know what Borneo was.

Annamae had had enough of Howard's foolishness. She was going to interpret dreams this one last time tonight and then leave when everyone had retired to their tents for the night.

And not only that. She had waited longer than she had earlier planned because she wasn't going alone. She was going to take the child with her and, she hoped, help him find his way back to his people.

One thing in her favor was the fact that the child could speak English. He had told her his name was Gray Stone, and she had told him her plan, encouraging him to be patient.

After thanking her for her kindness, he had pleaded with her to also take the cub from these horrible people. He had told her that no bear should be chained in a cage, just as no Blackfoot brave should be.

She had known that if she took not only Gray Stone, but also the cub, she would make Howard doubly angry.

But she had seen the love the child had

for the cub and promised him that, yes, they would release the cub and take him back to the area where he had been captured, which was somewhere close to where Gray Stone made his home.

When Annamae heard footsteps and looked up to see who had entered her tent, she grimaced. It was none other than that nasty man Reuben Jones, who was still following the carnival in order to torment her.

But knowing that this was the last time she would have to confront the man with the pockmarked face, Annamae conjured up a smile.

But she could not help shuddering when she caught him staring at her breasts beneath the pretty cotton dress she wore. Although she was small, his eyes always went there, mentally undressing her.

"Do you have another dream you want interpreted?" Annamae asked, sighing heavily as his beady eyes looked into hers, and a sly smile appeared on his thin lips.

"It was about me and you," Reuben said. He chuckled beneath his breath. "I dreamed of you last night. You were totally nude, and my hands were touching your —"

Insulted, enraged, and unable to listen to any more of this man's filthy thoughts,

Annamae moved quickly to her feet and pointed to the entranceway. "Get out," she said between clenched teeth. "Do you hear me? Get . . . out . . . of . . . here."

Reuben stood up, glared at her, then swept up the coins he had placed on the table upon entering the tent. "You never give me my money's worth," he growled. "I should go and tattle on you, but I won't. There'll be a next time, and by damn, feisty lady, you'd best sit and hear what I have to say, or . . ."

"Or what?" Annamae said, leaning into his face. She laughed. "You don't frighten me."

"You'd better think on that," Reuben said stiffly, then turned and stormed from the tent.

Annamae's heart was racing, because she could not help feeling threatened by Reuben.

But this would be her last encounter with him. When he came to the next town to have a "dream" interpreted, he would discover that she was far, far from that place — and him.

Inhaling a nervous breath, Annamae went back to her chair and waited for her next customer, her mind once again went to Gray Stone, and what she was planning to do tonight after everyone was asleep.

Yes, she would do her best to return the child to his home, even though that would delay her plan of going to Missouri to seek out her blood kin.

She was frightened at the thought of approaching an Indian village. But Gray Stone had told her more than once that his people were peaceful and that she would be looked upon as a heroine for having returned their chief's nephew to his home.

Yet although Gray Stone had reassured her time and again, Annamae just could not get past the fact that her parents were killed by Indians. What if this child's people saw her not as a heroine, but as an enemy, one of the white race who had taken so much from them?

She forced a smile as a young man of perhaps fourteen years of age came into her tent holding in his outstretched hand several coins.

"Can you really interpret dreams?" he asked, his dark eyes wide.

"Sit down, young man, and tell me your dream. After I interpret it, you can judge the accuracy of my insights," Annamae said, waving the young man toward the chair opposite her.

"Now please begin," she urged, finding it

hard to listen when her mind was elsewhere . . . on her escape plans!

CHAPTER SEVEN

As Cougar entered his village on his midnight black stallion he found his sister awaiting him at the outskirts of the encampment.

He dreaded telling Morning Flower that he had not brought home good news about her son. But after one look at Cougar, Morning Flower divined the outcome of the search.

Her son had not been found.

Without exchanging one word with her brother, Morning Flower turned and fled to her tepee, wailing in sorrow.

Cougar hurried on into the village and dismounted.

After putting his horse in his corral, Cougar knew what he must do. He went to his shaman's lodge, calling the man's name at the doorway.

White Thunder stepped outside, his eyes going to Morning Flower's tepee. He had heard her sobs, but he thought that Cougar would be the best person to console Morning Flower at this time. He was a devoted brother to her, and his words would mean more to her now than those of their village shaman.

"You go to her," White Thunder said quietly. "Talk with her. Encourage her. Then if you need me, I shall come."

Cougar nodded and walked to his sister's tepee, not stopping to announce himself, but instead stepping inside. He found Morning Flower on her knees beside the lodge fire, no longer wailing, but instead rocking back and forth with a strange sort of look in her eyes. She was humming something soft beneath her breath as she rocked.

"My sister, although I did not bring good news to you about your son, it is too soon to grieve," Cougar said softly. "True grieving should come when all hope is lost. I do not believe that it is lost for my nephew. The search for Gray Stone will resume at daybreak tomorrow. He is a fine, smart young brave. He knows of ways to survive."

Morning Flower wiped the tears from her eyes, stopped rocking, and gazed intently at Cougar. "My brother, if my child was alive, he would show himself to me in some way," she said, her voice weak. "He would do this, for surely he can feel my sorrow. He would not want me to hurt like this. He would somehow let me know that he was alive. No, my son is not alive. He has gone to the Sand Hills, where all Blackfoot spirits retire after death. My brother, I would rather join my son there than stay here in my lodge, mourning him. He would comfort me there. I would comfort him there. That is what mothers and sons do."

Hearing her talking like that sent a shaft of coldness through Cougar's heart. He could feel that she had given up, not only that her son was alive, but also that there was any point in living without him.

"My sister, do not talk such foolishness," Cougar said, kneeling beside her. When he tried to wrap her within his arms, she stiffened and did not allow it.

"Morning Flower, again I urge you not to talk with such lack of faith," Cougar softly encouraged. "You were born from the same womb as I. Surely you have the same strength as I."

Yes, he told her this, yet he knew what he said was not true. His sister was weak in many ways, especially when it came to having faith in the goodness of life.

"No," Morning Flower cried. "I have never had the strength or courage that you were born with. Never will I. So please go and leave me to my mourning."

"But, my sister, listen to what I say," Cougar begged, trying one last time to make her see the situation as he did. He feared that she was truly slipping away from him and all reality. "You are so loved. You are so needed. Do not give up on life. You sleep now. When you awaken tomorrow, after I have gone to search for Gray Stone again, you surely will have reason to rejoice. I will search until I find him. I promise you that."

"My brother, I know that you truly believe you can find Gray Stone, yet I cannot see it the same way," Morning Flower said, sobbing. "Please leave me to my prayers. Please leave me to do as I see fit."

Cougar stood, hesitated, then turned and left her lodge with a heavy, even fearful heart. He knew that she was acting and speaking from her deep grief. But he had never seen her in such a state, and he feared for her safety.

When he stepped outside he found a crowd of his people there, their eyes on him. He knew they were as concerned about his sister as he. "Pray for her," was all that he said; then he went to his lodge, where he sat by his lodge fire and prayed to the Great Mystery himself.

After a while, the deep stillness of the night was broken by the mournful howls of a wolf in the forest of aspens and cedar trees.

This call was answered by another, and then another, until they all united into a chorus of long howls.

Alarm leaped into Cougar's heart when a breeze fluttered his entrance flap, then brushed across his face, causing a chill to ride his spine.

"No!" he cried, then ran to his sister's lodge. Inside, he found what he had feared.

The breeze in his lodge had been his sister's spirit coming to say good-bye, for she lay dead on her blankets, her arms bleeding where she had slashed them with her knife.

Never strong in spirit or body, she had given up on life. Her grieving for her son had proved too much for her.

What stunned Cougar was that before his sister had taken the knife to her body, she had taken the time to clothe herself in her favorite robe of soft-tanned fawn skin with beaded stripes, readying herself for her own burial.

Cougar bent low and gathered his sister's body into his arms and cried, then chanted.

The chants drew White Thunder there. He stopped just inside the entrance flap, then went to Cougar and his sister. He took a handful of sage from a small bag at his waist and purified Morning Flower as he sprinkled it over her body, praying that her journey to the Sand Hills would not be a long one. He prayed that she would finally find peace and the beginning of a new and happier life there, since she had never known true happiness on earth.

White Thunder then left, promising to return soon to prepare Morning Flower for burial. He would be aided by several women of the village, for Cougar must leave again to search one last time for his nephew. He had promised his sister that he would do this. Even while she lay dead on her bed of blankets, he would keep this promise to her.

He gently laid her across her blankets, then knelt beside her and touched her cheek. "My beloved sister, I promise you that I will find Gray Stone and bring him safely home," he said, his voice drawn. "I will not rest until I have my nephew back home again, for I do not have the same lack of faith that you had. I see my nephew too clearly in my heart ever to stop believing that he is still alive."

He stood, looked through his tears down at his sister's quiet body, then left the tepee.

Once outside, he faced the full congregation of his people. They already knew his sister's fate, for their shaman had spread the word.

"She has found solace in death," was all that he could say. Then he ran from the village until he reached his private place of prayer.

He knelt there and prayed, and would stay there with his prayers until daybreak, when he would resume his search.

His sister would be mourned for as long as they could wait before burying her. Cougar hoped he could find Gray Stone so that his nephew could say a final good-bye to his mother before she was placed with her ancestors in their clan's burial grounds.

Chapter Eight

She'd done it! She'd made a successful escape from Howard and his carnival. Annamae smiled as she gazed over at the youngster who rode bareback on the pony she had stolen for him.

She gazed ahead, keeping her own stolen horse going at a steady trot. She was glad that she had found a saddle for her horse, for she had never ridden bareback.

She was also glad to have left other reminders of her carnival life behind. The dream books and candle, all of which had been props as she was forced to pretend to be someone she was not.

She had no supernatural insight into dreams!

She was ready for a new, honest life away from the carnival.

She smiled when she thought of her careful escape. Not only had she stolen animals, but also food, which now hung in a bag at the left side of the brown mare. At the bottom of the bag were the few clothes she owned.

She was glad that she had thought about her comfort at night, when the air grew cooler. She had tied some blankets on the backs of the mare and the child's pony.

She glanced at the right side of her horse, where another bag hung. In it was the bear cub, comfortably warm, only his head exposed.

It seemed content, as though it somehow realized that it had been saved from a horrible life at the carnival.

In time, when it was larger, it would have been trained to perform. She was sure the cub would have been whipped if it did not cooperate, as were the other animals in the carnival.

"You will be all right now," Annamae whispered. "I won't let anyone take you from us. When I get the child close to his home, I will release you to find your own."

Thinking of bears, which would be large and wild, and other four-legged creatures that could be a threat to their safety, Annamae glanced at the rifle she had secured in a gun boot on one side of the horse.

She had taken enough bullets to protect them until she reached Gray Stone's village.

She also had a knife sheathed at her waist.

Yes, she was very proud of what she had achieved, because she had never been an adventurous sort of person. She had always been tiny, "fragile," her father had called her.

She had even thought ahead and realized how harsh the sun could be on the hottest days. She wore one of her bonnets, the wide brim helping to shade her face from the rays of the sun.

She gazed heavenward. By the sun's position in the sky, she calculated that it must nearly be noon. The growling of her stomach attested to that, but she was afraid to stop just yet. Once she and Gray Stone and the cub were discovered gone, a search party would quickly be formed.

She again glanced over at Gray Stone, who seemed lost in thought. Perhaps he was thinking of the mother he had spoken of so fondly. When he had told her that his father had died at the hands of renegades, she had again been reminded of her own loss.

The discovery that they had lost parents in the same way seemed to bring her and the child closer together. They felt comfortable with each other. She was growing fonder of him as each moment passed, for he was such a sweet, thoughtful brave, and always had a smile for her when they looked at each other.

She hoped the route that Gray Stone had suggested would lead her to higher, hard-to-reach places as they traveled onward, so that Howard would not dare to follow. He was not an outdoors type of person. He was a coward in many ways. So when he saw the roughness of the terrain, he might give up his search.

Until only moments ago, Annamae and Gray Stone had shared conversation. He had told her all about his people.

She had told him about her unfortunate life, but her joy now that she was finally free.

She smiled when she remembered how Gray Stone had asked her if she was a woman shaman. Apparently, it was the shaman who interpreted dreams for the Blackfoot people.

She had seen a look of disappointment in his eyes when she quickly cleared up that confusion. She might have commanded more respect among his people if she were a shaman, but she was only a young woman whose life had been torn apart by a group of Shawnee renegades, and then made to pretend she could interpret dreams.

Finally, now she was free to be whomever she wished to be!

"Are you certain I will be welcome when we arrive at your village?" she suddenly blurted out, drawing Gray Stone's eyes to her.

"I'm white," she went on. "Surely your people hate all whites."

"Although you are white, you will be more than welcome," Gray Stone said, giving her a wide smile. "Remember that you are my heroine. You shall be seen as a heroine by my people, and especially by my uncle, who is our chief."

The reminder that his uncle was a powerful chief renewed the fear inside Annamae's heart, despite Gray Stone's confidence that all would be well.

"I think it's time to stop and eat," Annamae said, quickly changing the subject. "Are you hungry?"

"Very," Gray Stone said, drawing rein when Annamae halted her steed. He smiled down at the cub. "I think I know someone else who is eager to eat, too."

"Yes, all babies need food to grow," Annamae said, reaching over and stroking the cub's head. "I'm so glad that he trusts us."

"We are treating him with kindness. That is why he trusts us," Gray Stone said, dismounting. "He senses that we are taking him home."

Annamae dismounted and led her horse close to a nearby stream, where she tied the reins to a low limb while Gray Stone secured his pony.

"Grab the bag with the food in it, and I shall bring a blanket and the cub," Annamae said, trying to sound nonchalant, even though she felt uneasy. Although she thought Gray Stone had led them high enough to prevent Howard from following them, there was always the chance that he would be so angry he would go to any lengths to find her, the child, and the cub.

Trying not to think about it, Annamae spread out a blanket and sat down beside Gray Stone, who held the cub on his lap, stroking its light brown fur. She reached inside the bag and brought out a few items, placing them on the blanket between herself and Gray Stone.

"Are you familiar with cheese?" she asked as she unwrapped a chunk that she had stolen from the food wagon.

"Cheese?" Gray Stone asked, arching an eyebrow. "No. I have never eaten cheese."

"Take some," Annamae said, tearing off a corner and handing it to him. She watched him take a bite, smiling when she saw by the look in his eyes that he liked it.

"Here's some bread," she said, taking a slice from a freshly baked loaf that she had stolen from the cook's wagon and handing it to the child. "It's good with cheese."

She eyed the cub, which was hungrily watching Gray Stone eat.

Annamae took a piece of baked wild turkey from the bag and broke it into several small chunks, placing them beside Gray Stone.

The cub crawled from his lap and had soon gobbled up the turkey. It stretched out contentedly on its belly beside Gray Stone and fell fast asleep.

"Do you see where I am pointing?" Gray Stone asked, now munching on a small piece of turkey meat.

"Yes," Annamae said, slicing small pieces of apple onto a napkin. She gazed into the distances where fog lay heavily over the landscape. "I see. I also see fog."

"Sometimes it is foggy where I live, but most times it is not," Gray Stone said. "I do miss my home so much."

"How much farther do you think it is?" Annamae murmured.

"It is hard to tell, because I do not know how far we have traveled," Gray Stone said, his voice breaking. "I am but a young brave who does not yet know how to calculate travel time. My uncle knows all of these things."

"That is because he is a mature adult and you are still a child," Annamae said, drawing his eyes quickly to her again.

"I was on my vision quest when I saw the carnival from the bluff where I was sitting," Gray Stone said softly. "Had I succeeded with my quest, I would now be called an adult, not a child. But I was drawn from my quest when I saw the tents and animals. Curiosity drew me away from a task that should have been more important to me."

"You will go on another vision quest," Annamae said, having heard about such things. "When you arrive home, you can start it all over again."

"Yes, I do plan to," Gray Stone said, nodding. Tears filled his eyes. "I know how much worry I have brought into my mother's heart by venturing away to see the tents and animals of the carnival."

"Your mother will forgive you, for you are but a child with an adventurous heart," Annamae murmured.

"But you do not know my mother," Gray Stone said, sighing heavily. "She worries about me so much. She does not only worry about me, but about everything. I am afraid that worrying will be the reason for her demise."

"Everyone is different," Annamae said, trying to reassure him. "Some worry. Some don't. And no one I know who was a worrier died because of it. Your mother will be just fine, and when she sees you, she will realize that worrying did no good, and maybe she won't worry so much anymore."

Annamae looked over her shoulder, gazing back in the direction they had just traveled from. She began gathering together their things so they could resume travel.

"We must hurry onward," she said as Gray Stone helped her place the blanket and food back on the horse. He hugged the cub, then put him back in the bag so that his head was the only thing one could see.

"Sleep, sweet cub," Gray Stone said. "When you awake again, we will be even closer to our homes."

He mounted his pony as Annamae mounted her mare, and the trip was resumed.

They soon came to fields of golden flowers. These were a sea of color, a feast for the senses, with their sweet and intoxicating fragrance.

"I will savor and remember this place forever," Annamae said to Gray Stone. "It is as though we are traveling through paradise."

"Often my uncle calls our home paradise," Gray Stone said, his voice breaking.

"We will be there soon," Annamae reassured him. "Soon, Gray Stone. Soon."

They traveled onward.

When they passed a lovely lake they heard and saw olive-backed thrushes singing along the shores.

In lofty pines were winter wrens and myrtle warblers.

In the open glades, doves, ruffled grouse, chirping sparrows, and flickers flitted about.

And then suddenly the cub awakened and wiggled its way out of the bag.

It fell to the ground, then romped away, seeming determined to get somewhere.

"Where is he going?" Gray Stone said, quickly drawing rein, while Annamae did likewise.

"Do you think he senses that he is near his home?" Annamae asked, lifting the skirt of her dress and running after the cub, with Gray Stone huffing and puffing beside her as he tried to keep up with her.

"No, we are too far from where he lived," Gray Stone said, stopping when he finally saw where the cub had gone. "Honey. He has found a beehive just dripping with honey."

As the cub attacked the beehive and got all sticky with the honey, and the bees starting buzzing Gray Stone went pale. He had just remembered something: if he, himself, got stung by a bee, he would be horribly sick. It had happened one other time. He had never been so ill as then.

"I must leave this place," he blurted out, looking desperately at Annamae. "If I am stung, I will get terribly ill."

But just as they turned and started running back toward their horses, the bees went wild. They scattered in all directions, the cub whining and smacking at them with a paw.

Hearing the cub's distress, and realizing that it was being stung, Gray Stone stopped and turned to see, wishing he could help the cub.

"Come on, Gray Stone," Annamae cried, taking his hand and urging him to hurry onward. "There's nothing you can do for the cub. You are the one we must think about. My father was allergic to bees. I saw him so sick one time, I thought he was going to die."

Before they could get to the horses or find cover from the bees, the insects had swarmed over them. Both Annamae and

Gray Stone were stung several times before the bees finally retreated.

The cub came bounding toward them, its nose swollen from stings, crying as a baby would after the same sort of attack.

"Finally they are gone," Annamae said, stopping to look at the young brave. Ignoring her own stings, she hurriedly tended to Gray Stone's.

She began removing the stingers, but grew cold inside when she saw how swollen Gray Stone's face suddenly became, his eyes almost shut from the swelling.

"Oh, no. Gray Stone, what am I to do?" Annamae cried, her heart skipping several beats when he suddenly collapsed at her feet, unconscious.

Truly panicking now, Annamae lifted him and carried him over to a stream and bathed his face.

But he was still unconscious.

"Oh, Lord, what am I to do?" she cried. She had no medicine. And he couldn't travel like this. She felt she had done more harm now than good for the child by taking him with her. She knew that some people died from such reactions to bee stings.

Again she lifted him. She carried him to where there was a slight overhang of rock, where they might be sheltered for the night.

Sobbing and feeling, oh, so terribly helpless, Annamae built a fire. She was oblivious to her own pain. All she could think about was Gray Stone, who was still in a frighteningly deep sleep.

The cub came and nestled next to Gray Stone and fell asleep, apparently recovered from its own bee stings.

Trembling in fear for the child, Annamae finally removed her own stingers, and when night fell with its mysterious sounds — the laughing of loons, hooting of owls, and howling of wolves — Annamae could not fight off exhaustion any longer. She fell asleep, tears wet on her cheeks, for she was afraid that when she woke up, Gray Stone might be dead.

In her sleep she had a dream. Reuben was in it, chasing her, his pock-scarred face leaning down into hers. She suddenly awakened in a sweat.

Sitting up quickly, she looked all around her, afraid that Reuben was actually there, as he had been in her dream.

But fortunately he wasn't.

She reminded herself that she shouldn't worry about her dreams. They were nothing but figments of her imagination. She was not a true interpreter of dreams, nor could whatever she dreamed come true!

She crawled over to Gray Stone and gazed down at him. She gently shook his arm, feeling ill inside when he still would not awaken. That meant he must be unconscious, not only asleep!

She gazed heavenward, "Oh, Lord, what am I to do?" she cried. "Please send help, for I cannot save him alone."

She would even welcome Howard Becker at this moment if it meant help could be given to Gray Stone!

CHAPTER NINE

"Ellie!"

Ellie stopped brushing her hair when she heard the panic in her husband's voice. She knew that something terrible must have happened to get him so upset.

Her first thought was that one of the elephants had gotten loose again. It had happened more than once, and it always took days to find the escaped animal.

She prayed to herself that it was a simpler problem so they could get on with their day's activities and then ready themselves to leave for the next town bright and early tomorrow.

Dressed in a full-length cotton dress with long sleeves — she always wore long-sleeved dresses to hide her hefty upper arms — and with her golden hair shining from the brushing and hanging long to her waist, she ran from her tent. She found Howard standing outside Annamae's tent.

His face was red with rage.

His hands were doubled into tight fists at his sides.

A cold fear spread through Ellie, for she could not help thinking the worst. Annamae had been griping of late, and had even gone as far as saying she wanted to leave the carnival.

Oh, surely she had not fled in the middle of the night.

She ran up to Howard, her eyes questioning him.

"She's not the only one that's disappeared. The Indian brat and the bear cub are missing, too," Howard grumbled. He looked past Ellie at Snake Man as he came running and panting from the horse corral.

"One horse and one pony are gone," Snake Man said, his forked tongue making him lisp as he spoke. "So are several blankets from the horse tent, as well as an expensive saddle."

"Lord," Ellie gasped, turning pale.

"And so she's done it," Howard said, kneading his brow. "That ungrateful wench. After all we did for her, she takes to stealing from us? I wonder how much money she held back from what she made each night? Surely she planned this getaway for some time and calculated very well what she'd need in order to be comfortable while searchin' for some other fool to take her in."

He looked quickly at his tent, then at Ellie. "She probably even sneaked out one of my rifles when we didn't notice," he said. "Maybe yesterday, while I was checking out everything before the performances."

"But you'd surely have missed it," Ellie said, feeling torn about Annamae's betrayal.

A part of Ellie had truly grown to love Annamae, for who wouldn't? She had the sweetest disposition of anyone Ellie had ever known. It had been a pleasure to see to her happiness.

The only thing that clouded her sunny disposition was Howard's insistence that Annamae pretend to interpret dreams. Ellie knew that Annamae had not enjoyed duping people.

But Ellie had to remember just how much money the child had brought into the carnival. She and Howard were doubly rich now because of Annamae.

"Could it have been Indians that did this?" Ellie suddenly blurted out, paling at the thought. "If they discovered how we were using the young brave, they might have come to rescue him. They could have seen Annamae and decided to take her, too, and even the cub. Oh, Lord, if it is savages, how are they treating Annamae?"

"Ellie, just think about what you're saying," Howard said, peering into her eyes. "They'd not only have taken their young savage back, but they'd have killed us all in our sleep for having stolen the child."

"Not if they are from a peaceful band of Indians," Ellie murmured. "Perhaps the Blackfoot?"

"Hogwash," Howard said sharply. "No Indians came in the night and took Annamae, or the child, and especially not the bear cub. It's Annamae. She did this. She's turned her back on us after all we did for her. Well, if she felt confident enough to go out on her own, good riddance to bad rubbish. I'll find me another pretty young lady to take up the job of interpreting dreams. Annamae isn't the only pretty thing on two legs, you know."

"Howard, please go and find Annamae," Ellie pleaded. "Even if she did go out on her own, she's probably finding it isn't as easy as she thought it'd be, living away from the comforts of her tent."

"Let her squirm when she gets lost. Maybe then she'll realize how asinine it was to have lit out on her own," Howard barked out. "She'll come back begging us to take her in again. You'll see."

"Howard, don't be so heartless," Ellie said, placing her fists on her hips. "Gather together several men and go now and find her. And . . . if she has been taken by Indians, sneak in and steal her away from them. Or are you a coward?"

"The fact that Annamae stole my rifle from right beneath my nose, and took one of my prized steeds and even a pony, surely proves that Indians didn't do this," Howard said, again kneading his brow. "It points to her having planned this escape very, very carefully."

He tightened his jaw and glared at Ellie. "I won't go for her . . . at least not yet," he said. "If, by chance, Indians are involved somehow, and they left us alive after taking their young brave back, what would happen if I went after them? They would probably kill all of us, except maybe you, Ellie. They might want you for one of their brides."

Ellie gasped and placed her hands on her cheeks. "Don't say such things as that," she said, her voice trembling.

"As I said before, Ellie, I'm not going to hurry after Annamae," Howard said. "I've got some thinking to do about this. But one thing for sure: we're getting out of here as fast as we can."

He looked over at Snake Man. "Spread the word," he said tightly. "Tell everyone to prepare for departure. Now, Snake Man. Hurry. We don't want to hang around here any longer than we have to."

"Howard, if you leave and Annamae changes her mind and wants to come back to us, she won't have the chance to," Ellie said, her voice breaking. "Please, just go and find her, and then we can resume our lives as we always have. Uprooting the carnival and leaving now is the worst thing you can do as far as Annamae is concerned."

"I make the rules around here, and I say we're leaving," Howard shouted. His voice softened as he went to Ellie and drew her into his embrace. "Ellie, please see the sense in my decision. There are only a few here at our carnival who have sense enough to realize what's happened. Otherwise all we have left are the freaks who bring people in who pay good money to see them. But that's all they are fit for — gawking at. Otherwise, we're not a strong enough group to do much of anything about Annamae. The freaks don't even have enough brains to understand what has happened, much less mount a horse to help me hunt for Annamae."

"But don't you see, Howard?" Ellie said, leaning away from him in order to gaze into his eyes. "Those who can ride would be willing to follow you. And they won't even know the danger of what they will be doing. They won't even realize that if Annamae has been taken by Indians, their scalps could be taken as well as their lives if they interfere."

"Honey, I know how you feel about Annamae, but for now, we're heading out for another town," Howard said, reaching his hands to her long, golden hair and smoothing it away from her round face. "But I promise I'll think more on looking for Annamae. We won't be going all that far this time, honey. The next town we're visiting is just around the bend."

"But, Howard, if she tries to find us, will she know where you were planning to go?" Ellie still fretted.

"I'll tell you what I'll do," Howard said, tiring of the discussion. "We'll get settled in at the next town, and then, I promise, I'll leave and search for Annamae. You will stay behind in charge of things. Just see that everyone performs as usual while I'm gone. I'll only be taking a few men with me, and, except for Snake Man, none of those I'll take are a part of the acts. They'll mainly be the ones who care for the tents and animals."

Relieved, Ellie flung herself into her husband's arms. "Thank you, thank you," she breathed. "Oh, Howard, I love you so much."

Chapter Ten

Determined not to give up the search for his nephew just yet, and hoping that Gray Stone would be able to see his mother one last time before she joined her ancestors in the Turtle Clan's burial grounds, Cougar continued traveling onward beneath the bright full moon. Something told him not to stop just yet, not even to rest for the night. It was as though someone were beckoning to him to go at least a little farther.

It was then that he saw a campfire up ahead. He drew rein and stopped, his warriors following his lead and stopping as well.

"Dismount," he said in a voice only they could hear. "We will go the rest of the way on foot to see whose camp this is."

They dismounted and, each with a rifle in hand, moved stealthily through the darkness toward the fire. When they got close enough to see who lay sleeping beside the fire, Cougar's heart seemed to stop inside his chest. Although his nephew's face and eyes were swollen, Gray Stone was still recognizable to him.

The necklace he wore proved his identity to any who might question it. Gray Stone's mother had made the necklace for him to wear as a good-luck amulet while on his vision quest.

After seeing that there was only one other person at the camp besides Gray Stone, and that it was a mere woman, Cougar ran into the camp.

Annamae awakened with a start when she heard Cougar's cry of despair as he dropped to his knees beside Gray Stone. It was obvious just how terribly ill the child was.

Almost certain this was Chief Cougar, Annamae started to leap up. She was afraid she might be somehow blamed for the child's condition, and she wanted to run away, but was stopped when a warrior grabbed her and held her tightly as Cougar tried to awaken Gray Stone.

"He was stung by many bees," Annamae said, her voice trembling. "I had no medicine to help him and . . . and . . . he was too ill to travel on the pony. I . . . I . . . wish I could have helped him."

Cougar turned a sharp gaze her way. His

105

eyes widened when, by the fire's glow, he recognized her. She was the woman he had seen that day he had gone to investigate the strange collection of tents, people, and animals.

Now he was stunned by a resemblance he had not noticed before.

Although the woman's skin was white, and she was much older than Dancing Dove had been when he had last seen her, everything else about this woman reminded him of his young love. She had the same long, flowing black hair, the same dark brown eyes, round face, and petite form. He could not help wondering if this woman's skin was as soft as his Dancing Dove's had been.

As he stared at Annamae, she returned his captivated gaze. He wore a beaded buckskin shirt, leggings, and moccasins. He had a noble countenance, and his shoulders were broad and well formed. In every way he was a magnificent speciman of manhood. His manner was earnest and dignified, and as he knelt beside his nephew, his long black hair fell loose over his shoulders and down behind him to his waist.

In every way he was the handsomest man she had ever seen, and she knew that he was good and honest. Gray Stone had told her that he was.

She also knew the depth of the love that Gray Stone had for Chief Cougar. Judging by the way the chief was reacting to the child's illness, she believed that he loved the child in the same deep way.

Because Gray Stone had spoken so highly of his uncle and of his kindness, Annamae hoped Chief Cougar would show mercy to her. For until Gray Stone awakened, if he ever did, Cougar had only Annamae's word about what had happened. She was afraid that he might hate all whites — and she was white!

Cougar shook his head to clear it of the powerful notion that this woman resembled his young love. He had finally been able to put Dancing Dove from his mind so that he could fully concentrate on finding a woman to love and marry. It would do him no good to become fascinated by a woman who reminded him so much of her.

No. He could not allow himself to compare the two. Instead he felt an instant contempt for the white woman. There could be only one reason why she was with his nephew. She must have conspired with others to lure Gray Stone to the tents to use him somehow.

Perhaps after she had talked Gray Stone into going with her, she had gotten lost. It might be that his nephew had become disoriented as well, or had pretended to be in order to keep her from taking him to the place of tents and strange animals.

"Tie her," Cougar commanded, looking at his best friend, Four Clouds, who was one of two warriors who held her arms.

That order sent ice through Annamae's veins. "Why would you do that?" she asked, her eyes wide. "I am a friend of Gray Stone. I was helping the child when he was stung by bees. Even I was stung."

For a moment or two Annamae had seen Cougar staring at her as though he knew her. But suddenly his expression had changed to one of contempt.

"I do not have time for any more words from you, especially lies," Cougar said stiffly. He waited for Four Clouds to tie her wrists with a thin buckskin thong, then ordered, "You have her tied. Now silence her."

Annamae felt the color drain from her face, for she believed that he meant the warrior to kill her.

She was so relieved when she was only gagged, her knees went rubbery and weak.

"Four Clouds, stand by her," Cougar said, frowning at Annamae. "Do not give her any idea that she might be able to escape."

Four Clouds nodded and stood even closer to Annamae, one hand on her arm.

She trembled as she looked slowly up into Four Clouds's eyes, relieved when she did not see anger or contempt there, but instead something akin to kindness.

Her eyes were drawn back to Cougar, who stalked off into the darkness, then returned quickly with what looked like herbs. She watched him pick up one of the small food containers that she had washed after eating. He placed the herbs in it, along with some water, then put it near the fire for a while to steep.

After enough time had passed to warm the mixture, he removed it from the fire and began dabbing the liquid over Gray Stone's swollen face.

"Prepare a travois for my nephew," Cougar said, glancing up at his warriors. "We will return Gray Stone to our village on the travois so that our shaman can treat him. I only wish that White Thunder were here now. My nephew needs our shaman's strength, his powers, to survive."

The bear cub, which had remained hidden after the arrival of the warriors, came suddenly from the bushes and snuggled next to Annamae's legs.

She questioned Four Clouds with her

eyes, and when he nodded, she stooped closer to the cub.

She knelt, and the cub stood on its hind legs to get closer to her, since she could not reach out and take him onto her lap. He slowly licked one of her cheeks, then settled down beside her, content just to have her there with him.

Cougar's eyebrows rose when he saw the mutual love the bear cub and the white woman had for each other. He wondered how it had happened that a woman could have become this close to a cub, and why the cub trusted her so much.

He didn't ask the woman, though, because he felt any words that passed her lips would be lies.

But again, as he gazed at her in the fire's glow, he found himself drawn to her.

He forced himself to look away from her.

He was glad that the travois was made and ready for travel. He gently lifted his nephew into his arms, alarmed when even that didn't draw him from his deep sleep.

He carried Gray Stone to the travois and wrapped him in blankets. As he was kneeling beside him, the bear cub came and climbed onto the travois with Gray Stone, snuggling lovingly against him.

Annamae was afraid of what might happen to her now. It was obvious that no one believed anything she had said thus far, least of all the powerful Blackfoot chief.

As Cougar knelt beside the travois, making sure Gray Stone was wrapped snugly enough, Annamae studied the man the child loved so dearly. From his piercing glance and the firm expression on his face, she inferred that he was accustomed to command. And as she had seen before, he was a man who had a natural dignity of manner.

Although he had been stern with her, she saw a puzzling look in his eyes as he gazed at her.

And, ah, she could not help noticing how handsome he was!

But she would not let herself be fooled by this man in any respect. Suddenly she was thrown back in time to that day when her parents were massacred by Indians. She broke out in a cold sweat as she relived it all over again. She came back to the present only when she realized that Cougar was gazing at her curiously.

"Four Clouds, gather the woman's supplies together and place them on her steed," Cougar said, forcing himself to look away from her.

For a moment he had seen her thinking about something that had made her break out in a sweat.

He wondered what might have happened to her to cause such pain in her eyes.

He hoped to have answers soon as to who she was, and what had prompted her to take his nephew from his vision quest.

After Four Clouds had her blankets, travel bag, and all her belongings secured on her horse, he led Annamae to the animal.

Annamae managed to work the gag away from her mouth. "How do you expect me to ride while my wrists are tied?" she said, her voice breaking as she turned her eyes toward the chief. "Please, oh, please untie these bonds?"

She paled when he turned a slow gaze her way and paused, giving her that same stern look she had seen when he had told his warriors what to do with her.

She wasn't sure she wanted to know what else he had planned!

CHAPTER ELEVEN

"Four Clouds, untie the woman," Cougar suddenly ordered after gazing at Annamae. He was shaken by the pleading in her lovely dark eyes.

But he had to make himself remember who she was!

She was white.

She was his enemy!

Annamae gasped and gazed in wonder at Cougar. "You . . . are . . . going to release me?" she asked, relieved that he seemed to understand her role in helping his nephew escape imprisonment.

Tears fell from her eyes as Four Clouds came to her and untied the thong.

She rubbed her wrists as the rawhide fell to the ground. "Oh, thank you, thank you," she said, relieved that her future did not seem so bleak now. If this powerful chief finally believed what she had said about helping his nephew, then he would surely treat her well and allow her to move on with her life.

She had an aunt in St. Louis, Missouri. She hoped to stay there until she could find some employment, although she had no skills except the cooking and housekeeping her mother had taught her.

Perhaps she could become someone's housekeeper. . . .

"Four Clouds, rekindle the fire," Cougar said bluntly. "You and the others will then leave the woman alone beside it and go into hiding. You will watch to see who comes back to the campsite when they think it is safe. Then you will attack, but make certain the woman is not harmed. Bring her to me."

"What?" Annamae gasped, the color having drained from her face. He wasn't releasing her at all; nor did he believe her. He still saw her as a liar. "What do you mean? There was no one here but me and Gray Stone . . . and the cub. Please, oh, please, believe me."

Four Clouds stepped up to Cougar as his chief sat tall and straight-backed in his saddle. "Do you truly believe others were here before we arrived?" he asked tightly. "You believe they heard our horses and fled, leaving the woman and Gray Stone alone?"

"I do believe this woman and my nephew were not traveling alone," Cougar said

114

tightly. He gazed at Annamae, whose tears were now streaming down her pink cheeks, her eyes still pleading with him.

It was hard to see her as someone who could be part of such a plot as this, where a mere child was the target.

There was so much about her that suggested she was a woman of kind heart. Yet he had to make certain.

He pointed to several warriors. "Stay behind with Four Clouds," he said curtly. He pointed to those who would ride with him. "You come with me."

"So we are to hide and wait?" Four Clouds asked.

"I believe that others were with this woman," Cougar said. "I believe they are cowards who are far enough away by now that they do not know what we are planning. When they feel it is safe, they will come back to the woman. When they do, you will be close by, ready to ambush them."

"How can I make you believe that there was no one else?" Annamae said, wiping tears from her eyes. "I saved your nephew. Do you hear me? I . . . saved . . . him. He was going to be put on display in a cage at the carnival and . . . and . . . called the Wild Boy from Borneo. I could not allow that to happen. I was unhappy at the carnival myself, so I decided to leave. When I left, I took your nephew and the bear cub, which was also imprisoned behind bars at the carnival."

"The Wild Boy from Borneo?" Cougar repeated, his eyebrows lifting. "What sort of name is that?"

"It is horrible . . . a disgrace," Annamae said, feeling that she might be gaining ground with Cougar. "Just as what I was made to do was disgraceful. I . . . I . . . had to leave, and Gray Stone was more than glad to leave with me."

"He was in a cage?" Cougar demanded, rage filling his veins.

"Yes, but don't you see?" Annamae pleaded. "He is now free, except . . . except . . . for how ill he became from the bee stings. I was unable to help him. I am so glad you came along. You can take him home, so your shaman can care for him."

"How do you know of my shaman?" Cougar asked, leaning down so that he could look more directly into her eyes.

"Gray Stone told me a great deal about his people, much of it about you, his chieftain uncle," Annamae said. "He is so proud to be your nephew, and felt terrible that he had left his vision quest to go explore

116

the carnival."

What the woman said sounded logical, yet there was a chance she was just using his nephew's words to her own advantage. Possibly while Gray Stone was telling her these things, he was pleading for his life!

"Four Clouds, add wood to the fire; then go into hiding with the others," Cougar growled out. "You will know how long to wait. *You will know* when the time is right to conclude whether others are coming back to join the woman."

"My name is Annamae," she said stiffly. "I am not just a woman. I . . . I . . . have a name, and I am innocent of plotting against Gray Stone. I have grown to love the child. He is as fond of me. I pray that he will be well again."

Cougar leaned even closer to her face. "I warn you not to cry out. Do not reveal the truth that my warriors are close by, ready to ambush those who return, or you will die along with the others immediately," he said harshly.

Annamae took a step away from him, although his nearness aroused something other than fear in her heart. She was in awe of this handsome chief, although she should loathe him for what he was doing to her.

But she knew that soon he would learn

the truth about her and would surely apologize.

And as far as his actually harming her, as he warned he would do if forced, she did not believe he was capable of killing a woman. There was too much in his eyes that spoke of kindness.

And Gray Stone had told her that his uncle always tried to keep peace between his people and whites. He had told her how gentle and kind a leader he was.

Cougar gave her one long last look, then sank his heels into the flanks of his stallion and rode off with the others. The travois was dragged behind one of his warrior's steeds, while those who were left disappeared into the forest after the fire was burning high again.

Annamae sank down onto a blanket beside the fire.

She shivered.

She drew a blanket up around her shoulders.

Oh, Lord, she had never felt so alone.

How long would she be forced to sit there alone in the dark? When would the warriors who were made to stay behind come out again and take her to Cougar and sweet Gray Stone?

She missed both Gray Stone and the cub.

She looked over her shoulder in the direction she had last seen the travois.

"I hope you will make it, Gray Stone," she said, tears again falling from her eyes. "If not, I will feel so responsible."

"Damn it all to hell," a voice whispered in the night not far from where Annamae sat.

Yes, there were other eyes in the darkness besides those of the warriors who were keeping vigil.

It was Reuben Jones.

After he had heard about Annamae's disappearance, he had been searching diligently for her. But just as he had found her, the Indians had appeared.

He had seen it all, and knew that this was not the time to make himself known to Annamae. He would die an instant death if the warriors saw him.

"This isn't the right time, but now that I have finally found you, I won't let you get far from my sight," Reuben whispered, clutching his rifle. "Sooner or later, you will be with me again."

He smiled crookedly. "My pretty Annamae, my sweet interpreter of dreams, ol' Reuben here will save you from the redskins," he whispered. "There'll come a time when I'll get that opportunity, and when I do, pretty thing, I'll grab it."

And when he did finally get her to himself, he'd never let her go again.

His plans for her had nothing to do with the interpretation of dreams. She was going to be his wife . . . his plaything!

No, he could not have Annamae to himself tonight, but he would soon.

He could not live without her.

She was his destiny . . . he hers.

He wiped a stream of drool from the corner of his mouth, then smeared it on the side of his breeches leg.

"Just look at you, my love," he whispered. "An angel. You're my angel!"

CHAPTER TWELVE

The memory of the nightmare she had had again during the night was vividly clear. It was the same dream that had plagued her for so long now: of her parents being killed by renegades. Annamae scarcely touched the food that had been given to her for her morning meal.

The warriors who had been assigned to her sat beside the campfire with her, occasionally gazing at her, and then at the bowl of berries she had scarcely touched.

Four Clouds suddenly broke the silence as the sun came through the trees overhead, casting streams of golden light down onto Annamae. "Eat," he said flatly. "We will not stop for food again for a while. You must keep up your strength."

"I'm not hungry," Annamae said, swallowing hard. She *was* hungry — starving in fact. But she just couldn't stomach eating anything, not under these circumstances.

121

"All I want is my freedom," she blurted out. "I've done nothing wrong. Let me go."

"We will all leave soon, but together," Four Clouds said, chewing the last of the berries that were in his mouth. "My chief awaits our arrival and he will be looking for you at my side, so that is where you will be."

He stood up over her. "You awakened with a start," he said, searching her eyes. "I saw a look of fear in your eyes. Is that fear because of what is happening to you now, or from something that happened to you in the past?"

Even knowing that it usually helped to talk about the nightmare, Annamae remained quiet.

"You do not wish to talk? Then stay silent," Four Clouds said, walking away from her toward a stream that shone like silver beneath the sun.

He knelt beside it and cupped some water into his hands, then brought some water back and splashed the fire with it.

The flames sputtered and sizzled as parts of it were extinguished.

Then another warrior came and kicked dirt onto it, putting out the remaining flames.

"Come with me," Four Clouds said, offering a hand to Annamae. "Take up the blanket you slept upon and come with me. It is time to travel onward."

"I just wish you would listen to reason," Annamae said, ignoring his hand. She sighed as she stood up and gathered the blanket into her arms. "I'm only in the way. The one you should be thinking about is the child. You should be glad that I was able to help him flee the carnival. You should be thanking me, not forcing me to go with you."

"Gray Stone is ill because of you," Four Clouds said, leading Annamae's horse, toward her. "Secure the blanket, then mount the steed. And make haste. My chief awaits our arrival."

"He wouldn't be waiting if he had believed what I told him about Gray Stone," Annamae said, shoving the blanket inside the travel bag that hung at the side of her horse. "It was just a big waste of your time to stay behind with me. I was traveling alone with Gray Stone. No one was with us."

"No person with white skin can be trusted to speak true, and your skin is white," Four Clouds grumbled. He handed her the reins. "Mount the steed. Now."

Annamae gazed into his midnight dark eyes, and her anger dissipated somewhat

123

when she recalled the same dark eyes of another warrior, and, ah, the handsomeness of that warrior's face.

She could not help being intrigued by Chief Cougar.

Although he had spoken only words of anger and distrust to her, there had been something else in the depths of his eyes when he had gazed at her.

She felt that he wanted to believe her.

She wondered if he could have the same sort of feelings for her that she had had at times for him. When she stood so close to him she could smell his manliness, a smell of the forest, the wind, and the sun!

She wondered if he had gathered the smell of her own flesh and hair all around him, enjoying them?

Realizing it was foolish to be thinking such things about a man who seemed to want to hate her, Annamae mounted her mare. She rode away from the campsite with the warriors, Four Clouds in the lead.

"How far ahead of us do you think he is?" Annamae asked, bringing her mount up beside Four Clouds.

"Far enough, yet we will soon catch up with him," Four Clouds said, glaring at her. "Ride in silence. Conversing with a white woman is not something that interests me.

Keep . . . quiet."

They rode until the sun reached the highest part of the sky, and Annamae realized that it was noon. She was hungry, because she had not eaten the breakfast food that had been offered to her.

She felt a blush rise to her cheeks when she heard her own stomach growling; it was so loud, even Four Clouds heard. He glanced into her eyes, and then at her belly, then straight ahead again.

Just as they rounded a bend where the trees parted so they could ride through a tall stand of aspen, they spotted Chief Cougar and the others.

Annamae experienced a mixture of many emotions.

She was glad to have finally caught up with Cougar, and she was anxious to see how Gray Stone was faring.

As she rode up closer and could see the travois more clearly, she saw the bear cub nestled close to Gray Stone, who was asleep.

Then her eyes went to Cougar as he stopped his warriors and wheeled his horse around to face her. His eyes moved to hers, and he gazed intently into them.

Four Clouds rode up to Cougar. "No one came," he said quietly. "It has been proved that the woman was riding alone with Gray

Stone, or if not, those who had been with her became cowardly and decided to abandon her."

"How can I convince you that Gray Stone and I were riding alone?" she said, sighing heavily. She leaned so that she could look past Cougar at the sleeping child.

She straightened her back and gazed into Cougar's dark eyes. "How is he?" she asked. "He . . . he . . . is so still."

"He sleeps, and until we reach our home and he is examined by our shaman, there is no way to know how he truly is," Cougar said, beginning to believe now that this woman truly did care for Gray Stone. There was genuine concern not only in her voice, but in her eyes, when she asked about him.

So much of himself wanted to believe her, yet another part of him still told him to be wary of her and her story.

What was certain was his anxiety about his nephew. Until he knew that Gray Stone was going to be all right, the resentment he felt toward the woman was still there.

"We must travel onward," he said, motioning with a hand for his warriors to ride again in the direction of their village. He turned his gaze back to Annamae. "You will ride at my side so that I can keep an eye on you, for you will travel unbound now. But if you give me reason to, I shall bind your wrists, and perhaps even put a gag around your mouth."

"Oh, please don't do either," Annamae begged. "I promise you that I won't try to flee; nor will I talk anymore. I just want to hurry and get Gray Stone where he can be cared for."

Cougar gave her another lenghty stare, then turned his eyes forward as he rode onward.

Annamae rode quietly beside him. She could sense his occasional glances and wasn't sure how to feel about them.

Was he looking at her to make certain she wasn't going to try to flee?

Or was it something else that drew his eyes to her, as hers were drawn to him so often?

She couldn't seem to get enough of looking at him, even though he was her captor, and she his captive.

In time . . . yes, in time he would know the truth about everything. When his nephew awakened and told Cougar about her courage, surely everything would change between them.

But then another thought came to her, and a fearful coldness seemed to enter her heart.

What if the child never regained consciousness? What if he died?

If he did die, would Cougar see her as the one to blame?

CHAPTER THIRTEEN

After traveling for some time, Annamae found herself crossing a rich meadow as she rode beside Chief Cougar.

The meadow was very lovely in the soft evening light, with its long, waving grass and brilliant wild flowers. The air above it was filled with the songs of larks and thrushes.

The sun was sinking behind Mount Hope, lighting up the somber cloud masses with splendid color, while its rays streamed to the sides, forming a magnificent sunburst.

As she rounded a bend with the others, Annamae suddenly saw a scene she would never forget. In this luxuriant tract of meadow, and on the shore of a river, lay Chief Cougar's Blackfoot tribal camp, pitched in the form of an enormous circle.

The undulating ridge that surrounded it was brilliant with blue lupines and velvety sunflowers.

Great herds of horses dotted the green hillsides, contentedly feeding on the rich bunch grass.

Smoke from the evening fires was rising above the lodges.

A faint breeze, laden with a pleasant fragrance from the meadows, brought the sounds of an Indian village . . . shouts of men and women, crying of children, and the slow, measured beat of an Indian tom-tom.

Annamae could hardly take her eyes off what she was looking at, for never had she seen an Indian village before.

The cluster of tepees was so picturesque, each with its own painted decorations.

The blue smoke rising from their tops was perfectly reflected on the surface of the beautiful, serene river.

In the deepening twilight, the great cluster of Indian lodges, each surely about twenty-five feet in diameter, showed ghostly white against the darkening blue of the eastern sky.

As it grew quickly darker, Annamae thought the flickering lights of the many outside fires resembled fireflies in the summer dusk. Sweet grass was burning on the hot coals, its incense rising to the sky.

When the people in the village became

aware of the approaching horses and realized who it was, they came running to
greet Cougar and his warriors, stopping
only when they caught sight of the travois.

Cougar drew rein. "My people, we have
found Gray Stone, but not before he became
ill," he reported. "I have brought him home
to be treated by White Thunder. Say many
prayers that our shaman's medicine will
make him well soon."

The people began to chant softly as they
followed Cougar and the others into the village. As they walked, many of them cast
Annamae wary glances.

She was very uncomfortable beneath such
scrutiny, and was glad when Cougar took
her inside a tepee that sat a little away from
the others.

"Sit beside the fire," Cougar said, motioning with a hand toward the lodge fire and
the blankets spread around it. "I must go
and fully explain things to my people."

He started to leave, then turned and gazed
down at Annamae again as she slowly
lowered herself onto the blankets. "The
tepee you are in is being watched," he said
gruffly. "Do not attempt to escape."

"I . . . won't . . ." Annamae promised,
glancing away from him when he continued
to gaze at her. His midnight dark eyes had

not been filled with anger, but instead with something vastly different.

She hoped that in time he would reveal those feelings for her.

Suddenly he left, leaving her alone with her thoughts, fears, and hunger. She still had not eaten, and she felt emptier inside than she had ever before in her life. This emptiness came not only from hunger, but also from loneliness.

Ever since her parents' and her brother's murder she had been without a true family. From then on, the world had changed drastically for her. All she had wanted was to be like her mother; to find a man who loved her, one whom she loved with every fiber of her being.

"But now what is going to happen to me?" she whispered, tears filling her eyes once again.

She could not help herself; she was becoming more afraid by the minute, since she was now surrounded by a village full of Indians.

"And what about Gray Stone?" she whispered, trembling at the very thought of that sweet child not being able to smile again, or enjoy the love he had for the bear cub.

Her thoughts were interrupted when Cougar came back to the lodge and went to the opposite side of the fire from her. She felt the heat of a blush, for he was dressed differently from before. He was now wearing only a brief breechclout, which somewhat embarrassed Annamae, because so much of his body was not covered.

His physique, his muscles, and his sculpted face again made her aware of feelings she knew she should not have. His beautiful dark eyes bored into hers as he sank to his haunches beside the fire.

"How is Gray Stone?" she blurted out.

"The child hovers somewhere between life and death," Cougar said tightly. "Our people's shaman sits with him. He knows all that one must know about the mysteries of life and death. If at all possible, he will bring Gray Stone back to us."

"How long will we have to wait to know?" Annamae asked softly. "In the short time I've known Gray Stone, I have grown so fond of him."

Cougar wondered how sincere her words were, but all he could think about was the child and where his spirit might be at this very moment.

"My spirit left my body one time," he found himself suddenly saying, feeling the need to talk about things he scarcely shared with anyone.

"It . . . did . . . ?" Annamae said, her eyes widening in wonder. "How . . . is that possible? And if it did, how is it that you are alive?"

"One day, sometime ago, in a skirmish with renegade Ute, I was wounded," Cougar said, gazing intently into the flames of the fire, reliving the event as he spoke of it. "When I fell from my steed and lay on the ground beside it, I felt my spirit starting for the Sand Hills. But as I was departing, I turned and saw my friends and relatives mourning over my body. I did not want to bring sadness into their hearts, so I did not remain long in the spirit world, but returned again to my body."

"That is incredible." Annamae gasped. She leaned forward as Cougar's eyes lifted and he gazed deeply into hers. "You were actually dead and then came back to life? And . . . I have never heard of . . . the Sand Hills."

"My Blackfoot people believe that after death, the spirit goes eastward to the Sand Hills, a very dreary, alkali country on the plains," Cougar said softly, touched that she seemed so interested in what he was talking about. "It is inhabited by the ghosts of people and of animals, which exist together very much the same as in life. It is surrounded by quicksand so that the living cannot enter."

Then he noticed that Annamae winced as she touched one of the places where the bees had stung her. Up until now she had not complained about being uncomfortable, and he had not asked. He was too consumed with worries about Gray Stone and getting him home to even consider the woman's discomfort.

"I see that you are uncomfortable," Cougar blurted out. "I shall go for medicine for you."

Surprised that he would do this, she only stared at him as he left. When he came back, he knelt close beside her and very gently applied a creamy substance to the stings on Annamae's face and hands.

Again he was catapulted back in time, to when he had promised his Dancing Dove that they would be married when they grew up. He had always loved to touch her face and hands. They were so soft, as soft as this white woman's.

He was shaken by how his mind could go from one place to another so quickly, and how he could remember so vividly the young love of long ago.

He must forget.

He must separate his impressions of these

two women — the one with him now, and the one he had lost.

He was inexorably drawn to this white woman's loveliness and sweetness. Yet what if she was partially responsible for what had happened to Gray Stone?

What if she was a person of deceit who would say one thing when she had done another?

He had to be careful not to be lured into the trap of loving this woman, when, perhaps, she should be despised.

Annamae couldn't believe how gentle Cougar was to her, his hands so strong and powerful, yet so careful.

She was very aware of his magnificent presence.

She hoped he could, in time, believe her.

She prayed that Gray Stone would live. Besides herself, only he knew the truth about how they had happened to be together.

"The pain has been taken away so quickly by whatever you applied to the stings," Annamae blurted out. "Thank you."

Cougar nodded and set what remained of the medicine aside, to be applied later, then sat down across the fire from her again.

"Where are the carnival men who were with you and Gray Stone?" he asked after a moment's silence. "My warriors said they never returned where you were camping with Gray Stone. Was that because they felt you were not worth the trouble?"

He hated saying the words, but had to find a way to rouse her anger so that she would speak the truth to him. When women were angered, there usually was not any way to hold back their words!

"You still believe there were men with me?" Annamae said, sighing heavily. "You are so wrong. I will tell you again that there were no men. I helped the child escape that horrible carnival. I took Gray Stone away in order to save his life. As I said before, I took him from a cage in which he was being held captive."

She looked quickly at the entrance flap as it fluttered suddenly. A moment later the cub bounced inside and came to her and snuggled on her lap.

"I also saved the cub's life," she said, softly stroking its furry head.

"You are lying," Cougar accused. "No man would dare cage a Blackfoot child."

"Not only was Gray Stone caged, but also the cub," Annamae murmured. The cub's eyes looked up into hers trustingly. "I released them both and escaped the carnival people with them, for, you see, I was unhappy there myself. Leaving as I did was the only way I could get away from those people."

Frustrated because he wanted what she said to be true, but didn't know if it was, Cougar stood up over her and placed his fists on his hips. "You are a skilled liar," he said between clenched teeth. "Lie to me again and I will silence you."

She was numbed by his words and shrank away from him as he stalked out of the tepee.

"Oh, sweet cub, what am I to do?" she whispered, blinking back tears. "I cannot help being afraid. Gray Stone has to live, or I might not survive either."

A lovely Indian woman suddenly appeared in the tepee, carrying a tray of food.

Altlhough Annamae was starving, she could not eat immediately. She gazed pleadingly into the maiden's eyes. "What is to become of me if Gray Stone dies?" she asked guardedly.

"It is not for me to say," the woman said softly. "Gray Stone's mother died while he was gone. All of my people think you are responsible for her death, since you were the one who had the child. You see, the disappearance of Gray Stone was the sole reason his mother died. She died of heartbreak because she believed her son was dead and had traveled to the Sand Hills. She . . . wanted to join him there."

"No," Annamae gasped, recalling Cougar's description of the Sand Hills.

The woman went to the entrance flap, held it aside, then turned to Annamae. "I cannot say what will become of you," she murmured, then disappeared into the darkness.

A chill raced up and down Annamae's spine.

She knew for certain now that everything depended on Gray Stone.

He must live!

If not, surely she would die as well.

She took the cub into her arms and went to the entrance flap, holding it partially open.

She looked outside and saw the crowd that stood in the moonlight before one of the tepees.

She heard slow chants, prayers, and wails.

She knew then that Gray Stone was no better.

Sobbing, she turned and went back to sit by the fire again.

"Surely he is dying," she whispered to herself. "Or else why would everyone be behaving in such a way?"

She hung her head as tears fell onto the cub's face as it gazed up at her. "Little cub, I believe I might be living my own last moments of life," she murmured. "I might not even have another tomorrow!"

CHAPTER FOURTEEN

After she finished eating the food that had been left for her, Annamae realized that the sounds of wailing, chanting, and praying had increased.

When the maiden returned to get the empty wooden platter, she explained what was happening outside the shaman's tepee. The people were holding a ceremony in Gray Stone's honor, hoping that it might help him become well.

After the maiden left, Annamae decided she would like to see what she could of the ceremony. She crept from the tepee, glad that the warrior who was guarding her allowed at least that. But he put his arm out, stopping her from going any farther.

So she sat down just outside her tepee, the cub soon joining her and, snuggling again on her lap. It was as though he sensed what was happening, that his friend Gray Stone still was not well.

"He will be better soon," Annamae whispered to the cub. "He must."

What she saw was a huge outdoor fire that had been lit in the center of the village not far from the shaman's lodge.

The crowd, which seemed to her to be the entire population of this village, stood together just past the fire, their eyes directed at something that, from her vantage point, Annamae could not see.

Then as the crowd shifted to one side, Annamae gasped when she saw that Gray Stone lay on blankets just outside the shaman's lodge. The shaman was standing over him, while Cougar sat on the far side of Gray Stone.

Annamae strained her neck to try to get a better look at Gray Stone. A keen sadness entered her heart as she remembered that the child's mother was dead, and he did not even know it yet.

When he awakened, he had not only to fight to get better, but he also had to be told about his mother.

The worst thing was that he would have to be told that his mother had died by her own hand.

Annamae was afraid that he would blame himself, since he had chosen to leave the place where he ought to have stayed for his vision quest.

Annamae hoped that she would be able to go to him to comfort him at that time, and reassure him that he was not at fault. Howard Becker was the one to blame.

She hoped the child would see it that way. If not, he would have to live with a heavy guilt forevermore.

Unable to see Gray Stone well, or Cougar, Annamae peered through the darkness, wishing the glow of the huge outdoor fire illuminated the scene better.

At this moment the shaman, White Thunder, was standing over Gray Stone, his manner dignified and grave.

He was wearing only a breechclout; his long hair, tinged with gray, fell loose over his bare shoulders.

From his neck hung a medicine whistle made from the wing bone of an eagle. At the back of his head a single eagle feather stood erect, and he wore around his waist strips of otter skin with small bells attached.

Across his bare breast was a beaded mink skin, with small bells fastened to its paws and one also to its mouth.

With a forked stick covered with paint, White Thunder selected a live coal from the fire and placed it on the ground in front of Gray Stone.

He then took dried sweetgrass from a small buckskin bag and held it aloft, to command attention. As a signal that he was ready to begin the ceremony, he placed the sweetgrass upon the hot coal. As it rose, the smoke filled the air with a pleasing fragrance.

A young brave then brought a small buckskin bag, which he gave to White Thunder. The shaman took from the bag some red clay, the sacred paint that the Blackfoot believed gave White Thunder his power to ward off sickness and to bring long life.

As the people stood quietly by, watching, White Thunder painted his chin, representing the sun's daily course through the heavens.

He then painted his forehead, which represented the rising sun. Finally, he painted his cheeks, representing the setting sun.

He then took a beaver skin and passed it down both sides of his head, shoulders and arms, to the hands, ending with an upward movement.

After he recited a prayer, he unrolled a bundle containing buffalo and elk hides, which were spread out before him, between himself and the child.

Drummers in the distance began beating a steady rhythm on their tom-toms as the people began to chant and sing along with White Thunder. Their chief sat quietly by, watching Gray Stone and silently praying for him.

The first chant the people and White Thunder sang was about a porcupine sitting on a hill and watching a beaver at work. The porcupine said, "I will take my bow and arrow and kill you. . . ."

But the beaver jumped into the stream and swam off under the water and escaped.

They also sang the song of the war eagle, describing how it soared high in the air above the mountain peaks and at times swooped down toward the earth to seek its prey.

White Thunder rose and began dancing around the fire, singing at intervals, and at other times blowing on his medicine whistle.

And then all was silent.

White Thunder went to kneel beside Gray Stone.

He placed a hand on the child's brow and began to pray. "Hear us, Great Spirit in the sun. Pity us and help us. Listen and grant this child his life. Look down in pity on this sick child. Grant me the power to drive out the evil spirit and give him back his health!"

Annamae felt the mystery of the moment. For the first time, she believed that Gray Stone would survive.

As everyone began slowly rising and dispersing, Annamae continued to watch.

When Cougar rose and knelt beside Gray Stone to carry him back inside the shaman's lodge, Annamae knew the ceremony was over. Now all they could do was wait to see if their Great Spirit had listened and would grant them what they had prayed so hard for.

Tears in her eyes, she rose slowly to her feet, the cub in her arms, and returned inside her own assigned tepee.

She sat down beside the fire again, hoping that tomorrow would bring the miracle they all wanted so badly.

"Please let it happen," she prayed, gazing heavenward through the smoke hole over-head.

When she saw a brightly flashing star, seemingly standing out from the rest, she smiled. It made her feel better to know that she had something to gaze at. She would not feel as alone as she would have without it.

Sorely tired as he prepared to spend another night beneath the stars, Howard stopped, startled, when he saw the glow of a huge outdoor fire in the distant sky. He had been searching for what seemed an eternity for Annamae, and had decided to turn back at dawn tomorrow and give up on ever finding her.

Yet now he wondered if his patience had paid off.

Could that fire be from the very village that the escaped Indian boy was from?

Could the child be there even now?

Would Annamae be with him?

The thought that he might be this close to an Indian village frightened Howard. If the savages knew that he had imprisoned the child, there was no telling what they would do to him.

Yet for Annamae's sake, and for Ellie's, because his wife wanted Annamae back, he had to go on. He had to find out if she was there. If he hadn't agreed to the search, Ellie never would have let him have another peaceful night of sleep. She would have pestered and pestered him. Besides, he wouldn't have wanted to look like a coward.

He turned to those who were traveling with him. He drew rein and stopped his steed. "Do you see that glow in the sky?" he asked as the others stopped as well. "I believe we've found us an Indian village.

And I think it's near the spot where we were camped when I first caught the boy."

He nodded from man to man. "We'll travel onward, gents," he said. He frowned. "I know you're afraid. So am I. But isn't getting Annamae back with us worth it?"

"Not if we lose our scalps in the process," Snake Man said.

"You knew the risks when you agreed to come with me," Howard barked out. "Now get some spine and follow me. I'm pretty sure Annamae is not far from us now. We must at least go and take a gander and see if I'm right . . . or wrong."

Following Howard's lead, they all rode onward.

CHAPTER FIFTEEN

After a restless night, Annamae stared into the flames of the fire in her tepee. Beside her was an empty bowl that had held the breakfast stew she'd just finished.

She had decided she must eat in order to keep up her strength instead of brooding and worrying so much.

She must start thinking positively.

If she showed courage despite her circumstances, perhaps Cougar would let her live; perhaps he would even let her leave and go on her way to Missouri.

Sudden happy shouts coming from outside her tepee interrupted Annamae's thoughts.

She looked toward the closed entrance flap, her pulse racing as the shouts of happiness continued.

"Can it be . . . ?" she whispered as she hurried to the flap and shoved it aside.

Her eyes widened when she saw a crowd

gathering just outside the shaman's lodge. She was sure that Gray Stone's condition had improved, and keen relief washed over Annamae.

Gray Stone must have awakened!

He was going to be all right!

Tears rushed to Annamae's eyes. The child would now be able to clear her of blame, but even more important, Gray Stone would live. She had grown to love the child during the short time she had been with him.

Eager to go to him, she stepped outside, just in time to see Cougar walking toward her.

She stopped and waited for him. Her eyes locked with his after she wiped the tears from her own.

In them she saw a softness . . . a caring . . . and did she also see a look of apology?

Her heart pounded as he reached her and stopped.

"Gray Stone is all right," he said thickly. "And . . . after he heard that you were here, he told me the truth about your kindness. He has asked to see you."

"Oh, I am so glad that he is all right," Annamae said softly. "I just wish that terrible day had never happened. Had it not been for the cub finding the beehive, Gray

Stone wouldn't have been stung. Oh, I'm so glad he is going to be fine."

"I want to apologize for not believing you," Cougar said, his eyes searching hers. "For what you have done for my nephew, releasing him from captivity, you will be paid well in horses and pelts. You can choose which horses and which pelts. I want you to have the best."

"I want nothing for what I did," Annamae said, feeling overwhelmed by relief that Cougar finally believed her. "I . . . I . . . want nothing except to see Gray Stone."

"I insist that you be paid well," Cougar said, his voice drawn.

Annamae smiled softly at him, then walked with Cougar toward the crowd, which parted to make way for their chief and the woman they now knew had saved Gray Stone from a torturous life at the hands of the carnival people.

Annamae turned to Cougar as they stopped just outside the shaman's tepee. "Does Gray Stone know about his mother?" she asked, gazing into Cougar's eyes.

"No, he has not been told," Cougar said, placing a gentle hand on her shoulder. His gesture drew soft gasps from his people. They were clearly shocked that he should be so attentive to a white woman. "But he will be soon. I wanted to make certain he was strong enough to hear such a thing. But it must be soon, for we have delayed her burial for too long as it is."

"I won't say anything to him about it," Annamae murmured. "I just want to go and hug him and tell him that I love him."

"Enter now, for he eagerly awaits you," Cougar said, holding back the entrance flap for her.

Just as Annamae turned to step inside, the cub scooted past her, almost tripping her in its rush to be with Gray Stone. It was as though the animal knew that the child was awake and eager to see the cub, as well.

Smiling, Annamae went inside.

She stopped as she gazed down at Gray Stone, who was holding the cub in his arms. It was such a sweetly familiar picture to see Gray Stone and the cub together. They had grown so fond of each other before the incident with the bees.

Now they could be together again, as often as each liked.

Annamae took another step into the tepee so that Gray Stone could see her.

"Annamae," Gray Stone said, reaching a hand out for her. "I did not mean to frighten you by staying asleep for so long. But I am going to be all right. I am weak, but soon I will be strong again, as I was before the stings."

Annamae went and sat down beside his bed of blankets. The shaman remained where he was sitting on the other side of the fire.

"Gray Stone, I was so afraid for you," she said, her voice breaking. She placed a gentle hand on his cheek, where the stings were no longer visible. "But here you are, almost as good as new."

"Thank you for all you did for me," Gray Stone said, his voice breaking. He gazed at her face carefully. "Did my shaman doctor your stings as well? I no longer see them."

"No, not your shaman, but instead your uncle," Annamae said, touched anew as she recalled the gentle way Cougar had applied the medicine to her stings. "At least in that respect he was kind to me. Otherwise, he believed me guilty for what happened to you. He . . . he . . . even believed that I plotted with others in order to capture you for the carnival."

"I know, but he believes differently now," Gray Stone said softly. "I told him everything — about how I was caught by the evil man, and how you set me free and chanced everything to help me find my way home."

Annamae suddenly felt a heavy hand on

her shoulder.

She turned her eyes up and found Cougar there.

She blushed, for she saw that he was no longer guarded with her. Instead he was smiling at her.

"We must leave now and let my nephew rest," Cougar said. "It will be a few sunrises before he is well enough to leave his bed."

"Yes," Gray Stone said, looking past Cougar and Annamae toward the entrance flap. "My mother must know by now that I am all right."

He then gazed up into Cougar's eyes. "Where is she?" he asked softly. "Has no one told her yet that I am well?"

Cougar and Annamae gave each other troubled glances, and then White Thunder came to stand on the other side of Gray Stone's bed of blankets. "I will speak with him now," he said thickly.

Cougar nodded, took Annamae by the hand, and left the tepee with her.

Before they had walked even a few feet from the shaman's lodge, a cry of despair came from it.

"I hope that the news about his mother doesn't make him ill all over again," Annamae said, looking over her shoulder at the closed flap. "I know the pain of losing a mother."

She turned her eyes forward, lowered them, then said, "Also my father and baby brother."

"I am sad for you that you have had to experience such losses," Cougar said, placing a hand at her elbow and guiding her toward his lodge. "For I, too, know the heartache that comes with losing family — first my father and mother, and then my beloved sister."

"Life is hard too often," Annamae said, her eyes widening when she realized that he wasn't taking her to the tepee that had been her home since she had come to his village, but instead, to his own.

She was very aware of his people watching, and she wondered how they felt about his taking her to his own lodge.

But things had changed. They all knew her role in saving Gray Stone from a dreadful life at the carnival. They surely saw her in a different light now than when she was being held captive.

She immediately noticed the difference between this tepee and the first one she'd been in. Cougar's was much, much larger, and it sat away from the others.

As they stepped inside, Annamae gasped. Every inch of the inside of the lodge was painted.

When Cougar saw her stop and stare at the paintings, he led her on inside, then stopped and motioned with a hand toward them.

"I have painted the top of my lodge yellow like the sunlight, with clusters of the seven stars painted on both sides, which represent the north, whence the blizzards come," he explained. "At the back I have painted a red disk for the sun, to the center of which I attached the tail of the sacred buffalo. As you see, at the bottom I have painted the rolling ridges of the prairie, with their rounded tops and broad yellow bands."

He took her hand and led her farther into the tepee, stopping when they reached the fire pit.

He again gestured with a hand toward more paintings. "Beneath the yellow top and on the four sides, where the four main lodge poles stand, I painted four green claws with yellow legs, which represent the thunderbird," he said. "Above the entranceway, which is made of spotted buffalo calfskin, is a buffalo head painted red, with black horns and eyes in green, the color of ice."

"I see tails of horses tied at either side over the entrance flap," Annamae said, fascinated by the decorations. "There are also bunches of crow feathers, with small bells attached that tinkled when we came through the entrance flap. It is all so beautiful."

"And meaningful," Cougar said, leading her down to sit on a thick layer of pelts beside the fire. He then sat beside her. "Does it offend you or frighten you?"

"No, just the opposite," Annamae murmured. "I find it entrancing and beautiful."

A soft voice spoke from beyond the entranceway, announcing that food had been brought to them.

"Enter," Cougar said, smiling at one of the village maidens, who had brought a tray of food.

After she set it down and left, Cougar slid the platter closer to Annamae. "Eat," he said, taking a piece of cooked venison from the platter.

Annamae smiled at him and took a piece of meat herself, then fell into an awkward silence.

Cougar felt the sudden awkwardness, for now that he knew Annamae was innocent of any wrongdoing toward his nephew, he knew that he could allow himself to explore his feelings for her.

He had been attracted to her even before he knew for certain that she was a good, caring person. He had seen her tenderness toward the cub and the affection in her eyes whenever she spoke of Gray Stone.

But he had not allowed himself to think of anything beyond her guilt. He hadn't wanted to end up a fool for caring about her if she was bad.

She had been a part of a carnival troop, hadn't she?

But now he knew why. Gray Stone had told him.

She had been raised by those who owned the carnival and had had no choice but to participate.

He did wonder, though, about her dream interpretations, for Gray Stone had told him about them.

He wouldn't ask her about them just now. Perhaps he wouldn't even want to know the answers. Perhaps he had been too quick to put aside his doubts about her.

"I will escort you to your tepee now. You are free to leave the village whenever you wish to," Cougar blurted out. He needed to put some distance between himself and Annamae.

He saw a strange look in her eyes and was not certain how to interpret it.

"All right," Annamae said, stunned that he was ushering her from his lodge so abruptly.

Had she said something wrong?

Or was it because she had not said enough?

They left his lodge and walked to hers, stopping just outside the entrance flap.

When he gazed into her eyes, then hurried away, Annamae was even more confused by his attitude.

How did this powerful chief really feel toward her?

And . . . how could she tell him that she didn't want to leave his village?

She had no one out there who cared whether she lived or died, and even if she did make it to Missouri, she wondered whether she would be welcome at her aunt's house.

No. She truly had no one left in the world who cared for her.

"Except for Gray Stone . . ." she whispered. "And perhaps even . . . Cougar . . . ?"

CHAPTER SIXTEEN

With the dawn, a light breeze came from Mount Hope, making a low humming sound in the tightly stretched canvas of the tepee.

Annamae had just eaten her morning meal. The maiden who had brought her food had explained to her what the meal consisted of.

The maiden had said that she herself had prepared this soup for Annamae. She had pounded dried venison almost to a flour and kept it in water until the nourishing juices were extracted, then mixed some pounded maize into it.

After Annamae was alone, she had truly enjoyed the soup, finding it rich and tasty to the tongue.

Once she had finished breakfast, she put on a clean dress taken from her travel bag, and brushed her long black hair until it shone by the light of the morning fire.

How different her circumstances were today from what they had been yesterday. The day before she had been so afraid that she might not get out of this village alive, and here she was, free to go, and . . . and . . . yes, she had fallen in love with the handsome Blackfoot chief.

She had known she had feelings for Cougar even when she was not sure whether or not he would allow her to live.

From the beginning, there had just been something about him that had spoken to her heart.

And now?

The way he looked at her made her insides melt, for she was almost certain that he felt something for her, too.

Annamae looked slowly around her. She was alone in the tepee where she had been held prisoner, but now she was free to come and go as she pleased.

She stared into the flames of the fire, deep in thought about what course she should take now.

She did not want to leave the village.

She so easily saw herself adjusting to this life, even though it was vastly different from that which she had always known.

It was certain that if she could adjust to living the life of a carnival person, she could learn the ways of the Indian people.

Suddenly her thoughts were disturbed when the cub rushed through the entrance flap and playfully batted at Annamae's arm with a paw.

"You need to be played with, don't you?" Annamae murmured, grabbing him and rolling him over onto his back so she could tickle his belly. "Is Gray Stone resting? Is that why you are here with me, instead of with him?"

She could not help worrying about Gray Stone after hearing his cry of despair the day before.

She hadn't seen the boy since, for although she loved him dearly and felt protective of him, the people of this village did not realize the closeness she and Gray Stone felt for each other. No one had thought to tell her what was happening now.

"I wonder if he is truly all right?" Annamae whispered to herself, wishing she could march right over to the shaman's lodge and demand to see Gray Stone and talk with him.

But she knew she could not interfere in such a way, especially now. Gray Stone was surely being prepared for the funeral rites of his mother, which Annamae knew were to be held tomorrow.

"Tomorrow," she murmured, shivering at the thought of being part of such a sad event.

Were Blackfoot funeral rites different from the funerals of white people? Would she even be allowed to participate?

Her eyes were drawn quickly to the entrance flap when a familiar voice spoke her name from outside.

Annamae moved to her feet and went to hold the entrance flap aside. She found the same lovely maiden who had attended her since her arrival at the village. But this time she held something besides food.

Stretched out across her arms lay a lovely Indian dress, pure white, with beads in different-colored designs across the front. On top of the dress rested moccasins with the same beaded design.

"I have brought a dress and moccasins for you to wear tomorrow at the funeral rites of Gray Stone's mother," the woman said. "My chief asked me to bring these to you."

"Yes, tomorrow," Annamae said softly, searching the woman's lovely dark eyes. "And I am to be there?"

"Yes," the woman said, holding the dress and moccasins out to Annamae.

Annamae swallowed hard as she accepted them. "How is Gray Stone doing, now that he knows his mother is . . . gone?" she asked.

"He understands death and how to accept it, for he gave up his father to the Sand Hills, too," the woman murmured.

"Yes, the Sand Hills," Annamae said, nodding. She recalled Cougar's explanation of the Sand Hills, where those who died joined those who had gone on before them.

She looked quickly at the woman again. "You have never told me your name," she said softly.

"Blue Blossom," the woman replied, smiling shyly; then she turned and left without speaking another word.

"Blue Blossom . . ." Annamae repeated, going back to the fire.

She knelt and spread the dress out before her on the bulrush mats that covered the earthen floor.

"This is so beautiful," she whispered. "And . . . and . . . Cougar himself wants me to wear it?"

The cub came and pranced across the dress before Annamae could stop him.

"Shame on you," she said, whisking him up and into her arms.

She carried him to the other side of the fire and placed him on a blanket. "Stay there," she said softly, yet with an air of command that the cub now understood.

164

"Rest. We'll play later."

She went back to the dress and gently lifted it into her arms. Taking it to the back of the tepee, she folded it carefully and laid it down on the mats, placing the moccasins on it.

She knelt there and ran her fingers slowly across the beads. They were so beautiful.

She almost felt it would be wrong to wear something so beautiful to a funeral.

Shivers of dread encompassed her as she thought of her parents and where they lay buried, oh, so alone, in the ground. She had not been able to attend those burials, for she had fainted after seeing the massacre.

When Howard and Ellie had came upon the scene, they had been kind enough to bury Annamae's mother and father and brother before traveling onward.

Sighing, Annamae sat down again beside the fire, again lost in thoughts of what lay ahead for her.

She had no idea of the customs that would be involved in an Indian burial.

And she hated to think of Gray Stone's sorrow. When she was allowed to go to him, she would do everything she could to re-assure him that what had happened was no one's fault except Howard Becker's.

The hours passed slowly for Annamae.

She was alone the rest of the day, except for when her meals were brought to her by Blue Blossom, who stayed only long enough to hand the food over to Annamae and to retrieve the dirty dishes.

And now it was dark.

The moon cast a white sheen down the smoke hole overhead, and when Annamae looked upward she saw not only the full moon, but also the glitter of stars.

When night fell, she sought out the one bright star she'd seen before. She spoke to it, as though she were speaking to those she'd lost.

"Tomorrow Gray Stone will know the full extent of his loss," she whispered. "When his mother is lowered into the ground, he will understand that he'll never see her again, or be held by her."

She wiped tears from her eyes. "I miss you all so much," she murmured.

Suddenly she flinched. Somewhere in the distance several wolves howled in unison at the moon, and owls hooted eerily from a nearby tree.

The cub sensed Annamae's discomfort and came to her, crawling onto her lap.

"Do you, too, miss your mother and father?" Annamae asked, stroking the cub's grayish brown fur. "Do you wish to go back to them?"

She brought the cub up closer to her face and kissed the tip of his nose. "I promise you, sweetie, if at all possible I will help you find your way back home," Annamae reassured him. "In time I hope I can keep that promise, for I know that even though Gray Stone and I love you so much, you would be much better off with those of your own kind. If we can't find your parents, at least you can live the life of a wild bear."

The cub growled softly, making Annamae laugh.

"Listen to you," she said, cuddling the cub close in her arms. "You are sounding so fierce tonight."

In the dark shadows of the mountain, eyes gleamed as they gazed at the tepee in which Annamae now slept so soundly, the cub still in her arms.

"Gotcha," Howard said, glaring at the tepee, where the fire cast soft light on the inside cover of the lodge.

He had watched earlier, when the fire was brighter. He could make out Annamae's outline against the fabric of the tepee.

But he could no longer see her. He had watched her stretch out near the fire, and knew she must be asleep by now.

He had sent his men to check on the Blackfoot warriors who stood as sentries at various places on the outskirts of the village. They had also spotted the night herder, who stood not far away in the darkness, watching the horses.

Thus far, Howard and his men were safe, for they had not been seen.

And now all that Howard could think about was getting Annamae and hightailing it out of there.

Yes, this was the night he was going to steal her away. Surely she had discovered that life with him and the carnival was not all that bad, after all.

Anything would be better than living with savages!

He just felt fortunate that she was not harmed in any way. When he had seen her coming and going from one of the tepees, he had noticed nothing wrong with her, except that she looked a mite too content for someone who was surrounded by people who would as soon kill her as look at her.

He wondered about the child. If he could, he would like to take him back to the carnival.

But it was probably too risky to chance that. He would have to be content with Annamae, and by God, tonight he would

168

have her!

"I'll go on alone," he whispered to Snake Man, who sent the word down the line to the others who had accompanied Howard on his search for their dream interpreter.

She was too important to the carnival to be lost.

"Be careful," Snake Man whispered back. "I don't want to part with my scalp. Remember that."

Howard nodded and scooted along the ground in the direction of Annamae's tepee.

Another set of eyes gleamed in the dark. Reuben was well hidden in his hiding place, observing Howard and his men.

"He's gone and spoiled my plan," Reuben grumbled to himself. "I was going to get her tonight myself. Now Howard has beat me to it."

He smiled crookedly as a spiral of drool crept from his mouth and down across his chin. "Let him do the hard part — get Annamae — and then I'll do the rest," he said. "Yep, Howard Becker and the others will die as soon as Annamae is safely away from the village."

He settled in behind the bushes, where he was making his camp. "Yep, for now I'll wait," he whispered. "And then ol' Reuben'll kill those carnival fellas, one by one, as they sleep. Finally Annamae will be all mine!"

CHAPTER SEVENTEEN

Annamae tossed in her sleep, shivering and moaning, as she became caught up in a terrible dream that Reuben was there in the tepee with her, threatening her.

Suddenly she awakened, beads of cold sweat on her brow. She was so glad it was only a dream. She never wanted to see that horrible man again, and doubted that she would, unless . . .

"Annamae?"

A voice speaking her name in the tepee made Annamae's breath quicken.

She turned quickly and gasped when she saw Howard Becker standing there at the back of the tepee, where he had made a long slit in the buckskin covering.

Before she could say anything he was there, a hand clasped over her mouth.

"Shh," he said in a low voice.

When she reached up and tried to jerk his hand away, she found that she could not

171

move it.

"I don't like to do this to you, Annamae, but I can't chance your screaming," Howard said, peering into her frightened eyes. "I've come to rescue you from the savages, Annamae. Come on. I've made a slit large enough for both of us to get through. We're leaving this hellhole of a place where the savages have kept you captive."

The word *captive* made her eyes widen even more. She was no longer a captive. She now wanted to stay in the Blackfoot village.

She wanted . . . a future with Chief Cougar and his nephew, Gray Stone!

She wanted to play a major role in all of the Blackfoot people's lives, because she wanted to be their chief's . . . bride!

Yes!

She wanted to marry him!

If her intuition was right, Cougar cared for her deeply, hopefully enough to ask her to be his bride.

Although in the white world she knew that it was forbidden for a white woman to love an Indian, she could not help loving him. She wanted him with every fiber of her being.

But now? With Howard Becker interfering in her life once again? Oh, how could it be happening?

And he wouldn't even allow her to speak for herself, not while he held his hand so tightly over her mouth.

"Now that you know who is rescuing you, you have no reason to scream, so I'll remove my hand," Howard said softly, dropping his hand away from her mouth. "Come on, Annamae. Time is wastin'. I was lucky to have made it into the village without being seen. I only hope we can leave with as much luck. That damn moon. It's at its fullest tonight."

"How did you make it into the village without being caught? Sentries are posted everywhere," Annamae said, gazing intently into his eyes to guage his mood. She knew how ugly he could become when he did not get his way with someone.

She had grown used to avoiding him on those days when he was angry. It had been such a wonderful feeling to run away from him altogether.

And now he was there once again, a part of her life and a threat to her happiness.

"Luck was with me. I guess the savage sentries were asleep on the job," Howard said. He reached for her and drew her into his embrace. "Lord, Annamae, I'm so glad that I've found you."

Not wanting to be anywhere near this

man, Annamae wiggled her way free. "Maybe you didn't see the sentries, Howard, but they are there, and they're not the sort who would fall asleep on the job," she said tightly. "Believe me, they saw you. You've made a terrible mistake coming here like this."

"Annamae, we're wastin' time talking," Howard said, reaching out and taking her by an arm. "Come on. Let's get out of here. It gives me the creeps being in an Indian village. I'm going to get you away from this place. Don't you see, pretty thing? Once again I'm saving your life."

"No, Howard, I'm not going anywhere with you," Annamae said, yanking herself free. "I hated carnival life. I fled from it on my own. I wasn't forced to go, especially not by Chief Cougar."

"You had said you wanted to leave, but I didn't believe you," Howard said, searching her eyes. "Honey, oh, precious Annamae, tell me you're jesting. Come on. I don't like being here so close to those who surely enjoy taking scalps. Look at your hair. It's so pretty. In time the savages might even take it from you."

"You are so wrong about these people," Annamae said, sighing heavily. "Yes, it's true that some Indians take scalps, but not this

174

tribe. They are a people of peace. Why on earth do you think I'm all right? Because they chose not to harm me. I was treated decently from the beginning."

"And you are choosing to stay with them instead of your own people?" Howard demanded, running his fingers through his thick red hair. "Annamae, they've done something to your brain. You are not talkin' sense. And, by damn, you are going with me tonight. I won't allow you to stay. Do you hear? I won't allow it."

"You are not in a position to tell me what I can or cannot do," Annamae said, placing her fists on her hips. "I'm a free woman now, Howard. Know that I am grateful to you for caring for me after my parents died. But I grew so tired of that life you gave me. I no longer wanted to pretend I knew about dreams when I took all my knowledge from books. I felt cheap doing that, Howard. I felt like a thief."

"But, Annamae, why did you sneak off in the dead of the night?" Howard asked. "Why did you steal the boy and the bear and two horses? Did you hate us so much?"

"It wasn't hate, Howard," Annamae said softly. "It was just that I wanted more out of life than what I was doing. I wanted a life of my own."

"Ellie was sure you were abducted," Howard said, scratching his brow. "You weren't taken as a way to get back at me for stealin' the Indian boy from right beneath the Indians' noses?"

"No Indian abducted me," Annamae said. "It was time for me to move on, and when I saw the child in that cage, I had to help him escape. I wanted not only to free myself, but also to take the child back to his home, and eventually release the cub close to where his home might have been."

"You are talking such hogwash," Howard grumbled. "I saw you being guarded by a savage outside this very tepee."

"Yes, I was at first, but finally, after the Blackfoot people learned the truth about what happened, that I was bringing their young brave home, I was released. I can leave the village anytime I want," Annamae said. "And as the person who locked Gray Stone in a cage, Howard, you're in hot water just being here. You'd better leave now, while you have the chance."

She gasped when his eyes narrowed angrily and he grabbed her tightly by the wrist. "Not without you, I'm not," he snarled. "Come on. I won't ask you again. I'll drag you if I have to."

"Howard, no matter what you do, I'm not

going anywhere with you," Annamae cried. "If you don't release me I'll scream. You know what would happen then."

"You wouldn't dare," Howard said, half dragging her toward the slit in the wall of the tepee.

"Unhand the woman."

Cougar's powerful, commanding voice made Howard gasp and turn with Annamae. The Blackfoot chief was standing in his breechclout just inside the entranceway.

At first Howard just stood there, frozen to the floor from fear, his hand still gripping Annamae's wrist.

Then he turned and yanked hard on Annamae's arm, stopping only when a heavy hand fell on his shoulder. The weight of that grip yanked him away from Annamae.

"I told you to unhand the woman," Cougar growled out as he twisted Howard's arm behind his back.

Howard went pale and began to tremble when he heard screams of fear outside the lodge. The men who had come with him on what had proved to be a misguided venture had surely also been caught.

Annamae looked at Cougar, and then at Howard. She was stunned silent, because she truly had no idea what Cougar's next move might be.

He had caught a man, the very man who had stolen his nephew away, trying to force Annamae to leave the village.

"Annamae, don't just stand there; say something on my behalf," Howard cried as sweat ran from his forehead and down his cheeks. "Tell him who I am. Tell him what I did for you after your parents were murdered. Tell him how grateful you are for what I did. Tell him, Annamae. Oh, Lord, speak up. Tell him I'm only here because I thought you were being held captive. I wanted to save you. Now do what you can to save me. You owe me, Annamae. You . . . owe . . . me."

Annamae saw the dilemma that Howard was in. Although she had grown to dislike the man terribly, and never wanted to be with him and his carnival group again, she could not help worrying about his welfare.

She would never forget that he had taken her in and cared for her after her family was slaughtered.

"Cougar, please let Howard go," Annamae blurted out. "Yes, he was wrong to capture Gray Stone and place him in a cage, but he has seen the error of his ways."

She turned quickly to Howard. "You have, haven't you?" she asked, hoping that he would say the right thing. For even though Cougar was known for his peaceful ways, surely he felt a need for vengeance against this man who had placed his nephew behind bars.

"Yes, certainly," Howard said, breathing fast. His heart was pounding so hard he was afraid it might leap from his chest.

He tried to turn so that he could face Cougar, but the Indian was holding him too tightly. His wrist was throbbing from the hard grip. "Please let me go," he pleaded. "I promise to leave quickly. And I am truly sorry about having taken the boy."

Howard gazed at Annamae again. "Please, oh, please, let me and those who are with me go. And also Annamae," he blurted out. "She doesn't belong here. She is white. No white woman should live with redskins."

"Annamae wants to go nowhere with you," Cougar said, finally releasing his grip on Howard.

But he placed his hands on the man's shoulders and quickly turned Howard to face him.

He spoke down into Howard's face. "Annamae stays," he said flatly.

Howard gazed with fear into Cougar's dark, hate-filled eyes. When Cougar lowered his hands from his shoulders, he turned again and looked pleadingly at Annamae.

"Annamae, don't you have something to say?" he said, his voice breaking. "Didn't you hear the Indian say you were staying with him and his people? Can't you see they are keeping you to pay me back for locking up the boy? Tell them you want to leave, after all. You don't belong here, Annamae. Your skin is white. It is forbidden for a white woman to live among redskins."

When Annamae didn't respond, Howard turned even paler. Clearly she did not want to leave.

The Indian, he thought suddenly to himself. Yes, the Indian! He was handsome. Had she fallen in love with him?

"Annamae, I beg of you, tell the Indian that you want to go," Howard said, trying one more time to make her see sense.

"No, I won't," Annamae said, boldly holding her chin up in defiance of Howard. "And especially not with you. Like I said before, Howard, I want no part of carnival life ever again. Didn't my leaving prove that to you?"

Then she stepped past Howard and stood directly in front of Cougar. She gazed into his dark eyes. "I do want to stay," she murmured. "But will you please let Howard go? You'll never see him again. Nor will I.

Howard is going far away, out of Indian territory."

She turned to Howard. "You are, aren't you?" she asked, searching his eyes.

He glared at her for a moment, then nodded. "Sure, yes, I will leave, and when I get back to my people, we will most certainly go onward, as far away from Indians as we can get," he said. Yet there was no true apology or conviction in his voice.

"Neither you nor those with you are going anywhere," Cougar said, stepping past Annamae and standing tall over Howard. "You leave this tepee now, from the front, not the back, where you wrongfully cut into the buckskin covering. You will join the others outside by the large outdoor fire."

"Others . . . ?" Howard gulped out as he gazed fearfully into Cougar's eyes.

"Yes, others," Cougar said flatly. "Those who came with you to steal Annamae away, and perhaps even my nephew, have been taken captive."

"No," Howard cried. "Never your nephew. All I want is Annamae . . . and . . . my freedom, as well the freedom of my men."

Annamae was beginning to be truly afraid for Howard and the others. He had no idea of the string of events, all bad, that had been set in motion when he locked up Gray

Stone that evening.

Gray Stone had been badly injured while escaping Howard's clutches and could have died, and the child's mother had killed herself out of despair that she would never see her beloved son again.

Yes, Annamae now felt that Howard might not get out of this village alive, although Cougar seemed too gentle a man to out-and-out kill men unless faced with danger to himself or his people.

As Howard crept past her and Cougar toward the closed entrance flap, Annamae moved to Cougar. "What are your plans for Howard and the others?" she asked quietly.

"The white men are now my captives," Cougar said. "They will be made to see the sadness they created by caging my nephew. They will be made to witness my sister's burial."

Trembling, Howard brushed past Cougar and Annamae and stepped outside.

He stopped there and looked at his men, apology in his eyes.

Yes, after hearing Cougar call the child his nephew, Howard now truly understood the danger he was in. He felt trapped, and he saw that Annamae had no control over the situation.

For the first time in his life, Howard felt

182

completely helpless.

Annamae walked with Cougar out of the tepee.

She stood back and watched, horrified, as the men she knew so well — and liked — were all tied together. Their ankles were bound, and then they were all staked to the ground.

She cringed when some of the men cried and begged, while others kept silent, too afraid to speak.

Annamae knew that she could say nothing that would help them. She had to wait and see what their end would be. She was afraid now, for the first time, of Cougar.

She clung to what he had said in the hope that this was all he would require of his captives . . . that after they witnessed the burial of Gray Stone's precious mother, Cougar's need for vengeance would be satisfied. She prayed that he would then release them so they could go back to their own families.

"Annamae . . . Annamae . . . !" Howard pleaded, his voice sounding foreign to her, for she had never seen him afraid of anything, or anyone. . . .

CHAPTER EIGHTEEN

The sun was hidden by large, white puffy clouds.

The air was sweet and pure, with the scent of pine wafting through the air from the nearby forest.

Birds flitted playfully here and there.

A deer's dark eyes could be seen as the animal peered through a break in the berry bushes that he was feasting upon, watching the slow procession of Blackfoot people, whose destination was their burial grounds.

There were two travois being carried ahead of the procession; one was for Gray Stone, who was still too weak to walk, and the other was for his mother, who was wrapped in her burial attire.

Chief Cougar and White Thunder led the procession, and only now and then could Annamae get a glimpse of Cougar.

After Cougar had forced Howard and the other men to stand tied to stakes the whole night long, he seemed very different from the kind and gentle man she had known . . . up until now.

He had said they were tied there in order to witness Gray Stone's sorrow.

Oh, surely once the funeral was over they would be released!

She tried not to think about Cougar at all, just wanting to get the burial rites behind her so that she could make a decision about her future. She no longer felt she could ever truly love Cougar in the way she had before. He had proved to be someone quite different from the person she'd thought he was.

Blue Blossom had came to Annamae before the people gathered outside for the funeral rites. She had helped Annamae with her hair after Annamae had dressed herself in the lovely beaded dress and moccasins. At the same time an elderly woman, who was skilled at sewing, had worked quietly nearby, repairing the damage to the tepee that had been done by Howard Becker.

A chill swept through Annamae when she thought of the way Howard and his friends had looked this morning. It had been a shock to see the shape they were in.

It was obvious that they had not been allowed to relieve themselves. Their clothes were wet and soiled with urine.

And when Howard caught her standing there, looking at him, he did not give her a pleading look. He glared at her as though she were the enemy.

It took her only a minute to realize why. She already had on the Indian dress and moccasins, and her long black hair hung in braids down her back, all of which made her look like an Indian maiden!

Her heart pounding, she had stepped quickly back inside the tepee.

She still could not believe that Cougar could be so inhumane toward Howard and the others. She felt so bad for them.

She knew Howard had done wrong by putting Gray Stone in a cage as though he were an animal. But even so, he should not be treated in such a way.

Still, Annamae knew that some Indians might have done much worse to their prisoners. Howard might even be dead were he among Indians who hated whites with a passion.

As she continued walking with the others, Annamae thought of the things that Blue Blossom had told her about the Blackfoot people and their thoughts on death.

Blue Blossom had said that the Blackfoot

believed that when people died, their spirits did not always start at once for the other world.

Some actually felt lonely and were unwilling to leave home and friends. They wandered near their old haunts; some were actually seen hovering near!

Blue Blossom had told Annamae that sometimes, as a loved one sat by the cold body of the deceased, he or she might become alarmed by a sudden cold blast of air, which was the spirit of the departed one entering the door and standing close by.

Annamae was drawn from her thoughts when the procession stopped.

She gazed at the spot where Gray Stone's mother's resting place would be.

The death lodge made to receive Morning Flower's body was pitched in a dense thicket, where it would not be disturbed by heavy winds.

New poles had been used to pin the bottom of the lodge securely to the ground, and once Morning Flower was placed inside, it would be tightly laced at the front with rawhide, so that no wild animals could enter and defile her body.

Beneath Morning Flower's wrappings of blankets, she wore her most beloved clothes, for it was said that the dead traveled to the

Sand Hills in the clothes they were buried in.

Everyone slowly made a circle around the tiny lodge as Gray Stone's mother was momentarily placed on the ground just in front of the entranceway.

Gray Stone was helped from the travois so that he could kneel beside his mother while White Thunder came and sprinkled sage across Morning Flower's body, to purify it.

And then he also sprinkled sage onto Gray Stone's and Cougar's heads, as a sign that their sorrows were ended and they would now begin life anew without their loved one.

Few words were said over the body, and as Cougar and three of his warriors placed Morning Flower in her final resting place, slow chanting began, accompanied by the beating of drums from somewhere distant and the sweet sound of a flute being softly played.

Once Morning Flower's lodge was laced tightly closed, the procession turned and made its way back to the village.

When the prisoners came into sight again, Annamae gave Howard a glance, then looked away when she found him glaring at her. She was sure now that he saw her as a traitor, although she had had nothing to do with Cougar's decision to place Howard and the men there.

She only hoped that now that the burial was over, Howard and his men would be freed.

She realized now that she saw Cougar in a different light today. She felt foolish for having allowed herself to fantasize about loving him. He was a man she truly did not know.

When she saw Gray Stone carried inside the shaman's lodge again, she hurried there.

White Thunder greeted her and swept a hand out as an invitation for her to enter.

She stepped inside while the shaman stayed outside in order to give her a few moments alone with Gray Stone. White Thunder seemed to understand the depths of the feelings that Annamae and Gray Stone had for each other.

Annamae was a little afraid that Gray Stone would be so distraught, he would not want to talk with her, but she was wrong. As she knelt beside the bed of blankets, with the fire pit at her back, Gray Stone smiled and reached a hand out for her.

"It is good that you are here," Gray Stone said, his eyes bloodshot from crying. "Thank you for being part of my mother's burial rites. It still does not seem real that . . . she . . . is gone."

"I know," Annamae said, taking his hand

and gently holding it. "I felt the same after my loved ones died. In time you will grow to accept her loss, but you will never forget your mother. Never."

"Nor my father," Gray Stone said, a sob catching in his throat. "And how are you, Annamae? You look so pretty in that dress." He laughed softly. "Even your hair. It seems natural that it should be braided."

"I like the braids, too," Annamae said, laughing softly herself, glad that the moment was light and sweet instead of filled with morbidity.

"Annamae, I spoke on the white men's behalf," Gray Stone blurted out as he leaned up on an elbow, his hand slowly sliding from Annamae's.

"You did?" Annamae said, her eyes widening.

"Before the rites for my mother, I met with my uncle in private," Gray Stone said. "I pleaded with my uncle to release the men. I said that if anything happened to them, and my people were responsible, it could only go ill for us. I asked my chieftain uncle to release the men and have them escorted far away with a warning never to come anywhere near you or our people again."

"Even me?" Annamae said, touched to the

very core of her being by this child's generous, loving nature.

"Especially you," Gray Stone said, easing himself back down onto the blankets.

Then he smiled at Annamae again. "But know this, Annamae: my uncle had already planned to let the men go," he said. "He feared repercussions, too."

Annamae heard footsteps behind her. She turned and saw Cougar coming into the tepee.

"The men are already gone," he said, smiling into her eyes as he knelt down beside her. "They were given food and escorted away."

So very relieved that Cougar had proven to be the man she had always thought him, Annamae flung herself into his arms.

"Thank you, oh, thank you," she murmured.

"You will never see that man who wronged both you and my nephew again," Cougar said, holding her near and dear to his heart. "He vowed to me that he would not bother you anymore."

She leaned away from Cougar and gazed into his eyes. "Howard was kind to have taken me in when I was orphaned, so I do have some feelings for him, but I truly do not care ever to see him again," she said.

"Annamae, do you want to be escorted somewhere now yourself?" Cougar asked, searching her eyes. "You are free to go."

Annamae's heart skipped a nervous beat.

She saw how deeply he was gazing into her eyes, and she could see a look of pleading on his face.

She believed that he truly did not want her to leave; and she certainly did not want to go.

"Would it be all right if I stay . . . for at least a little while, at least until Gray Stone is well again?" she murmured.

She didn't want to be bold enough to say that she never wanted to go, that she cared too much for Cougar to leave.

She had already forgotten those few hours when she had thought ill of him. She knew now that all along he was going to let the prisoners go.

Cougar's heart thumped wildly inside his chest. "Do you mean that you would like to stay with my people . . . or . . . their chief?" he asked thickly.

"Their chief . . ." Annamae murmured, smiling shyly into his eyes.

"That is good, that is good," Cougar said, drawing her back into his arms.

Their embrace was long and sweet; then Cougar placed an arm around her waist and turned to leave while Gray Stone watched, all smiles.

Annamae could sense Gray Stone's happiness over what he had just witnessed. She gave him a soft smile over her shoulder just as Cougar swept the entrance flap aside.

Gray Stone returned the smile, then welcomed the cub into his arms after the tiny animal brushed past Annamae and Cougar.

"Sweet cub, Annamae will stay forever, not only until I am fully well," he whispered to the little bear. "Nothing will keep her from my uncle's arms. Nothing!"

Despite his sorrow, he was feeling some peace and happiness today because he had so many who loved him. They would help fill the empty spaces in his heart left by his mother's death.

But he knew that in time, once he was well, he must say good-bye to another loved one: the cub. The bear had to be returned to the wild, for once it was grown, it would want to have a mate.

"I will miss you so," he whispered, cuddling the cub closer. "But I am grown-up enough to accept things as they come to me."

The cub growled, drawing a laugh from Gray Stone. "Your growl is growing up much faster than you are," he said, for each time the cub growled, it sounded more ferocious than the last!

CHAPTER NINETEEN

Just as Annamae and Cougar stepped from the shaman's lodge, Cougar turned to her. "Will you go with me to my tepee?" he asked thickly.

Annamae's pulse raced as she gazed up into his midnight dark eyes, seeing a desire there that made her feel weak, yet warm all over.

She would go with him anywhere now that she knew, without a doubt, that he had feelings for her.

She had gone with him before into his tepee, yet it seemed there was more to the invitation today than before.

She wasn't sure if it was wise to be alone with him now, feeling the way she did. Should he kiss her . . .

"Yes, I will go with you," she blurted out, the thought of being in his arms and being kissed by him beautifully sweet to imagine.

She had never loved a man before. While

traveling with the carnival, she had not had the opportunity for lengthy relationships. She was not attracted to any of the carnival men, and the only customer she saw repeatedly was that horrid man who followed the carnival in his strange pursuit of her.

Fortunately, Reuben was gone from her life forevermore, and she would be staying here at this village, where she could feel safe and . . . and . . . yes, even loved.

Cougar's smile was his only response when she agreed to go with him.

She walked beside him as though on a cloud until they reached his large tepee.

Once they were inside it, she turned, her heart beating rapidly, as she watched him secure the ties at the entranceway, ensuring total privacy.

Privacy for what? she wondered. One did not require the ties to be secured just to talk.

Could that mean . . . ?

Cougar turned to Annamae, placing his hands gently on her shoulders. "Earlier, you said that you wished to stay among my people, yet you did not say the word 'forever,' " he murmured, searching her eyes. "You said that you wanted to stay for a little while, until Gray Stone got well, yet in the same breath you also said that you wished to be here because of me. How can I determine the true meaning behind your words? Do you wish to stay forever? Do you wish to stay mainly because of me?"

He moved his hands to her waist and drew her closer to him, so close Annamae could feel his breath on her face as he went on.

"You must know that my heart feels warm toward you," he said thickly. "I sense that you feel the same. Am I right?"

Her knees now weak with a passion that was new to her, and feeling too breathless to respond to his question, she could only nod.

But that seemed enough for him, for he brought her even closer, their lips now meeting with a tenderness that made Annamae almost swoon from the ecstasy of the moment.

She twined her arms around his neck and returned the kiss, her lips trembling against his.

He fitted his body even closer to hers, as though he were molding himself against her, and she could feel the muscles of his thighs pressed against her. His hands made a slow descent down her back. She was lost to everything but the moment.

"I want you," he murmured huskily against her lips as he leaned enough away from her so that their eyes could meet. "And not just for a moment of loving, but forever. Will you be a part of my life . . . as my wife? I know the love you have for Gray Stone, and that which the child has for you. We can raise him together as our son."

Annamae was rendered speechless by the suddenness of his proposal, yet she knew without a doubt that what he asked of her, she also wanted.

But still she could not speak the words her heart was shouting at her to say. She was so filled with the wonder of the moment, the words just would not come from her mouth!

Seeing her hesitance, and understanding that his declaration was perhaps too sudden for her, Cougar gently framed her face between his hands. "Woman, I know this is all happening quickly, but I want to protect you from men like Howard Becker . . . from all evil white men. If you are my wife, not only will I protect you, but so will all of my people."

She was so deeply touched by the sincerity of his feelings for her, Annamae still could not speak. Instead, tears filled her eyes and then streamed down her flushed cheeks.

"Why do you cry?" Cougar asked, gently

wiping the tears from her cheeks with his hand.

"The tears are what my mother would call happy tears," Annamae said, smiling shyly through the moisture that still filled her eyes.

"If they are happy tears, does that mean you are happy because I have asked you to be my wife?" Cougar asked, searching her eyes. "Or is all of this too soon? Should I have waited longer?"

"Oh, no," Annamae murmured. "I am so glad that you didn't. I have fallen in love with you, too. I can't say exactly when. I just know that I do love you and . . . want . . . to marry you. I cannot think of anything more wonderful than to be able to awaken each morning in your arms."

He swept his arms around her waist and drew her against him. He kissed her again, this time with even more passion, then whispered against her lips, "Have you been with a man? I mean, have you shared your blankets with a man?"

Annamae felt the heat of a blush rush to her cheeks at his intimate question. "No," she replied bashfully as their eyes locked again. "I have never loved before. I have never wanted a man . . . until you."

"My body cries out for you," Cougar said huskily. "But is it too soon for you? Would you rather wait? I do wish to make you my wife as soon as possible. My life has been filled with the needs of my people, not my own needs. I ache to have a wife, to have a family. Will you be the woman to fill the aches inside my heart and body?"

"Yes, oh, yes, I ache for you, too," Annamae said, finding it unreal that she was actually saying such things to a man, especially a man who had first taken her as his captive, not his lover!

But she did love him, and surely had from the very moment their eyes first made contact, even though at that time he saw her as his enemy.

"I know nothing about being with a man in the way you are suggesting, yet I feel deep inside my soul that I wish to be with you," she murmured. Yet despite her words, she was a little afraid of what she was about to do with a man for the first time.

What if she was not skilled enough to please this powerful Blackfoot chief?

What if she disappointed him?

Would . . . he . . . still want her?

"No, I don't want to wait," she blurted out, trying to feel confident that she would know enough about making love once she began, for surely it was not something one had to practice.

She knew how much her parents loved each other and had watched them so very often retire to the privacy of their bedroom, holding hands.

When that door was closed, she knew that things were all right between them, for after a while she would always hear her mother's sweet laughter. Then her mother and father would creep past her closed bedroom door to go to the kitchen for a snack after making love.

"Please . . ." she whispered, gazing intently into his eyes. "Please show me the miracle of making love. I have never wanted to know until now."

She trembled with ecstasy as he stepped away from her, then slowly began undressing her, even taking the time to unbraid her hair so that it hung long and thick down her back.

Once she was perfectly nude, he stood before her, gazing at her body. Slowly he touched her all over. She closed her eyes and felt herself floating away into another world.

When he touched that very private place between her legs and slowly caressed her there, her eyes flew wide open. She felt wondrous feelings that she had never known existed.

The feeling was so deliciously sweet and wonderful, she almost melted into the bulrush mats beneath her bare feet.

And then he stepped away from her.

She blushed anew, as he removed his own clothes, item by item, until he, too, stood nude before her.

Although she had been with her father in close quarters at home, she had never seen him without his clothes.

And now, the first time she was seeing a man naked, she was entranced by his muscles, and by that part of him that surely separated him from all other men. For he was not at all small, but instead . . .

"Touch me," Cougar said huskily as he reached for her hand and placed it on his manhood, which seemed fully aroused and ready for lovemaking.

Annamae blushed anew. "I have never seen a man naked, let alone . . . touched one there," she said, feeling the heat of his manhood against the palm of her hand.

"It is yours, only yours," Cougar said thickly. "Move your hand now on me for a moment just as I caressed you."

Recalling the exquisite feeling of his hand and fingers moving across her bud of womanhood, creating sensations that made her seem to soar above herself, and hoping she could create the same feelings for him, she started moving her hand on him. She was glad when he emitted a soft groan, which proved that she was giving him the same sort of pleasure he had given her.

Cougar's breath quickened as the heat of his passion rose almost beyond the point of no return. Gently, he drew her hand away from him.

He placed his arms around her waist and lowered her to the blankets spread beside his lodge fire. He feasted his eyes on her beautiful, petite body. He had longed for this moment from the first time he'd seen her, even though he had not been certain whether she was his enemy or friend.

Now she was everything to him! Everything!

Her body was warm against his as he spread himself atop her, his lips on hers again, kissing her with a hot passion that made her moan. A raging hunger was fueling his desire as he held himself above her so that he could have full access to her body, to touch her, to caress her.

One hand went to a breast, and then his mouth ventured there. He rolled her nipple with his tongue, aware of how this action caused her to breathe raggedly and to tremble.

He slid his hands to her breasts, cupping them, seeing the contrast of his dark fingers on her white skin, a reminder of the separate world to which they each belonged.

But she was now his world, his life. And he could not wait any longer.

He lowered his lips to hers in a long and wondering kiss as his throbbing heat found the hot, moist place between her thighs.

Knowing that he was the first with her, he wanted this joining to be something she remembered with ecstasy all of her life. He hoped she would want it over and over again, as they fell into their intimate embraces each night.

Slowly he entered her, realizing that she was now scarcely breathing, while the raging hunger ate away at his insides.

Annamae was filled with a flood of emotions as she felt a man moving into her for the first time, the warmth of his manhood filling her secret place.

And then her mind splintered into a million sensations, first pain, and then bliss as he went past that place inside her that proved she had not been with a man before.

"Did I hurt you?" he whispered against her lips as his body became still.

"Only for a moment," she whispered back, realizing just how strangely husky her voice sounded.

"And now?" he asked, his eyes gazing into hers.

"I never knew such bliss could exist," Annamae murmured, reaching up and gently pushing some of his fallen hair back from his gorgeous face. "Love me, Cougar. Oh, please make love with me."

His lips fell hard against hers in an erotic, passionate kiss as his body began to move. He thrust himself into her over and over again.

Sometimes he moved slowly, with acute deliberation, and then he moved faster, with quicker, surer movements.

Ecstatic waves of pleasure splashed through Cougar. The euphoria that filled his entire being was almost more than he could bear. This woman, with her delicate beauty, was making him feel foreign to himself. He had never known such blissful joy as he was feeling now.

Annamae was almost beyond coherent thought as she moved her body with his, matching his steady strokes within her.

She twined her arms around his neck and clung to him, and then wrapped her legs around his waist, locking them together at her ankles as she rode him. She felt pressure building somewhere deep inside her, growing hotter and hotter, as if a fire were consuming her.

White-hot flames seemed to be roaring in Cougar's ears. His body tightened as he felt himself drawing near the wondrous release of total union.

He tried to bring his breathing under control, to wait for that last moment of bliss, then plunged himself more deeply inside her. He groaned against her lips as he let the euphoria fill him while his body and hers trembled together in an all-consuming climax.

Breathing hard, her eyes wide, and shaken by the intensity of her ecstasy, Annamae gazed at Cougar as he rolled away from her and stretched out on his back. He, too, was finding it hard to get his breath after the wondrous throes of lovemaking.

"It was so wonderful," Annamae murmured, finding it hard to believe what she had just experienced with this handsome Blackfoot chief. "I never knew it could be like that."

He turned to her and ran his fingers gently through her long hair. Then he leaned closer and swirled his tongue around one of her nipples, sucking it into his mouth.

Annamae closed her eyes in ecstasy when his mouth left her breast, making a wet, sensual path downward across her tummy.

When he bent lower and flicked his tongue across her tender womanhood, she sucked in a breath of total bliss, even though she felt that what he was doing might not be right.

But something that gave her such pleasure must be all right, for again she felt wild ripples of desire sweeping through her. Suddenly she felt again that total rush of pleasure that came from the depths of her soul, as his tongue continued to sweep back and forth across her womanhood.

She opened her eyes wide when he leaned away from her, a mischievous look in his midnight dark eyes.

"What you just did . . . ?" she murmured, blushing.

"It gave you pleasure, did it not?" he asked, gently stroking her with his fingers where his tongue had just been.

"Very much," she said, giggling. "My whole body is aflame from it."

"Then do not ever think of that part of our lovemaking as questionable," he said. "One day I shall show you what you can do with your tongue and lips to also give me the same sort of pleasure."

Just imagining it made Annamae blush.

Cougar caught the blush and swept her

into his arms, cuddling her close. "My woman, I love you," he said huskily. "I need you for always. We will marry soon."

Annamae was in a state of wonderment. So many unexpected things had happened to her since she had left the carnival, but these moments with Cougar were what she would always remember most prominently.

To have such a man love her seemed unreal!

"I long to be your wife," she murmured, clinging to him as he held her close.

"Soon, my woman, soon," Cougar whispered against her lips.

CHAPTER TWENTY

The Blackfoot warriors rode with Howard and his carnival friends beside a stream of clear water that flowed along one side of a meadow. A stand of pines grew tall and straight on the far bank, a forest of aspen trees at their left.

Reuben rode on his mare far enough behind this group so that he would not be seen. He had decided that he must find a way to ally himself with the carnival owner.

Reuben had watched what had transpired between Howard and the Indians, how Howard and the others had been tied together and left staked to the ground for an entire night.

At this very moment Howard and his men were being escorted far from the Blackfoot village by several warriors. Reuben wondered if the savages' plans were to take the prisoners far enough away from the village so that Annamae would not be aware of their fate. Chief Cougar might have given his warriors orders to kill the white men.

That was why it was important for Reuben to stay unseen as he followed the group. If the Indians detected his presence, he, too, could die a terrible death.

His heart pounded hard and drool streamed from the corners of his mouth as he caught one of the Indians suddenly looking over his shoulder at the trees where Reuben was trying to hide.

He grew cold inside when this Indian suddenly wheeled his horse around and rode hard in Reuben's direction, entering the forest not far from where Reuben had stopped.

Suddenly the Indian drew rein and dismounted.

Reuben let out a heavy sigh of relief when the Indian began relieving himself, proving his reason for separating himself from the others: he had needed to take care of a very personal chore.

But afraid the Indian might sense someone's presence — he'd heard that all Indians' senses were keener than any white man's — Reuben remained stiff and still, hoping his mare would do the same.

If it let out even a snort, Reuben was doomed.

But the animal behaved itself as Reuben

stroked its thick neck. Reuben's eyes followed the Indian's every movement as he rode out of the forest and soon rejoined the others.

"That was a close one," Reuben whispered to himself.

He wiped drool from the corner of his mouth with the back of his left hand, then continued on through the forest.

He thought back to how he had last seen Annamae.

He had watched as she walked among a funeral procession. He had been close enough to see the body taken into a tiny house, then laced inside.

Then after the funeral rites, he had watched Annamae return to the village and enter one lodge for a while, then go to another with the Indian chief.

Reuben hadn't had time to observe her any longer, for he had a plan that he hoped would end in his finally getting Annamae to himself. He had hurried after Howard, his carnival friends, and their Indian escorts.

From then on, Reuben had stayed hidden but had never let Howard out of his sight. Knowing that Howard must still want Annamae with him, Reuben had cooked up a plan to propose to the other man.

He would ask Howard to join him. Together they would succeed in getting Anna-mae.

"I'm coming to your rescue, sweet thing," he whispered to himself, chuckling.

Yes, he would include Howard and the others in his plan, but only until Annamae was freed from the savages. Then Reuben would kill the men while they slept.

Then it would be only Reuben and Anna-mae!

Although she would know that he had killed Howard and the others in order to have her all to himself, wouldn't she be grateful to him for rescuing her?

Howard was intent on taking her back to be a part of the carnival acts, and Reuben knew that she didn't want any part of that life anymore.

No doubt she hankered for a normal life with a husband and kids.

"Ol' Reuben'll give you both," he said, chuckling beneath his breath. "Yep, you can count on ol' Reuben."

His breath was stolen away when he heard something close by, like the rustling of leaves. The color drained from his face when he thought that there might be another Indian following the main group, keeping an eye on them, as a sentry might do.

If that was the case, the Indian would

certainly have already seen Reuben.

He flinched when the sudden shrill cries of a flock of blue jays assaulted his ears. The birds soared above his head, while their leader made himself obnoxious by sitting in the big fir tree close to Reuben and chatting incessantly.

Although he hated the racket the birds were causing, Reuben was relieved to know that there was no Indian creeping up behind him.

Sighing, he rode onward, then grew pale again when he saw that the Indians had noticed the blue jays' commotion.

The man who'd relieved himself earlier was peering in the direction of the noisy blue jays. Reuben knew that if the Indian looked carefully enough, he would see Reuben.

He brought his horse to a sudden stop. His breath caught in his throat while the Indian continued to gaze in the direction of the noisy birds.

"Lordy, lordy," Reuben whispered, as drool crept down one side of his chin.

He inched his way back into the darker shadows where the sun did not reach through the leaves overhead.

Fortunately, the blue jays flew out of the trees, now darting toward the stream to quench their thirst.

"But what's that damn savage going to do?" Reuben whispered, squinting his eyes as he continued watching the Indian, who still sat quietly on his steed, as the others continued riding onward, away from him.

When the Indian suddenly shrugged and wheeled his horse around to join the others, Reuben hung his head in relief. "I'm not sure if I can do this any longer," he said to his horse, stroking its neck. "I'm getting spooked, friend. Damn, damn spooked."

But to have a chance to see Annamae again, to make her his bride, he knew he would do anything, even face dirty savages.

His chin lifted, his eyes narrowed angrily, and he slapped his reins against the horse's rump and rode onward through the shadowed trees.

"Nothing is going to stop me," he said tightly to himself. "Especially not savages."

Yet he knew fear now.

"I've got to be more careful," he said, peering darkly ahead at Howard. "Soon we'll become partners. You just don't know it yet, do you?"

He chuckled and rode onward.

"But you will soon," he said, again wiping drool from his mouth. "I ain't lettin' no savages spoil my plan, especially the fun I'm going to have once I get Annamae all to myself."

CHAPTER
TWENTY-ONE

It was so good to feel free again, and to be on a horse for no other reasons than to have a good ride.

She glanced over at Cougar as he rode his midnight black stallion, relieved that he truly trusted her now, and even loved her.

A blush flooded her cheeks when she thought of making love with him. It was as though she had discovered another world in his arms, just as she had found such a different way of life among the Blackfoot.

Although she felt somewhat brazen to admit it, she could hardly wait for their next lovemaking. Surely she would be more skilled now than she was the first time.

She wanted only to please this wonderful man whom she loved with every beat of her heart.

And oh, how handsome he was in his fringed buckskin outfit today, his thick black hair hanging down to his waist and fluttering in the wind.

Cougar felt Annamae's eyes on him.

He turned to her, smiling when he saw the pink of her cheeks.

Was she thinking about last night and how they had soared to heaven and back while making love in each other's arms?

Soon, when they found a perfect place to make camp for the night, he would teach her more about how to please a man, as he would show her the many ways he knew to please a woman.

It was certain now that she had erased his first love from his heart, a first love who was far too young to have experienced love-making with him. He and his young love had spent their time together exploring the forest, the earth, the water, and all things that lived near their village.

Their times together had been light-hearted, yet both knew they loved each other in a special way, and believed they would one day be married and bring children into their world.

That was never to be, but now he had a woman he cherished even more than he had cherished Dancing Dove. He would allow no other man to come near Annamae again, or threaten her as Howard Becker had so carelessly done. The next time Cougar would not be as generous. Should Howard Becker ever venture close to Blackfoot country again, it would be the last thing he ever did.

"What are you thinking so hard about?" Annamae asked as she gazed deeply into Cougar's dark eyes. "You are smiling at me, yet I sense your mind has wandered elsewhere. I hope it wasn't to another woman."

Cougar knew that he had to tell Annamae about his first love before someone else mentioned Dancing Dove and their special feelings for each other.

But he did not feel that now was the time to tell her.

They would soon be married.

He wanted nothing, not even memories, to shadow that day.

He wanted it to be a day that would remain forever inside his woman's heart, one she could think about through the years with a joy that came of the wondrous bond between husband and wife.

"I was thinking about that white man who is even now being escorted far from my people's home," Cougar said, for in truth that was the exact person he had been thinking about just before she'd spoken.

"What about him?" Annamae asked, seeing that his eyes were not looking into hers, but instead taking in her whole appearance.

She did feel beautiful in a new dress that Blue Blossom had brought to her this morning. This was a soft-tanned buckskin dress that was ornamented with elk teeth, and her leggings and moccasins were decorated with porcupine quills.

Her hair flowed freely down her back, moving in the soft breeze of midmorning, and she felt that she could pass as an Indian maiden, at least from a distance. She was proud of that, for she wanted nothing more now than to be Blackfoot, even though she was not one by blood.

But surely when she became Cougar's wife, she could announce to all mankind that she was Blackfoot, through and through!

For a moment Cougar forgot what she had said, for his eyes were taking in her loveliness. Her oval face, her beautiful eyes, the shape of her body, which was so alluring in her formfitting dress, revealing to him the swell of her breasts beneath the buckskin fabric, nearly took his breath away.

He could only smile with pleasure as he watched her small feet, clad in dainty moccasins, kicking the horse's sides so she could keep up with him.

Ah, but was she not a vision of loveliness?

And she was his!

He thought of the way she gave her all to him when they were making love. His heart skipped several beats even now as he recalled her warm, soft body next to his.

"Cougar?" Annamae said, blushing anew as he took in everything about her. She truly believed that he found her as beautiful as she felt! "You mentioned Howard Becker. Are you still concerned about him? Do you still see him as a threat?"

Cougar shook his head to clear it. He was so entranced by her that he seemed to have lost all his senses, even his ability to talk.

"Not a threat, for before he could get anywhere near you again, he would die. But I do believe he still might try to get you away from me," Cougar said tightly. "You need not worry about him. He is the one who should be consumed with worry, for I will not tolerate his trying to interfere in your life again."

"Oh, surely he won't," Annamae said, understanding the meaning behind his words. Although he was a man of peace and kindness, he would not think twice now about killing Howard.

"If he is a smart man at all, he will heed this chief's warnings," Cougar said thickly. "But today is not the time to discuss this man. No time is right to discuss him. He is far away by now. After he is taken to his people, my warriors will return, and that will be the end of it."

"Yes, I agree that this isn't the time to talk about Howard Becker. We needn't discuss him ever again, because he surely knows it's best to forget me," Annamae murmured. "We are supposed to be enjoying ourselves as you prepare me to become the wife of a powerful Blackfoot chief, by teaching me the ways of your people."

They were passing through the foothills and riding alongside the great river. Soon they made a sharp turn left and began following a worn trail up the mountainside.

They passed through small areas of luxuriant bunch grass brilliant with wildflowers, then plunged into a dark forest of fir, spruce, and pine.

They traveled onward, for the moment not discussing anything, but instead absorbing the wonders of nature.

They passed into an open basin, both marveling at the variety and the brilliant color of the flowers there.

"What are those flowers?" Annamae said, breaking the silence and pointing. "Those over there."

"Those are camas, the flower most loved

by my mother. I remember walking among them with her when I was but a small child. Her grip on my hand was solid, so that I could not wander and get lost," Cougar said, momentarily thrown back in time to relive those happy moments with his mother.

He recalled other memories of being with his chieftain father. The times with him were spent learning how to ride, to shoot bows and arrows, and how to gentle the first pony his father had given him.

Such thoughts of being with his parents, who were now waiting for him in the Sand Hills, made him happy more than sad, for it was those memories that sustained him when he ached inside to see his mother and father again.

Those days were long gone, and it was now time for him to make memories for his own children, the children who would be born to him and Annamae.

"Do you wish to have many children?" he suddenly blurted out.

The question took Annamae off guard. She looked quickly at Cougar. "Do you?" she asked, searching his eyes. "For, wonderful man, however many children you want, I want the same."

That answer seemed perfect, as she was

perfect, and Cougar smiled widely.

He rode onward with her through the wildflowers, their colors vivid and breathtaking. There was the violet-red of the wild geranium, the violet-blue of the Western virgin's bower, and the yellow of wild parsley.

"Tell me. . . ."

Annamae was about to urge him to talk about his people's customs, but stopped to ask about another unfamiliar flower. "What is that circular cluster of flowers?" she asked, pointing to them.

"My people call them by the name dusty stars," Cougar said, stopping his horse. "They are called dusty stars because they emit a puff of dust when pressed. They are supposed to be meteors that have fallen from the sky and spring up into puffballs in a single night."

"Truly?" Annamae said, amazed at what he had told her. "I must press one of them."

She laughed softly as she dismounted and went to kneel beside the cluster of flowers.

When she touched one of them slightly, a spray of what looked like dust came from it, causing Annamae to giggle.

She pressed one and then another, stopping only when Cougar came and took her into his arms.

He pulled her body against his and held her close, then gave her an all-consuming kiss.

He then leaned slightly away from her, yet still close enough so that their breath intermingled. "Would you like to make love among the flowers?" he asked huskily.

"Do you mean the puffballs?" Annamae said, her eyes twinkling. She giggled. "We might be covered with dust once we are done."

"No, I do not mean right here. Look there, to the right of the flowers." He pointed at several large indentations in the earth. "Those are bear prints, so this would not be a good place to lie down. But over by the river, I see a thick bed of moss that would feel good to your back," he said, reaching up and twining his fingers through her long black hair. "We then can talk as the sun moves toward the horizon. That would be a perfect place to make camp for the night. The horses can graze amid the tall grass and have plenty of water."

"Do you mean to turn them free?" Annamae asked, her eyes widening.

"As free as you and I," Cougar said, smiling into her eyes.

"Won't they run away?" she asked, glancing over her shoulder at his black stallion, and then at her strawberry roan, a gift this morning from Cougar.

"They have been trained," Cougar said, walking away from her.

She followed him as he led the horses over to the river, then removed their saddles and travel bags.

Once their reins were off, he gently slapped each on the rump and watched alongside Annamae as they trotted away. They did not go far before stopping to snort and munch contentedly on the grass.

"It's interesting that you can trust those horses so much; if they ran away, we'd have quite a distance to walk," Annamae said, surprised that the horses could be trained not to leave their masters behind.

"We will not have to walk," Cougar reassured her, chuckling softly.

He took the travel bags and blankets and placed them beside the river, then spread the blankets across the beautifully thick green moss.

He turned to Annamae and slowly undressed her until she was standing totally nude before his feasting eyes.

She had no fear of someone coming along, for they had come quite a distance and had yet to see anything but animals, flowers, and birds.

She could not help blushing when he removed his own clothes, then reached his arms out for her.

But without hesitation, forgetting her timid side, she went to him. She sighed with rapture as he swept her against him, his powerful arms holding her as he gently lowered her to the blankets.

After she was stretched out before him, he lay over her, blanketing her with his body, surrounding her with his hard, strong arms.

His eyes were dark with need as one hand started its descent on her body until he had found the soft mound of hair at the juncture of her thighs.

She gasped and trembled with pleasure, slowly tossing her head back and forth as his fingers parted the feathering of hair. He pleasured her there, slowly caressing, causing the passion to build within her.

And then with quick, eager fingers, his free hand was in her hair, bringing her lips to his. His mouth bore down on hers, exploding with raw passion, as his kisses became hot and demanding.

He urged her lips open as his kiss grew more and more passionate, far more demanding than she could recall him being before. But she enjoyed this difference.

Her body was responding, on fire with

need of him. When she felt his heat enter her, where she was throbbing unmercifully, everything but her passion was forgotten.

He molded her close.

She moved when he moved.

She sighed when he sighed.

She moaned when he moaned as she clung to his powerful shoulders.

Cougar's eyes were hollow pits of passion as he paused for a moment to gaze down at her. "My woman . . ." he said huskily; then again his mouth covered hers with reckless passion until they both found the ultimate pleasure.

Their bodies quaked and rocked and trembled, then lay still, the two seeming to be one as they clung to each other.

"I love you so," Annamae whispered against his cheek. "I have never been so happy. Thank you for bringing this happiness into my world."

"Our world," he said huskily. "Our world. We are now as one."

"Yes, oh, yes . . ." she murmured. "We . . . are . . . as one, forever and ever."

CHAPTER
TWENTY-TWO

Annamae had never felt so content in her entire life. She had just shared a meal of roasted rabbit with Cougar, close to the campfire that he had built before darkness had fallen.

Only moments after the fire had been built, he had crept away long enough to catch and kill the rabbit. Nothing but the bones now remained after the cooked, tender meat had been eagerly eaten.

A dessert of berries had followed, leaving Annamae and Cougar pleasantly full and ready to spend the night alone together.

Soon after the meal was finished, Cougar had spread their bed of blankets on the prairie grass close to the small fire. Now they lay snuggled together beneath the magnificent canopy of a night that was spangled with stars.

He had said that he had built a smaller campfire than usual; it was more convenient for cooking the rabbit. He had also told her that white men's fires were always too large and wasteful.

He had used small pine sticks that gave out an abundance of light and heat. He had explained to her how he could distinguish the different odors of burning firewood. Birch and cottonwood gave off a sweet fragrance, while the pine had a resiny scent. He knew very well the disagreeable odor of alder, called *mic-cisa-misa,* which meant "stink wood."

Their horses still roamed loose in the rich pasture not far from where Annamae and Cougar lay on their backs gazing into the wondrous beauty of the heavens. Their clothes were back on now, for warmth; though it was summer, during the early part of morning the temperature would be cool.

"Lying here like this, with the sky so broad and beautiful, I feel an overwhelming sense of the infinity of God's universe and my own smallness by comparison," Annamae murmured, still gazing heavenward.

"I feel it, too," Cougar said, turning his eyes to her and feasting once again on her loveliness.

Earlier, while they were still sitting beside the fire, he had gently wrapped a blanket of brilliant scarlet around her shoulders. It had since fallen away and now lay around her.

"Such moments as this are a reminder of just who we are, and where we came from, and where we are meant to go," Cougar then said.

He turned his eyes heavenward again, then pointed to one star in particular. "Do you see that much brighter star in the northeast part of the heavens?" he asked.

"Yes," Annamae murmured. "I watched it rising with remarkable brilliance over the tops of the tall spruces and pines across the river from where we have made our camp."

"That star, which is called the Dog Star, is used by Blackfoot warriors on nights when we are away from our village, to lead us safely back to our loved ones," Cougar said.

He then turned his gaze to Annamae again. "You have never told me about your dream interpretations. My nephew mentioned them to me," he blurted out. "How is it that you have that skill? Were you born with it?"

She turned her eyes quickly toward him. "Didn't Gray Stone tell you how it was done?" she asked, searching his eyes by the fire's glow. "I explained it all to him."

"No," Cougar said. "He said it was best that you tell me. Why did he feel that way?

Are your dreams born of superstition, or reality?"

"Neither," Annamae said, smiling softly at him. "As you know, Howard and Ellie Becker rescued me after my family was slaughtered by renegades. I grew up with them, feeling safe, yet out of place. I had never even seen a carnival before they made me part of one."

"So after giving you a home with them, they asked more of you?" Cougar encouraged.

"Yes, in time they did," Annamae said, lowering her eyes, for she felt ashamed of her role in the traveling carnival.

She looked quickly at him again. "When I grew old enough to draw attention, Howard wanted me to become an interpreter of dreams," she murmured. "I learned everything from books. So when people came to me, wanting answers about why they had this dream or that, I knew what to say, because I had studied a vast number of books about dreams."

"So you were not born with the skill. You were forced to pretend that you could do this thing," Cougar said, reaching over and smoothing some of her fallen hair back from her eyes.

"Yes, it was forced on me," she said,

remembering those times when she had to tolerate such men as Reuben Jones. The thought made her visibly shiver, and she told Cougar all about the disgusting man.

Cougar picked up the edges of the scarlet blanket and brought them back around her shoulders.

"You never have to interpret a dream again," he said. "You never have to be put in the position of tolerating men such as that Reuben person you just mentioned. You are safe in all ways now with me."

"I know," Annamae said, moving closer to him. "But . . ."

"But?" Cougar said, arching an eyebrow. He sensed she had more to say about the dreams and interpretations.

"Sometimes, when I was told a dream, I was stunned to realize that I could interpret it, even though I had not read anything about it in a book," she said, almost shyly. She gazed into his eyes. "I . . . I . . . have never admitted this to anyone, not even to myself. Sometimes I have dreams myself that later come true. When I remember having done this, I brush the thought out of my mind right away because it makes me feel as though I'm a stranger to my self."

She gazed into his eyes even more intently. "Should I be concerned at having such a power as that?"

Cougar was quiet for a moment as he contemplated her revelation. These powers she spoke of might be regarded by his people as frightening.

For himself, he found nothing threatening about her abilities. There was too much sweetness and gentleness about her for him to worry she might have a dark side.

"Do not concern yourself over this. You have carried this secret quietly inside your heart for too long," he encouraged. He placed a gentle hand on her cheek. "I feel honored that you shared this with me. I will not tell anyone. It will be something sacred between us."

"Sacred?" Annamae said, lifting an eyebrow.

"Something as unique as what you can do should be held sacred and secret from anyone but yourself, and now me, since I will be your husband," he said. "I can tell that it disturbs you to know you have such powers; it will be to your benefit not to tell anyone else."

"Do you urge me to keep quiet because it is truly for my own benefit, or yours?" Annamae asked. "Do you think if your people knew of my ability, it might change their opinion of me? Do you think they might become afraid and mistrusting? Do you think they would disapprove of my becoming your wife?"

"I do not say anything that is a half-truth, so when I said it was for your benefit that you keep this to yourself, that is exactly what I meant," Cougar said, slowly nodding.

"I'm sorry I doubted your word," Annamae said, snuggling against him.

"Have you had dreams of late that concern you?" Cougar asked, sweeping an arm around her and holding her closer. "Or would you rather not tell me if you have?"

"I will not keep anything from you ever again, and, yes, I have been having troubled dreams," Annamae said softly. She turned and gazed into his eyes. "I dream too much about Reuben stalking me, as he did while I was part of the carnival group. I sometimes awaken in a sweat, thinking he is standing over me as I sleep."

"He would never have the chance to get that close to you. Do not fret any longer over that dream," Cougar reassured her.

"I just wish I could forget he ever existed, for he was such a troubling sort of man," Annamae said, again shivering. "And when he talked, he drooled. It was so horrible."

Then she sat farther away from him and

turned to face him. "But I am concerned about something else, too," she said, her voice drawn.

"And what is that?" he asked, seeing the fear in her eyes.

"Those huge footprints we saw not long before we chose this place for our campsite," she admitted.

She looked guardedly from side to side, then into the dense darkness of the forest behind them.

Then she gazed into his eyes again. "Do you think we are in danger of that bear coming in the night while we are asleep?" she asked, her voice breaking. "After being around the bear cub, I forgot that it one day will grow into something as large as that bear whose prints are imbedded in the ground. Perhaps we should free the cub before he gets more attached and decides not to leave. I know that it is impossible for him to stay with us indefinitely."

"As for the prints that we saw, we are safe enough, for should a bear come near where we are camping, the horses would let us know," Cougar reassured her. "You would hear a snorting noise from the horses like you have never heard before."

She looked over her shoulder at the two horses, which were still contentedly grazing nearby, though there was nothing to keep them in place.

Then she smiled at Cougar. "Yes, I see what you mean," she murmured. "So I guess I can relax, can't I?"

"We will have to consider the cub's welfare more carefully when we return home," Cougar said, reaching out for Annamae, and drawing her close to him again. "I know that Gray Stone will be disappointed at having to take the cub back to where it was found, but it must be done, and soon."

"I, too, will be sad to see it left behind," Annamae said. "But I know it will be the right thing to do."

She turned to him again. "White Thunder, your shaman, truly amazes me," she said softly. "He seems to know so much about everything, especially how to make medicines of all kinds out of mere plants. Can you explain to me a little about his powers? Or is it something you are not to talk about?"

"I can talk about anything and everything with you, for soon you will play an important role in my people's lives. You will be my wife," Cougar said. "White Thunder is someone who performs miracles that even I am in awe of. You see, we believe our medicine man can control the weather, heal the sick, and exorcise evil spirits by means of incantations and magic arts. He is really more of a magician than the sort of medical doctor that your people are familiar with."

"Do you think he would say that I should be exorcised of evil spirits because of my ability to interpret some dreams?" Annamae asked, searching his eyes.

Cougar laughed.

He framed her face between his hands and brought her lips close to his.

He kissed her softly, then gathered her into his arms and sat her on his lap, facing him. "There is not one hair on your head that is evil." He chuckled. "And as far as what White Thunder thinks of you? He sees you as special, as do I, and approves of your becoming my wife."

"Thank goodness." Annamae sighed. "I do want all of your people's approval, especially White Thunder's." She smiled into his eyes. "Please tell me more about what shamans do."

"I think it is good that you are interested in what White Thunder does," Cougar said. "I will tell you more about a shaman's duties, and then some of our beliefs, but I see weariness in your eyes and feel that we should sleep soon. In the morning we will return home. And then preparations for our marriage will begin."

"It is all so unreal" — Annamae sighed — "that I am going to become your wife. My life has changed entirely since I left the carnival, and this new life is one I adore."

"The longer you are with my people, the more you will see how wrong the white man is about people of my skin color," Cougar said, his voice drawn. "As for our shaman . . . when a shaman is making medicine, he is performing mysterious ceremonies or otherwise controlling supernatural powers to avert the malevolence of evil spirits."

He reached over and shoved another piece of wood on the fire. "The sun, as the great center of power and the upholder of all things, is the Blackfoot's supreme object of worship," he murmured. "Every bud and leaf and blossom turns its face toward the sun as the source of its life and growth — the berries we eat are reddened and ripened under its warmth; men and animals alike thrive under its sustaining light. In the darkness and cold of winter nature retires into silence and sleep."

"You have spoken of the supernatural more than once tonight," Annamae said, somewhat afraid even to ask about it, yet needing to know as much as she could before becoming Cougar's wife.

"The Blackfoot people are firm believers in the supernatural and in the control of human affairs by both good and evil powers in the invisible world," Cougar softly explained. "You see, the Great Spirit — or Great Mystery, as we call it — is everywhere and in everything: in the mountains, plains, wind, water, trees, and all birds and animals."

He paused, then said, "Some birds and animals, such as the grizzly bear, buffalo, eagle, and raven, are worshipped because they possess a larger amount of good power than the others, and so when a Blackfoot is in peril, he naturally prays to them for assistance."

"If grizzly bears are worshipped, then why is it also feared?" Annamae asked, again recalling the huge prints of the bear that they had seen earlier.

"All animals must fight for their existence, as do grizzly bears when they feel they are threatened. It is only natural for them to do what they must to survive," Cougar explained.

He saw Annamae suddenly yawn and stretch, and knew that it was time to stop talking so that she could get her rest before the trip home tomorrow.

"Enough talk for tonight," Cougar said,

lifting her into his arms and stretching her out on the blankets.

She twined her arms around his neck. She smiled into his midnight dark eyes. "Do you truly think we should sleep, or . . . ?" Her eyes twinkled mischievously.

"We will sleep now, and at sunrise tomorrow we might do something else," he said, his own eyes filled with mischief.

It was hard not to take what she offered, but he knew that her rest was necessary. They had a lifetime of loving ahead of them!

She looked to her left, then at Cougar again. "Do you truly think we are safe here from the grizzly?" she asked, her voice breaking with fear she hated for him to hear.

"Yes, we are safe enough," he said, brushing soft kisses across her brow. "While with me, you are always safe."

"I do feel safe," she whispered.

He swept his arms around her and brought her up against him as he gave her an all-consuming kiss. Then he stretched out on the blanket beside her and watched her fall asleep, consumed with such love for her, he felt nothing else at this moment.

He bent low over her. "My woman, my love for you is stronger than the howling winds of winter!" he whispered against her cheek.

CHAPTER
TWENTY-THREE

The night was as black as black could be. The moon had hidden beneath a thick cover of clouds. Annamae was sleeping soundly, with no dreams to disturb her restful sleep.

Suddenly she was awakened from her deep slumber by hot breath against her cheek, and sensed the presence of a large animal standing over her.

Remembering the prints of the grizzly not far from where they had made camp, she felt a cold sweat come over her, and she was half-paralyzed with fear.

She could not even find the words to cry out for Cougar, for he, too, was in the same danger as she!

As she lay there awaiting what would surely be a horrible, slow death by a bear's mauling, she trembled in terror. The animal standing over her let out a grunting, snuffling sound close to her head.

Probably the grizzly had been prowling

about when she and Cougar had fallen asleep. It would have been drawn to the campsite by the scent of the bones left over from supper.

When it got there, the grizzly no doubt saw better pickings in the two humans it found.

More paralyzed by the moment, with a building fear, and realizing that Cougar's rifle was too far away for her to reach, Annamae finally found the courage to speak Cougar's name in a whisper.

When she got no response, she wondered if he was even still there. Surely the noise of the animal would have awakened him.

Yet . . . there she lay, alone, afraid, and not knowing what to do next except to await her fate.

No, she would not give up the wondrous new life she'd just found with Cougar! Annamae acted on an impulse. She pulled up her knees, and with all her strength she plunged her fists and feet simultaneously against the body of the brute.

Her attack was a complete surprise for the animal that stood over her. It seemed, if possible, even more frightened now than Annamae. Letting out a loud snort, it whinnied, turned, and galloped away.

The familiar sounds of a horse made

Annamae realize that it was not a bear that had come upon her and Cougar in the night, but instead one of their own horses!

Sighing with relief, now even finding humor in what had just happened, she sat up quickly and looked over at where Cougar had been sleeping.

He was gone! That was why he had not been awakened by the noise of the horse.

A different fear swept through Annamae as she realized that she was all alone.

She was only now aware of the hint of morning when she gazed across the river at the horizon. There were streaks of orange in the dark sky, which was lightening more and more each moment.

"Cougar!" Annamae cried out.

Hugging herself to ward off the chill of the morning, she stood up and gazed slowly around her.

It was then that she saw Cougar walking toward her, a pile of wood in his arms.

She was so relieved to see him, Annamae broke into a run and met him halfway.

The sky was light enough now for Cougar to see the alarm on Annamae's face as she gazed up at him.

"I should have awakened you and told you that I was going for wood for our morning cook fire," he said gently, feeling guilty for having caused her undue alarm. Had she thought that he had abandoned her?

"Cougar, something frightening just happened. Or maybe it was actually quite funny," Annamae said, beginning to see the humor in the incident.

"What happened?" Cougar asked, walking with her now toward the campfire, stopping when they reached it to let the wood tumble from his arms.

"I was awakened by an animal," Annamae said, bending to her knees to help him arrange the wood over the embers. She laughed. "At first I thought it was that grizzly bear whose footprints we saw. I thought it had come for its morning meal . . . namely us."

"What was it?" Cougar asked, glad when the flames caught hold and began to provide a pleasant warmth.

"A horse," Annamae said.

She looked over at their two mounts, which were contentedly grazing where they had been left, untethered.

Then she looked past them and noticed a small herd of wild horses making their way along the river.

"It was a wild horse," she blurted out, remembering how it had whinnied and snorted as it galloped away. "I imagine it sniffed me out in the night and was too curious not to come and investigate."

"But you are all right," Cougar said, placing his hands gently on her shoulders.

"Yes, but I imagine the horse may have a few sore ribs," she said. She laughed softly. "I don't know where I got the nerve to do what I did. I actually hit the horse with my fists and feet. It didn't stay around long after that."

"I have heard of such curiosity in wild horses, which do not normally go near humans," he said. He turned his eyes toward the two grazing steeds. "I am surprised the wild horses didn't try to lure your mare away to join them."

"I guess the horse found me more interesting," Annamae said. She leaned into Cougar's embrace. "I'm so glad it wasn't a bear. We wouldn't be standing together like this if it had been."

"Do not think any more about it, for you are safe. I was wrong to have left you even for a moment," he said thickly. "But you were so soundly sleeping, I did not want to disturb you to tell you that I was leaving to get firewood."

"You can't watch me every minute of your life," Annamae said, sighing. "You have your duties to your people. It is up to me to learn how to take care of myself in your absence."

"You seem to be doing all right," Cougar said softly, envisioning how it must have looked when she had attacked the horse with her fists and feet. "You thought quickly in a situation that could have been deadly. And I will never forget what you endured to bring my nephew back to his family and people."

"Yes, I am quite proud of myself," Annamae said, softly laughing. "And now, what are we going to do about eating?"

"While I was gathering wood I prepared a snare. A rabbit is caught in it even now," Cougar said, looking over his shoulder in the direction of the spot where he had seen the rabbit struggling to get free.

"I hate to see small animals killed, yet I know it must be done," Annamae said, stepping away from him as he removed his knife from its sheath. "I'll stay here. I'd rather not see the actual kill."

Cougar nodded and walked away from Annamae as she turned her eyes back to where the wild horses had been. They had fled farther away, and were now hidden from her sight.

"I've much to learn about being the wife of a proud Blackfoot chief," she murmured, nodding.

And she would.

She never wanted to disappoint Cougar, especially after they spoke vows and were husband and wife.

After Cougar brought the rabbit back to the camp and skinned it, and it was cooked a tempting brown, they shared a delicious meal. Afterward, they made certain the campfire was totally out, then mounted their steeds and rode back in the direction of the village.

Before they got very far, they caught sight of a band of mountain sheep quietly feeding above the timberline. Suddenly the sheep began scattering in all directions.

"Something frightened them," Cougar said, quickly taking his rifle from its gun boot at the side of his stallion. "And that something might be too close for comfort as far as we are concerned."

A dark form with an awkward gait appeared, following some of the sheep over the boulders.

"A grizzly." Annamae gasped, turning pale as she realized that if this grizzly had found their camp, she might not be riding alongside Cougar now, safe and alive.

"Stop your horse," Cougar said, drawing rein himself. "Make no sound or movement. We must make sure that the grizzly keeps its eyes on the scattering sheep, not us."

The grizzly stopped its chase when it came across a large patch of huckleberries. Annamae had thought it would begin feasting on the berries, but it seemed interested in something else. Oddly, the bear began tearing up the ground and turning over large stones.

"It prefers insects to the sheep or the huckleberries," Cougar said quietly as they both continued to watch the grizzly, which was now burrowing its nose into the earth, its large tongue eagerly lapping up whatever insects it had uncovered.

"The wind has shifted, carrying our scent away from the grizzly. While it is busy eating, we must go on our way and get as far as we can from that bear before it finishes its simple meal of insects," Cougar said.

"I'll just be glad when I see the smoke from your people's cook fires and know that we are almost home," Annamae murmured.

Cougar smiled over at her. "You just called my village your home," he said, pride in his voice. "It is good, my woman, that you consider yourself a part of my people even before we become husband and wife."

"I do feel that way, deep down inside," Annamae murmured. She reached up and ran her fingers through her hair, straightening out the tangles brought by the wind, which was beginning to pick up and grow colder.

Cougar gazed heavenward and saw dark clouds rolling in. "A storm seems to be following us," he said. He looked at Annamae, who was shivering.

He drew rein.

Annamae followed his lead and watched as he pulled the scarlet blanket from his travel bag, then reached over and slung it around her shoulders.

"Secure it beneath the belt of your dress and it will not blow away as we ride hard toward home. I want to be inside my lodge before the cold rain begins," he said, watching her slide the tail ends of the blanket beneath her belt, and secure it, as he had suggested.

Then they rode onward, now at a hard gallop.

"I enjoyed our outing so much," Annamae shouted over at him. "Even the scare I had when I thought a grizzly was visiting us."

"We will have such small adventures throughout our marriage, for I never want you to feel that life is dull while you are the wife of this Blackfoot chief. I often have duties to my people that must take me away from home," Cougar explained. "When I must go and parley with this tribe or that, sometimes even with white military people, I do not want you to feel rejected."

"I understand that duties come with being a powerful chief; it is the same for the president of the United States," Annamae said, seeing how mentioning the president brought a harsh gleam to Cougar's eyes.

She was sorry that she had brought him up, for she knew that many treaties between the government and the red man had been broken, most of the time due to decisions made by the president.

"It is understandable that you would make mention of the white chief, for he is the leader of the white people, as I am the leader of my people," Cougar said, his voice drawn. "I hope that when you are my wife, you will no longer think of that white chief as your leader. He speaks with a forked tongue to my people."

"My sole loyalty will be to you and your people," Annamae said, truly believing that she would feel that way. She knew of the hardships of all Indians in America, brought on mainly by the leaders of the country.

She regretted this state of affairs, for the Indians were the true first people of America!

Of course, she knew that she would be

seen as a traitor if any white people knew she felt that way.

She might even be regarded as a traitor for marrying a Blackfoot chief, but that didn't matter to her. Although a marriage between a white woman and an Indian was taboo, for her it would be wonderful!

CHAPTER
TWENTY-FOUR

Upon first awakening, Annamae had realized there was something different about the village.

There was a lot of activity outside Cougar's lodge, where she had slept contentedly all night, and the people of the village seemed unusually busy.

Late last evening, before she had finally fallen asleep, Cougar had told her that the meat supply would be replenished today. There were many black-tailed deer and elk along the river, and the warriors would leave home to hunt.

Now the young braves played games as they waited for the hunters' return.

The day had advanced, and the sun was sliding down from its midpoint in the sky, making its way toward the horizon. Annamae noticed that the young braves had stopped their games and kept a sharp lookout for the returning warriors, who would come home with their shoulders heavy-laden with a deer, or even two — one per shoulder!

Earlier, Gray Stone had surprised her by coming to Cougar's tepee. He was strong enough for a visit, and even now he was sitting with her beside the slow-burning fire in Cougar's fire pit. The boy chatted eagerly about anything and everything, while Annamae's eyes kept moving to the entrance flap. She was among those women who awaited the return of their men from the hunt.

Cougar had left at the crack of dawn with his warriors to do his part in replenishing their food supply.

"It is so good to be up and around," Gray Stone said, stroking the cub's fur as the animal lay cuddled on his lap.

Annamae watched how lovingly Gray Stone held the cub and could not help recalling how large and fearsome the full-grown grizzly bear had been.

She knew that the cub would be just as large one day, and dreaded having to tell Gray Stone that he would soon have to give his pet up to the wild.

"I could be so happy were it not for my mother's death," Gray Stone said, his voice breaking at the mention of his mother. He hung his head. "I knew she was not a strong person in many ways, but I never knew that she could be so weak in her mind as to take her own life. . . ."

Seeing how he stopped before saying anything else, Annamae reached over and ran her fingers through his thick black hair.

"I know how you feel, and it isn't easy to talk about," she murmured. "I lost my entire family all at once. The renegades changed my life forever."

Gray Stone looked quickly up at her. "But you have put your sadness behind you," he said softly. "You are going to marry my uncle. He will make sure you do not linger on that sad day of your life very often."

"I wish he could completely erase it from my mind, but that can never be," Annamae said, leaning away from Gray Stone to slide a piece of wood into the fire pit. "But he has lessened my hurt; that is certain."

"In time the hurt will lessen inside my heart, as well," Gray Stone said. "But it is too soon. I . . . miss . . . my mother so much."

He smiled down at the cub. "But I have the cub to help me during my time of sadness," he said.

Annamae thought again of the fierceness of the huge bear.

She gazed at the cub's claws. Her eyes

widened when she saw just how much thicker and longer they were now than on the day she had first seen him in the cage.

They could do much damage, even while the cub was just being playful.

Yes, soon the cub would have to be taken back to where it could find its way to those of its own kind.

She understood the hurt this new loss would bring to Gray Stone, but it would heal with time, just as he had recovered after the horrible days of being so ill from the bee stings.

"You and my uncle will soon marry?" Gray Stone asked, interrupting Annamae's quiet concerns.

"Yes, soon," Annamae said, blushing a little.

"It is so good that you will be a part of my life now," Gray Stone said. "Were you to go, I would have you also to mourn."

"I will be here for you forever," Annamae murmured, taking one of his hands and squeezing it gently. "Whatever you might need, all you must do is ask and I will do whatever I can to give it to you."

"Thank you," Gray Stone said, bashfully lowering his eyes.

Then he gazed at her again. "Tonight, after all warriors have returned from the hunt and everyone is filled with deer meat, there will be storytelling time," he said anxiously. "Will you sit with me?"

"Both Cougar and I will sit with you," Annamae said, slowly sliding her hand from his. "What sort of stories will be told?"

"All sorts," Gray Stone said, smiling at the thought of the camaraderie of storytelling time, when children and adults alike sat around the huge outdoor fire and listened to their storyteller's tales.

Annamae glanced at the closed entrance flap, hoping to hear the warriors return soon, for the day had been long without Cougar.

But Gray Stone was a wonderful substitute. He talked enough to keep Annamae from thinking about missing Cougar.

"Will you tell me about what to expect tonight?" she urged, so glad to have Gray Stone with her again, as they had been for a short while after escaping from the carnival.

"Storytelling always begins in the evening, just as the sky turns dark, and continues far into the night," Gray Stone said eagerly. He laughed softly. "You see, we Blackfoot are good talkers. Although we have one main storyteller, others join in and tell their own tales. Some go into minute details and give vivid descriptions of their experiences."

"Why are the stories told at night, instead of earlier in the day?" Annamae asked.

"We Blackfoot have always insisted they be told after dark," Gray Stone said, still stroking the cub's fur as it slept soundly across his lap, its legs outstretched in front and back.

"Stories told around the night fire fill everyone with both awe and dread," Gray Stone said, causing Annamae's eyes to widen in wonder. "You see, while the stories are being told, there are mysterious sounds in the air. The singing of the wood on the fire seems like voices from the spirit world. The wailing of the coyote in the distance sounds weird and ghostly."

Suddenly a gust of wind roared through the poles overhead, shaking the lodge, throwing the door flap open, and swirling the smoke.

Annamae gasped and grew pale. "What was that?" she asked.

"A spirit entered my uncle's lodge and left just as quickly," Gray Stone said, then laughed softly as he reached a comforting, reassuring hand to Annamae's arm. "Do not be afraid. It was truly only the wind."

Annamae laughed as she gazed up at the smoke hole, and then at the entrance flap, both of which seemed normal again. "For a moment there I thought we were no longer alone," she murmured. She glanced quickly at the entrance flap again when she heard shrill voices coming from the young braves outside the lodge, who were announcing the bringing in of a deer.

They all shouted "Woo-coo-hoo," in unison at the top of their voices. The call was repeated over and over again, proof that more than one warrior had arrived with a heavy burden of deer.

"Come and see," Gray Stone said, nudging the cub from his lap.

"Let me help you," Annamae said when she saw how much of a struggle it was for the child to get up.

She went to him and placed an arm around his waist until he was on his feet. Then they both left the lodge together, stopping outside to watch.

Several of the warriors had arrived together, bent over by their burden.

Then Annamae caught sight of Cougar. His fringed buckskin shirt was sprinkled with blood, his eyes were filled with pride because he carried two deer, one on each shoulder.

"How can they carry such a heavy load?" Annamae asked. She glanced at Gray Stone, and then again at Cougar, who stepped up to an elderly woman's lodge and dropped one of the deer just outside the entrance flap.

"Her husband is in the Sand Hills," Gray Stone quickly explained. "My uncle now hunts in place of her man."

"That is so kind," Annamae murmured, blushing when Cougar turned and looked directly into her eyes. He smiled as he came toward her with the other deer.

"Now he brings a deer to the woman who will soon be his wife," Gray Stone said, smiling at Annamae just as Cougar dropped the black-tailed deer at her feet.

"My woman, this prize is yours," Cougar said, seeing how her smile faded as she gazed at the bloody carcass that lay at her feet.

"Thank you," Annamae said, not knowing what else to say. She had no idea how to prepare this meat for eating.

She glanced around at how the other women were already busy butchering the meat that had been brought to them.

"The choicest pieces of game will be cooked and offered to the Great Mystery," Cougar said, realizing how new this all was to Annamae. Soon she would learn everything about the hunt and how the meat was prepared. He would see to it that she was taught every nuance of Blackfoot life.

Annamae's eyes were drawn to the young braves again. The singsong cheers were kept up as the game continued to be brought in until at last all hunters had returned. Happiness and contentment reigned absolute in a fashion she had never observed among white people, even in the best of circumstances.

Soon the men were lounging and smoking, the women actively engaged in the preparation of the evening meal.

She heard one of the women say, "Great Mystery, do thou partake of this venison and still be gracious to the Blackfoot."

"This time someone else will prepare our meat, but the next time, after we are married, you will be the one to do it," Cougar said as one of the women came and dragged the carcass away.

Annamae was astonished at how quickly the meat was prepared. Some women lowered the boiling pots of water and meat into their personal outdoor fires, while the fragrant roasting of venison filled the air.

The children had resumed their games as their mothers labored to prepare the meat for future meals.

And suddenly, it seemed, the world became shadowed by night, everyone's bellies were filled with venison, and the time for telling stories had arrived.

"Come, let us sit together," Cougar said as he ushered both Annamae and Gray Stone over to where he had already spread a thick pelt for their comfort.

Annamae watched the villagers as they found their own places beside the roaring fire. Then one older man took his place before them.

"He is the storyteller," Cougar quietly explained to Annamae. "Listen well. There are many truths in his stories, as well as amusing anecdotes."

The scent of the cooked meat was still heavy in the air, and racks of prepared meat stood in various spots around the village. Annamae sat contentedly between Cougar and Gray Stone, the cub once again asleep on the child's lap.

Annamae dreaded more and more the moment she would have to tell Gray Stone that it was time to return the cub to the wild. She wasn't certain how he would be able to say good-bye. . . .

Silence reigned throughout the crowd as the storyteller began his first tale. With his first words, the children moved in closer around him.

Annamae leaned forward and listened attentively, for she remembered the nights beside her family's fire, when her father would tell stories. She had always loved story time with her mama and papa!

"Long ago there was a small mouse who worked in the autumn at gathering beans," the storyteller began. "She went out every morning carrying a snakeskin as her bag. She worked hard at filling it with ground beans, then dragged it home with her teeth to where she kept her food stored for the long winter ahead. This mouse that worked so hard had a sister mouse who cared more for having fun. She liked to dance and sing. She did not go out and gather food, and suddenly the time was gone for gathering the beans. When this sister finally realized she needed to get her own beans, she didn't have a bag in which to carry them. So she went to her sister and begged for hers. Her sister asked why she didn't have her own bag. Where was she during the moon when the snakes cast off their skins? Her sister mouse said that she was there, but she was enjoying dancing too much to get herself a cast-off skin. Her sister told her that she must now suffer the punishment of her idleness, that this was the way it always seemed to be with the lazy and careless."

The storyteller looked from child to child.

"And so you see that it does not pay to be idle," he told them. "You should never expect someone else to do your work for you."

The stories continued long into the night, until the children's wide yawns revealed that it was time for sleep.

But before they all left, Cougar stepped up and took the storyteller's place before the crowd.

"My people, today has been a good day," he said, smiling from one to another as the outdoor fire cast shadows onto their attentive faces. "The hunt was good, the meat filling to our bellies, and the storytelling fascinating. But I have something else to give to you before you leave for your beds. I have news of this chief who is taking a bride."

Annamae blanched as she waited for the people's eyes to turn to her. Instead, all looked straight ahead at their chief, awaiting the words that would confirm what most already knew.

"I have been a long time without a woman in my heart," Cougar said, slowly looking at Annamae. "But there is one now who has brought much joy into my life and will bring the same into yours."

He gestured with a hand toward Annamae.

"This woman's skin is white, but with every breath she takes, she is as one with us," he said thickly.

He didn't ask her to join him, for he saw resentment in some of his people's eyes. In others, though, he saw acceptance.

He knew that in time all would accept this change in their chief's life, for Annamae had much joy to share.

He saw that many looked at Gray Stone, realizing that now he was going to be raised as their chief's son. It was plain to see how happy this news of their chief's upcoming marriage made him.

Gray Stone's reaction seemed to be what made his people accept the news, for they knew what the boy had just been through.

Suddenly Cougar went to Annamae and helped her up from the pelts.

When his people saw the love in her eyes for their chief as she smiled up at him, low chanting began. The people came, one by one, to embrace not only their chief, but also his future wife.

Annamae felt the weight of the world lifted from her shoulders, for during the storytelling, when she had time to think through all that was happening in her life, she had known a moment of fear, questioning whether she could really be accepted by

Cougar's people.

But now?

All fears and doubts were erased!

She was ready to become the wife of a powerful Blackfoot chief.

And she was ready to become a mother to sweet Gray Stone.

CHAPTER
TWENTY-FIVE

The day had been a glorious one for Annamae, beginning with her being dressed for
her marriage with Cougar.

Blue Blossom had made Annamae's dress
for her special day. It was a heavily beaded
tunic of soft-tanned fawn skin, worn with
matching leggings and moccasins that were
beautifully decorated with colored porcupine quills.

She wore white shells earrings and a
necklace of elk teeth and deer bones.

Her hair hung down her back in two
braids, each of which was tied at the ends
with small strips of hide.

The ceremony that made Annamae a wife
to her wonderfully handsome Blackfoot
chief was long past. The sun was just dip-
ping low in the western sky as she sat with
her husband, who wore a fringed buckskin
outfit, his own hair arranged in one long
braid down his back.

It was the height of the celebration now, and Annamae's bright and cheerful disposition radiated sunshine to all around her. She was watching a group of male dancers as they swayed and leaped around the huge outdoor fire in time with music being played on drums, rattles, and flutes.

This particular dance had a lively air, and as the women joined the men, they entered into it with spirit and dash, laughing merrily.

Annamae noticed a little girl about twelve years of age watching the dancers. As the dance reached its peak of merriment, the little girl's eyes were sparkling with excitement. Just then her mother stepped away from the dancers and went to her, snatched off the child's blanket that lay around her shoulders, and pushed the child into the circle of dancers.

At first the little girl cast her eyes demurely downward, but soon forgot herself and entered into the dance with animation, her lithe body swaying to and fro, her small moccasined feet keeping perfect time to the beating of the drums and shaking of the rattles.

Annamae was taken by how pretty the girl looked, with her shining black hair falling over her shoulders in striking contrast with the brilliant scarlet of her dress, which was beautifully fringed and decorated with beads. Her leggings were also beaded, and around her waist was a small belt closely studded with shiny, brass-headed tacks.

Cougar leaned over and whispered into Annamae's ear. "Come with me," he said, drawing her eyes quickly up to gaze into his. "The celebration will continue without us. It is time for us to retire to our lodge so that we can be alone for our own private celebration."

"But won't your people mind?" Annamae whispered. The music and dancing continued and the smell of cooked venison and corn was heavy in the air. "Shouldn't we join the feast when the women are ready to offer it?"

"The feast is for the others, not the bride and groom," Cougar said, taking her hand and urging her to her feet.

She smiled awkwardly down at Gray Stone, who sat with Blue Blossom, neither of them joining the dancers.

He gave her a knowing nod, their eyes momentarily meeting and holding. His look told her that what Cougar was suggesting was perhaps the way it always was for a new Blackfoot husband and wife during their marriage celebration.

She hurried to her feet and ran off, hand in hand, with Cougar. A moment later they were inside his tepee, the fire burning softly in the fire pit, with a pot of food hanging over the flames.

She noticed that the entire floor of the lodge was covered with plush, rich pelts, which must have been placed there after she had left to marry Cougar.

She believed that Blue Blossom was also responsible for that. The maiden had become a true friend to Annamae, a friend who seemed to think of everything.

"My wife," Cougar said, twining his arms around her waist. He drew her close as they inched nearer to the fire, where two bowls awaited them. They would eat and then . . .

"My husband," Annamae murmured, wrapping her arms around his neck. "My very handsome Blackfoot husband."

"Was today all you expected?" Cougar asked, his eyes searched hers. "Was there enough celebration to please you?"

"Everything was perfect, so much more, even, than I expected," Annamae said, her voice breaking with emotion. She had never thought she could be so happy, not after having lost her parents in such a horrible way, and then being at the mercy of a man like Howard Becker.

And then there was Reuben. He had made her life almost unbearable, for she never knew when he would suddenly arrive in her carnival tent, saying it was for a dream interpretation, when she knew all along it was just another opportunity for him to be alone with her.

She now no longer feared coming face-to-face with that man again. Surely he knew never to come anywhere near this Blackfoot village, especially after he heard that she was married to their chief. As nosy as he was, and as determined to have her for his own, she did not doubt that somehow he would hear about what had become of her.

No! He would not dare come and interfere!

"I see in your eyes that you are thinking of something or someone other than this moment and your new husband," Cougar said with a smile. "Do you wish to tell me about it?"

"I *was* thinking of someone else," Annamae said, nodding. "That horrible man who made my life miserable while I was a part of the carnival."

"The man named Howard Becker?" Cougar asked, slowly dropping his hands away from her. "Do you fear that he might try to steal you away again?"

"No, it wasn't Howard whom I was thinking about, but instead that man who stalked me when I traveled with the carnival," she murmured, dropping her arms from around his neck. "He showed up at every town the carnival visited."

"You are no longer a part of that carnival," Cougar said, gently placing his hands on her shoulders. "You are part of my village now, as one with my people. You are the wife of their chief. So do not worry about something that will never happen. That man would not dare come near our home."

"No, I don't think so either," Annamae murmured. "And thank you for making me feel so safe."

She put her arms around his neck again. "My husband," she said, smiling into his eyes. "That sounds so wonderful. It's as though I am in a dream." She giggled. "My darling, please don't pinch me and wake me up."

"You are very much awake and very much a Blackfoot chief's wife," Cougar said. Then he eased away from her and gazed down into the flames of the fire. "But . . ."

Annamae sensed something had suddenly changed between them. Almost afraid to know what had altered his mood so abruptly, she stood there for a moment longer, watching Cougar.

She thought that surely he would turn toward her at any moment and reassure her that nothing was wrong, that his sudden change of mood was caused by something that had happened today among his warriors that he did not want to talk about.

But then he did turn to her. He reached his hands out to her.

"There is something that I feel I must tell you," he said slowly, realizing how hesitant Annamae was to take his hands.

A sudden fear went through Annamae. She didn't understand why he was looking at her so strangely.

"What is it?" she asked, still not letting him take her hands.

She was suddenly afraid that things might not be as wonderful . . . as perfect . . . as she had thought.

"If you have something to tell me, please say it," she blurted out. "I have kept no secrets from you. Have you kept one from me? If so, please tell me now. Don't make me wonder what it might be."

"I know that I must, and I will," Cougar said, his voice drawn. "But it should have no effect on our feelings for each other; nor should it cause damage to our newly spoken wedding vows."

"Just please say it," Annamae said, her heart pounding. "Please?"

He stepped closer and forced her hands into his, holding them tightly. "My wife, I loved someone else long ago," he blurted out.

Annamae's eyes widened.

Her mouth dropped open.

Oh, Lord, had she been his second choice?

Had he loved someone even more dearly than he did her?

It must be so, or why would he feel the need to tell her about this other woman, especially on their wedding night?

She tried not to lose faith in his feelings for her, not until she heard the whole story. But as she waited for the truth, pieces of her heart seemed to be tearing away.

"I loved someone else, but, my wife, that was when I was a mere boy, with a boy's infatuations," Cougar said. "I never knew what true love was until I met you. I want nothing now but to fill your life with love and happiness."

Cougar's words caused a wave of keen relief to wash through Annamae.

She sighed, then eased her hands from his and placed them on his cheeks, framing his face between them.

"My darling, thank you for explaining this

to me," she said. "But you didn't have to. Surely that was so long ago."

"It was, and when her father took her and his clan far away from my own, that was our last good-bye," Cougar said. Should he tell her the full truth — that until he'd met Annamae, he could not get Dancing Dove from his mind or heart? No, he knew that she would not want to hear that.

He smiled into her eyes. "I knew that you would understand," he said. "And I am glad that I told you."

"I am too," Annamae said. Yet she did not truly understand why he had felt the need to tell her about his first love if it truly was so trivial a thing to him.

He took her hands from his face and held them close to his heart. His eyes moved slowly over her face, and then went to her hair. "But I must confess to you, there is much about you that reminds me of my past love," he said. "Your eyes, your hair, your round face, and . . . and . . . your soft skin."

Annamae was aghast at this newest revelation. Oh, Lord, surely if he saw so much that reminded him of his young love when he looked at Annamae, he had fallen in love with her for all the wrong reasons.

He saw his first love when he looked at her!

When he looked into Annamae's eyes, he saw another girl's adoring gaze. When he ran his hands across her arms, he was comparing her skin to another's.

"How could you?" she suddenly cried.

Tears spilled from her eyes as she yanked her hands from his. "You don't love me. You . . . love . . . her. In your heart, you married her. You finally . . . married . . . her!"

Stunned by Annamae's reaction, only now realizing how what he had just said must have sounded, Cougar reached out for her, but he was not quick enough. She had fled the tepee.

Annamae was blinded by tears as she ran toward the river, only scarcely aware that the celebration was continuing around the huge fire. She didn't even care if some of Cougar's people saw her flee her husband's lodge with tears in her eyes.

She could not help her reaction. She felt betrayed!

This man she adored and was married to, for life, had loved someone before he had loved her, and . . . and . . . apparently he saw that someone every time he looked at Annamae!

As she ran onward, she left behind a band of young men singing a wolf song together, reviving the custom of former days, when an expedition would be starting upon the warpath.

They stood in a circle, holding a hide between them, upon which they beat time with sticks.

They sang no words, but gave the wolf howl at regular intervals. Young women standing near joined in the wolf howl.

This song was very ancient, having been handed down through many generations of Blackfoot.

It was sung in time of danger, either hunting or upon the warpath, in the belief that the wolf would inspire the singer with his cunning. It was also sung at times of celebration such as when a powerful chief took a bride!

Cougar was aware of the meaning of the song and the dancing. He himself had joined in many times, imitating the wolf as he and his friends danced and sang together.

But tonight was different. He felt as though he might have lost the most important person in his life, even before he and Annamae had enjoyed their first night together as a married couple!

Twilight had faded into darkness.

The bright fires inside the many tepees revealed their weird decorations and the moving shadows of those within who had left the celebration to retire for the night, believing all was well in their chief's lodge.

"Nothing is right!" he cried to himself, hoping there was a way to make amends with Annamae. He must make his wife believe that when he gazed upon her, he saw no one but her.

Yes, when he'd first met Annamae he had made comparisons, but he had fallen in love with Annamae for herself, not for her resemblance to a long-lost love.

Now he must convince her of that, or lose her forever!

CHAPTER
TWENTY-SIX

Truly feeling betrayed, and, oh, so empty inside, Annamae ran alongside the river.

All she wanted now was to flee.

But where?

She had no idea.

She just wanted to get away from this place where she had lost her heart, and now her pride.

She felt like a fool for ever having believed that a man such as Cougar could truly love her.

Blinded by tears, she continued running onward beneath the great white moon and the glittering stars.

From somewhere to her left, amid the trees, she could hear the soft sound of an owl hooting into the night.

That made her lonesomeness twofold, for the call of an owl always made her feel lonely . . . lonely for her life before the renegades had slain her parents and baby brother.

Back home, there had been many barn owls that serenaded her family during the hours of night.

One morning, she had seen one that was pure white. A white owl had been rare in the area where she had lived.

They weren't so rare here in Montana. She had seen two flying together one early evening. . . .

"Annamae! Stop!"

Annamae's heart felt crushed when she heard Cougar shouting at her from behind, realizing that surely his people now knew she had fled their chief on their wedding night.

Oh, what would they think?

But that was not her concern any longer.

Finding a place to go without Cougar was her only worry now.

She suddenly tripped on a rock and found herself awkwardly falling to the ground, her head hitting first.

The impact momentarily took her breath away, and when she regained it, Cougar was there, sweeping her up and into his powerful arms.

He looked fuzzy at first when she gazed at him, her vision momentarily impaired by the fall.

But as she regained her sight, the moon's sheen on Cougar's handsome copper face showed her an expression that told her once again how foolish she was to love him. Even now, he could pretend too well that he cared about her.

"Let me down," she said, pummeling her fists against his hard chest. "I've had enough of you and your lies. I . . . I . . . want to leave this place and never see it or you again."

"I understand your reaction to what I said, but you must listen now to what I truly meant," Cougar said.

He held her firmly as she tried to squirm free. "Yes, I saw many things about you that reminded me of Dancing Dove, but it was you, not your resemblance to her, that I fell in love with," he said passionately. "I love you, not a memory. The reason I told you about her in the first place was because I felt I owed you an explanation . . . I wanted you to know that I did love someone before you. I was afraid that someone in the village might tell you about her. I wanted to be the one to tell you, not someone who might confuse you about the truth."

"No matter who told me, the truth is still there — that surely when you look into my eyes you see . . . Dancing Dove," she said, finding it so hard to say the name of someone who had meant so much to him.

Even the name was beautiful!

"When I look at you, I see the woman I love today," Cougar said thickly. "After I discovered my love for you, the woman of my youth faded into the wind. Please understand that what I say is true. I love you, only you, not some childhood fantasy. Had someone else told you of my childhood infatuation, would you have not felt that I had kept it from you for a reason?"

"Yes, all the wrong reasons," Annamae blurted out, her shoulders swaying with a sudden ecstasy she tried to fight off when he gently reached a thumb to her cheek and brushed away her tears."

Oh, she did love him so much!

She could never love anyone else.

He was her one and only love, for she had never before loved anyone else.

She wished now that she had. Maybe then, knowing about his young love would have been more understandable, more . . .

In the soft white light of the moon's glow, he searched her eyes. "Can you reach inside your heart and find a way to believe me?" he asked in a pleading tone. "This is our special night, our first as husband and wife. Let me take you to our lodge and prove just

how much I do love you. I want you, Annamae. My heart is dying with the fear that
you might never allow me to truly love you
again."

Annamae had listened hard and had allowed herself to measure every word of what
he had said to her about this young love he
had had so many years ago. She was feeling
foolish now for having made such a fuss
over his revelation.

She could see in his eyes how much he
loved her . . . Annamae!

Oh, Lord, she could hear it in his words.
His voice!

And she could feel it in the way he held
her so tenderly, close to his pounding heart.

"I do love you so much," she sobbed,
flinging her arms around his neck and moving her lips toward his.

He met her with an all-consuming kiss,
one more passionate than ever before,
because he knew now that she did believe
him and wanted to stay with him forever
and be his wife.

He knew that she wanted to raise Gray
Stone with him, as well as those children
they would bring together into this world.

"Take me home," she whispered against
his lips. "Please . . . take me home."

To avoid arousing curiosity, and not wanting his people to realize that their chief's wedding night had been momentarily spoiled by a misunderstanding, Cougar carried Annamae into the shadows of the trees until they reached the back of his tepee. Then they ran around to the entrance flap and darted inside.

The celebration continued on into the night as the dancers thumped their feet against the hard-packed earth around the great, roaring outdoor fire.

The children were allowed to stay up past their bedtime, singing and dancing and playing around the fire.

What remained of the food from the wedding feast had been carried inside the lodges of those women who had cooked the food. It was hung over the warm coals of their fires, to be eaten early the next morning as their first meal of the day.

Once back inside his tepee, Cougar eased Annamae down onto the plush pelts beside the fire, then went back to the entranceway and drew the flap tightly closed, fastening each tie securely.

Annamae's breath caught in her throat when she saw him turn to her. In his eyes was such love, she knew that nothing would ever make her doubt him again.

"Come to me," she said, her voice soft and

lilting as she held her hands out for him. "I want to prove to you how much I love you. Oh, husband, I am so sorry I ever doubted you. I shall make it up to you tonight and every night from here on."

A keen pleasure spread through her body when he came and knelt over her, his lips bearing hard down upon hers in a meltingly hot kiss as his fingers eagerly undressed her.

Soon her earrings and necklace were removed and her braids were untwined, her hair spread out beneath her as she lay nude on the soft, plush pelts. He stood up and undressed himself as she watched, and she blushed when she saw that part of him that would soon give her such pleasure.

The heat of his gaze scorched her as he came and knelt over her. Annamae wrapped her arms around his neck and brought his lips down to hers, melting inside when he kissed her with a fierce, possessive heat. His hands moved over her body, caressing her soft, vulnerable places until they tingled to his touch.

She gave herself up to the rapture when he moved his lips from her mouth to a nipple, rolling it with his tongue.

She arched her body up closer to his, and the very touch of his flesh against hers made Annamae moan with a longing she had never known until she had fallen in love with this wonderfully handsome and caring man.

A raging hunger washed through her, and she gasped with a keen pleasure when she felt him plunge his manhood into her. He withdrew and plunged again, until she became almost mindless with the desire he was arousing within her.

She seemed to know that her pleasure would be even greater if she placed her legs around his hips, and she moaned with ecstasy when she realized that she was right.

He was able to sink more deeply into her warmth, over and over again. He now held her as though in a vise, his lips pressed against her cheek, his breathing ragged.

She writhed in response to his each and every movement, his kisses firing her desire.

"My love," she whispered against his lips as he cradled her close with one arm, his free hand moving slowly over her, touching her where he knew she would feel the most pleasure.

The euphoria that was filling Cougar's entire being was reaching the point where he could hardly bear the waiting. He needed to reach the ultimate pleasure with this woman who was now his wife, the woman who would bear him strong sons and beautiful daughters!

He was overcome with feverish heat as her body moved rhythmically with his. He knew that the moment of sheer, total ecstasy was near, yet he paused to savor the taste and feel of her lips and the touch of her body for a while longer.

But when he tried to draw air into his lungs one more time as he awaited that moment of total bliss with his wife, he could only tremble and plunge himself more deeply inside her.

He soon realized that she had found that moment of no return as well. Her body trembled almost violently, and she clung to the rock hardness of his shoulders, crying out her pleasure at the very moment he finally found his.

When their bodies became quiet, yet still clinging together, his steel arms still enfolding her, Annamae sobbed against his lips.

"My dear, dear husband, you have made my life so full, so complete," she murmured. "I am so very content to be your wife. And I can tell that you are just as content."

"More than that," Cougar whispered against her lips. "I have never felt such complete happiness as now. My wife, my woman, at this moment you are all there is on this earth. Nothing else matters."

"Your people . . ." Annamae said, leaning a little away from him to search his eyes.

"Always my people," Cougar said huskily. "But that is a different sort of love. The loyalties are different." He leaned farther away from her. He softly brushed a strand of hair aside. "You are awesome in your beauty. You are my everything."

"As you are mine," Annamae said, realizing that while they were talking, one of his hands had traveled lower and was now stroking her where she was still tender from their frantic lovemaking.

She closed her eyes and moaned in ecstasy when the rhythmic pressure of his hand between her legs became almost torturous. Her need for him filled her again, and she yearned for his powerful manhood.

She opened her eyes and smiled into his as one of her hands went to his manhood, her fingers opening and wrapping about him. Slowly she moved her hand on him in a rhythm that she knew pleased him. She could see it in the look of dark passion in the depths of his eyes.

While she pleasured him in that way, his fingers caressed her swollen love bud, bringing to her such bliss she drew a ragged breath, closed her eyes, and let the feelings overwhelm her.

He touched her lips wonderingly with his own, then gave her a kiss so heated, her senses reeled.

She clung to his shoulders and gave herself up to this newest rapture, floating . . . floating . . . floating. . . .

CHAPTER
TWENTY-SEVEN

Tears of joy spilling from her eyes, Ellie watched Howard approaching on horseback with the others. She was so very glad that he had made it back to her alive.

Yet she didn't like the look of the Indians with her husband.

And where was Annamae?

Had Howard's attempts to get her back failed?

Was Annamae dead?

For the moment, though, Ellie was just happy that Howard had returned to her, no matter how. He was obviously not injured, and as their gazes met, he smiled reassuringly at her. Ellie sighed with a relief she had never felt before.

Then, with hands clasped in front of her, she watched as Howard and the other men who had accompanied him stopped and dismounted. One Indian rode up close to Howard, stopping and frowning.

She listened with a pounding heart as the Indian, speaking plain English, warned Howard to keep his distance from the Blackfoot people, especially their chief's woman.

Howard nodded and watched with the others as the Indian wheeled his horse around and rode off with his warrior companions.

Then Ellie broke into a run and didn't stop until she was clutched in her husband's arms. "Oh, Howard, it has been horrible not knowing how you were," she sobbed. "And what of Annamae?"

She could feel his arms tighten at the mention of Annamae.

He gently placed his hands on Ellie's shoulders and took a slow step away from her.

"Annamae is gone forever," he said. "And, Ellie, it is of her own choosing."

"What do you mean . . . of her own choosing?" Ellie asked. She searched his eyes. "Howard, what did that warrior mean when he warned you to stay away from his chief's woman?"

She placed a hand over her mouth. "No." She gasped. "Please don't tell me he was referring to Annamae."

"Exactly," Howard said, dropping his

hands to his sides. He turned to the others and shouted, "Pack your wagons. We're getting out of here."

Then he took one of Ellie's hands and walked with her toward their wagon, nodding a quiet hello to those members of his carnival crew who had stayed behind with Ellie, waiting.

Over his shoulder he watched as the men who had accompanied him on his fruitless venture went to their own loved ones, hugging and kissing, and some even crying.

"Are you saying Annamae truly wanted to stay behind because . . . because of an Indian?" Ellie asked, turning pale at the thought of Annamae actually being in love with a savage.

"Not just any Indian, Ellie," Howard said, helping Ellie into the wagon. "A chief, Ellie. Annamae stayed behind because of a Blackfoot chief."

"You mean she's in love with him?" Ellie gasped. "Howard, are you certain it was Annamae's decision to stay with the chief? Could she have been forced to say she would stay, while all along wanting to leave with you?"

"Ellie, if you had seen how Annamae acted when she caught me standing in her tepee, you'd know well enough how she feels about that Injun," Howard growled out.

An hour later the wagons were packed and everyone was ready to travel onward. Howard settled himself in the driver's seat of his own wagon, called Ellie to come forward and join him, then set his eyes forward and snapped his reins.

The horses responded immediately and moved into a gentle trot, the wagon wheels squeaking as they rolled across the soft sweetgrass.

Ellie reached over and grabbed the reins from Howard. She yanked hard on them and stopped the two horses.

"What in damnation are you doing?" Howard shouted, grabbing the reins back from her. "Ellie, has my absence caused you to go stark, raving mad? Why on earth did you take the reins and stop the horses?"

"Because we're not going anywhere but back in the direction of that Indian village," Ellie said in her most determined voice. She folded her arms angrily across her chest. "We're going to save Annamae. I won't stand for us not trying."

"In my absence you've surely gone loco," Howard said, frowning at her. "Didn't you hear anything I said? Didn't you hear the warrior's warning to stay away from his people, especially Annamae? If we were to show our faces there again, we'd not only lose our hair as quick as you can bat an eye, but we'd be dead."

"Not if only you and I went and asked for her," Ellie said, her jaw tight with determination. "Surely they could see that we were coming in peace. A woman's presence would make a lot of difference. I could plead Annamae's case by telling them that I've raised her as my daughter and I want her back."

"You are talking hogwash," Howard growled out.

Ellie grabbed the reins again, so that Howard would have to listen to what she said. "Howard, you're behaving like a coward," she said tightly. "And you know that's not the sort of man you are, or you wouldn't have sneaked into an Indian village in order to save Annamae."

"This is different, Ellie," Howard said, kneading his brow in frustration. "I've been warned, and by damn, I heed warnings, especially if they come directly from an Injun's mouth. You should've seen how we were treated after they discovered us there."

Ellie's eyes widened. "What do you mean?" she asked, her voice drawn. "How . . . were you treated?"

"The savages tied us to stakes in the middle of the village and left us there a long time without water or food, or . . . means to go and do personal things," he said, his voice cracking with embarrassment. He remembered that he had had no choice but to soil his breeches more than once during that awful night.

"I think you know what I mean," Howard said.

"No." Ellie gasped. "They wouldn't be that cruel."

"Yes, and I'm sure they enjoyed seeing our embarrassment," Howard replied. "But before we were told we were free to leave, they gave us clean clothes — as you can see, they are buckskins — and allowed us to bathe, and then fed us. At least they were that decent to us."

Even so, Howard had been eager to get as far as he could from that pack of savages.

"My Lord," Ellie said. "You are truly lucky to be alive."

"That's what I'm trying to tell you, Ellie," Howard said flatly. "Now, can we proceed and get as far from those redskins as possible before they have a change of heart and come for us again?"

"Yes, I do think that's best," Ellie said, then tightened her jaw as she glared directly into Howard's eyes. "But after we get everyone down the road a piece, we're leaving the crew, Howard, and returning to that Blackfoot village for Annamae. I'll do the talking this time."

"I know you're as stubborn as a mule, Ellie, but damn it, haven't you heard a word that I said?" Howard shouted, drawing everyone's attention to their argument. "It's too dangerous to go back there. And Annamae is content as she is. We're not going to interfere any longer in her life."

"You'd let her marry a savage?" Ellie gasped out. "You'd let her bear children to . . . a . . . savage?"

"If that's what she wants to do, hell, yes," Howard retorted. He turned quickly to the left when he heard the approach of a horse behind him.

He squinted his eyes as he looked at the man approaching him, then widened them. "Well, don't that beat all?" he said, raising an eyebrow. "If it ain't that no-good son of a gun Reuben Jones. What's he want, and how in the hell did he find us?"

Ellie sighed deeply. "Oh, Lord. Maybe he thinks Annamae is still with us. Why else would he show his pockmarked face to us again?"

"He's the sort that never gives up,"

Howard said, looking over his shoulder at the rifle he and Ellie always kept behind the seat of the wagon in case of sudden danger.

Reuben had never before caused that sort of trouble. What would he do now that Annamae wasn't there for him to torment any longer?

They waited until Reuben drew rein beside their wagon.

"What do you want?" Howard growled as he glared at Reuben, flinching with disgust when drool spilled from one corner of the beady-eyed man's mouth. "If it's Annamae you're seeking, you've wasted your time. Just turn around and go back where you came from."

"Annamae is exactly why I am here," Reuben said, resting his right hand on a holstered pistol at his right hip.

"Like I said, Reuben, you've wasted your time coming to get a glimpse of Annamae. You're even wasting my time, for she ain't here," Howard said, slowly nodding. "So, nitwit, you just get on outta here and leave us in peace."

"I know she ain't with you . . . nitwit," Reuben replied mockingly. "And I know exactly where she is." His gaze fell to where he recalled Howard had soiled himself when he was tied to a stake in the Indian village.

Reuben smiled at Howard. "I saw it all," he said. "I saw you tied at that village."

He snickered. "I even seen you pee your pants," he went on. "But I also saw Annamae there. Howard, I want the same thing you want . . . to get Annamae away from the Indians."

"Well, seems you're wrong about that," Howard replied, ignoring Reuben's insulting words. "Me and my men have been warned about getting near Annamae again, and if you think what happened before was bad just think what'd they do to us, you included, were we to go back there and cause Chief Cougar trouble again over Annamae. Over anything. Nope. I want nothing to do with whatever you have planned. You're nothing but trouble."

"Don't you see?" Reuben said. "I was there. I was that close to Annamae, and nothin' happened to me. If I could get that close before, I can do it again. But I need help. I can't rescue her all by myself. Tell the others what we're going to do; then come on with me. We'll get Annamae this time. I guarantee it."

Howard threw his head back in a fit of laughter, then solemnly stared into Reuben's eyes. "You can't guarantee anything but getting us all scalped and killed," he grumbled. He slung a hand in the air. "Get outta here, nitwit, and that's the last time I'll tell you. Be warned that if you come anywhere near me or my carnival crew you'll be sorry."

"You're a coward," Reuben said, glowering. "You're a yellow-bellied coward."

"If you're so brave, go and try to get Annamae yourself," Howard said flatly. "But I'll tell you one thing; I won't tempt fate again."

"Don't you care for Annamae at all?" Reuben asked, moving slow eyes over to Ellie. "Don't you? Surely you care for her. You took her in. You raised her as your child. Tell your husband he's wrong to leave her at the mercy of those savages."

Ellie's jaw tightened, for she saw this man as someone who never stopped interfering in things that were none of his business. Had he not arrived when he did, she truly believed she could have talked Howard into going for Annamae.

Now she wasn't sure about anything.

Just angry!

Reuben looked at Howard again. "Do you truly care so little for Annamae?" he demanded.

"Right now I care more for my own hide than I ever cared for Annamae," Howard

298

answered, drawing a gasp from his wife as she looked at him in disbelief. "She served me well enough, but now she's no longer my responsibility. She's gone, I tell you, so stop hanging around my carnival."

"I see no carnival here," Reuben said, laughing sarcastically. "And I've a right to be wherever I want to be." He leaned his face closer to Howard's. "Come on. Let's get together and go save Annamae. We could even seek help from the cavalry."

"I don't think you hear well enough," Howard said. He looked Reuben square in the eye. "Get outta here, or I won't be responsible for what I do to you. I've heard what you said today, but for the last time, you damn nitwit, get outta here!"

Reuben glowered again at Howard, then wheeled his horse around and rode away. It was all up to him now. He would get Annamae, or at least die trying.

He rode off in the direction of the Blackfoot village.

Howard frowned and snapped the reins against the horses' rumps. "That nitwit has no idea what fate awaits him if he tries the nonsense he says he's going to try," he said, ignoring Ellie's angry stare.

Without any warning, she gave him a slap across the face, causing him to look quickly at her, his eyes wide with shock.

"Reuben is right about you," she said, slowly shaking her head back and forth. "You're a coward. A yellow-bellied coward."

CHAPTER
TWENTY-EIGHT

The sounds of the Blackfoot village were comforting to Annamae as she sat alone beside her husband's fire pit, making moccasins of a discarded lodge covering, while Cougar was in council with his warriors.

She could hear the children laughing and playing, among them Gray Stone, who was well enough now to resume his normal activities.

Annamae knew that he would soon leave to achieve an unfinished goal . . . completing his vision quest.

She felt somewhat uncomfortable about his leaving, for he would be gone for four long days and nights.

But each time she began feeling uneasy about his vision quest, she reminded herself of his mother and why she had died. She had feared for her son's safety far too much. With that sad example in mind, Annamae cleared her own thoughts of any concern for what Gray Stone would soon do, for she did not want to be a fearful, overprotective mother.

And Cougar had reassured her that Gray Stone's quest was a natural thing for a young brave his age, that all young braves had their own vision quests to achieve, and they normally occurred without any mishaps.

It was certain that Gray Stone had brought on all that happened by not following the rules set down for the vision quest. Both Cougar and Annamae knew that Gray Stone would never do anything so misguided again!

Annamae paused for a moment in her sewing to gaze into the slowly burning flames of the fire, smiling when she thought of her husband.

It was now so natural to wake up in Cougar's arms each morning, savoring those moments with each other before they got up and began their day's activities.

This new world she had found was one of wondrous happiness and peace.

She had finally been able to put behind her everything that had caused her pain in the past. This was a new life for her, one that she cherished with every beat of her heart.

She placed a hand on her tummy, smiling at a dream she had had more than once recently. She had dreamed of being out in the forest, picking baskets of herbs with the other women, and finding a nest full of bird's eggs.

Having studied dreams, she knew the meaning of the bird's eggs. They meant the dreamer was with child!

"A baby," she whispered, sighing at the very thought of holding a child born of her and Cougar's special love.

She knew that since she had dreamed that same dream four nights in a row, it had to be true!

She beamed at the thought of being able to tell Cougar that she was with child. She was only waiting to be absolutely certain. Already she had missed her first monthly since her marriage to Cougar. If she went another couple of weeks without showing any blood, then she would know for certain that her dreams had told her the truth.

And because of those dreams, she had chosen today not to make moccasins for her or her husband, but for a baby.

She was doing this secretly, wanting to surprise Cougar with them, so she had a pair of moccasins that she was making for her husband, too. She kept them close by, so she could grab them if she heard him coming toward their tepee.

She would hide the child's moccasins beneath the end of her doeskin skirt and resume sewing the larger pair until he left.

Once their baby's first pair of moccasins was finished, she would know whether she was truly with child. If she was, she planned to reveal her news to Cougar in a unique way.

She would place the tiny, completed moccasins, beautifully designed with soft-colored beads, on her husband's dinner plate.

She giggled at the very thought of how he would react to such a gift.

He would slowly pick them up, gaze in wonder at them, and then look quickly at her with a huge smile. She knew he would understand the meaning behind the moccasins. He was as anxious for a child as she.

For the present they reveled in their relationship with Gray Stone. He was their child now, loved as much as if he had been born to them in the natural way.

Gray Stone's place in the tepee was at the far back, where he had moved his own belongings and his bed.

At night, when it was time to go to sleep, Annamae unrolled a blanket that her husband had strung between two lodge poles, so that the child have his privacy, and so would Annamae and Cougar.

But even so, they made certain Gray Stone was asleep before making love.

Feeling so content it sometimes frightened her, because she knew that life could change in a heartbeat, Annamae resumed her work on the tiny pair of moccasins.

Seeing the tanned white buffalo skin that she was using to make the moccasins reminded Annamae of all she had learned since becoming Cougar's wife.

Blue Blossom was not only Annamae's special friend, but now her teacher.

Each day she taught Annamae something new about their people's customs or everyday lives.

Blue Blossom had told Annamae that when a lodge covering was discarded so that a new one could be put up in its place, it was cut up for moccasins. The hide would not harden or shrink when the wearer went outside in the snow or rain, for the lodge covering had already been exposed to such extreme weather.

Annamae now knew that eight buffalo skins were required to make a small lodge, and from twenty to thirty to make a tepee as large as the one in which she now made her home with Cougar and Gray Stone.

She had been taught that the best poles for the tepees were made from slim, straight mountain pines, which the women cut and peeled and seasoned slowly, to keep them straight.

In time, Annamae would be making a new lodge for her family; she would be certain it was made correctly, so that it would hold up against all sorts of weather.

The weather today was mild and wonderful, and a sweet scent wafted through the open entrance flap. Annamae looked quickly toward the entranceway, her eyes widening when she heard a child cry out in pain.

Wanting to see what had happened, and to whom, she quickly slid her half-made moccasins inside her sewing basket, making sure they were hidden from view.

She then rushed outside just in time to see Cougar and White Thunder kneel down beside a little girl, who was crying, and whose mother was running toward her.

"What happened?" Annamae asked as she came up to her husband's side. He was holding the girl in his arms while White Thunder examined a bloody streak on her arm.

"The cub," Cougar said sadly, looking over his shoulder at Gray Stone who was holding the cub protectively in his arms, yet with a look of apology in his eyes.

"The cub?" Annamae asked, kneeling down beside Cougar as the child's mother watched White Thunder wash the blood from the wound, and then apply a treatment of his own making.

"It was playing with the children and, without realizing the lethality of its claws, scratched the child accidentally," Cougar said. "You know what that means, do you not?"

"I am afraid that I do," Annamae said, an ache filling her heart.

"We will leave soon to take the cub away," Cougar said, gently laying the child in her mother's arms.

Annamae turned and looked at Gray Stone as she rose to her feet beside Cougar. Tears came to her own eyes as she saw the special bond between the child and the animal. But they had all known from the very beginning that the cub would not be able to stay with Gray Stone.

And when Annamae recalled the huge grizzly bear she'd seen, she shivered at the thought that the cub might one day be as large and as dangerous.

"Yes, it must be done," she murmured, walking with Cougar over to Gray Stone, who still held the cub tightly in his arms.

"I know what you are talking about," Gray Stone said, nodding as Cougar placed a gentle hand on his bare shoulder. "And I understand."

He gazed quickly up at Cougar. "But I wish we did not have to do it," he said, his voice breaking. "I love him so much."

"As he loves you, Gray Stone," Cougar said, kneeling down beside Gray Stone.

Cougar reached out and stroked the cub's fur, yet his eyes were on the animal's sharp claws. "We are fortunate the child was not harmed more than she was today," he said. "Just look at those claws. And his teeth are very sharp, too."

"When must we do it?" Gray Stone asked.

"Now," Cougar said, his voice firm. "We cannot risk waiting any longer. Today a child was injured, but not as terribly as she could have been. The next time it could be deadly."

"But . . . today . . . ?" Gray Stone gulped out.

He winced when the cub squirmed free and leaped to the ground, running toward the group of children who had circled around Gray Stone.

"Oh, no," Gray Stone cried, leaping to his feet and running after the cub.

Having seen the wound the cub had inflicted on their friend, the children scattered, screaming in fear.

"You see?" Cougar said when he came up to Gray Stone, stopping him by placing a heavy hand on his arm. "Now. It must be done now. The children are too frightened of the cub to want to be near him."

"And that is so sad, for my cub would never purposely harm anyone," Gray Stone said, bending to one knee when the cub came back to him, seemingly hurt by the children's reaction to him.

"No, never purposely," Cougar said, gently patting Gray Stone on the head. "You are strong enough to travel now, so you will go with me. Let's get our things ready. We will leave before it gets dark. We can make camp somewhere between home and where I believe we should take the cub to release him."

Annamae came to Cougar's side. "I want to go, too," she murmured.

"I would not think of leaving without you," Cougar said, rising and drawing her gently into his arms. "I know how you feel about the cub. It is only right that you are there to say a final good-bye."

"Yes, a final good-bye," Annamae said, tears streaming from her eyes. . . .

CHAPTER
TWENTY-NINE

Morning was soft and pretty as the sun began rising slowly in the east, casting its orange light on the trees and the gently blowing grass of a meadow.

Elsewhere, where the trees grew thick along the embankment of a broad stream, birds were just awakening in the aspens, some scrambling from limb to limb, chirping, while others took sudden flight.

Not far away from the noisy chatter of the birds, the feel of cold steel at his temple awakened Howard with a start.

His heart thumped wildly in his chest. He was afraid to see who was standing over him, holding a gun at his head.

His first thought was that it was Indians, who had fooled him into believing he was free, leaving him with his wife and friends, while knowing all along they would not be far away, ready to take him captive again.

He wanted to cry out, to awaken the others to the danger facing them on this lovely early morning, but words seemed stuck in his throat, rendering him absolutely speechless.

So he just lay there, breathing hard, awaiting his fate. Most disturbing of all were thoughts of his wife, and how the savages would enjoy taking her long, lovely hair as their prize for their scalp poles.

"Please . . . please have mercy," Howard finally managed to say in a small, pitiful squeak of a voice. "Leave my wife in peace. She . . . she . . . doesn't deserve to die like this."

"And you bet your bottom dollar I'm not going to die anytime soon," he heard his wife say. She sounded as though she were standing right over him, instead of lying where she had spread her blankets the night before.

She had wanted to be closer to the fire, she had said, and he hated the heat from a campfire. So he had encouraged her to sleep where she chose, although he was hurt that she hadn't wanted to snuggle up next to him after they had been parted for so long.

"What did you just say?" Howard asked.

"You heard me," Ellie said, still holding the barrel of the rifle against her husband's right temple. "I'm not dying anytime soon,

311

but you might, if you don't change your mind about going for Annamae."

Suddenly realizing that the one holding him hostage was not an Indian, but instead his very own wife, Howard rolled quickly over on his back to find the barrel of the gun aimed directly at his nose.

"Ellie, what in tarnation do you think you're doing?" Howard demanded, starting to grab the rifle from her. He stopped when she dug the barrel into the bridge of his nose.

"Ellie, for God's sake, stop it," Howard said, his heart thumping just as hard now that he knew it wasn't Indians who were threatening him, but his wife.

"I'll stop it only when you agree to go for Annamae," Ellie said, very aware now that others were awake, and gawking disbelievingly at what she was doing.

She didn't glance their way, but shouted a warning that made her wonder at her own sanity.

"I can turn this firearm quickly on any of you who want to interfere in a husband and wife's disagreement," she said tightly. "If you don't like what you see, turn your eyes away. I've got to encourage my husband to do something today, and it seems this is the only way I can do it."

"Ellie, have you gone stark, raving mad?" Howard said, his eyes holding hers. "I didn't teach you how to shoot a gun, only to have you use it on me. Turn that barrel away from me. Lower the gun to your side. Then we can talk like decent people."

"Howard, yesterday I saw the true person you are. I knew right then that the responsibility of saving Annamae had fallen suddenly on my own shoulders. So here I am. I'm trying to convince you in the only way I know to go with me back to the Indian village and try to talk sense into those redskins' heads. Annamae deserves a second chance with us, and we're going to give it to her."

"And that second chance would be . . . ?" Howard asked sarcastically.

"Once she's back with us, she won't be forced to do things she doesn't want to do," Ellie said tightly. "She'd just be with us as our daughter, not a carnival worker forced to pretend to interpret dreams."

"All right, all right, enough, enough," Howard said, slowly raising a hand toward the rifle. He dropped it quickly back at his side when Ellie shoved the barrel even harder against his nose.

"Say it, Howard," Ellie said, searching his eyes. "Tell me you'll go with me to try to talk sense into those Indians about our Annamae. It will be just the two of us. That way we won't be seen as a threat."

"Ellie, didn't you hear them warning me never to come around again?" Howard asked, a cold sweat breaking out on his brow at the thought of what the Indians might do to him were he to disobey their orders.

"Yes, but that was only because they thought you might try to steal Annamae again," Ellie said, now slowly lowering the rifle to her side.

Howard leaped to his feet and leaned his face into Ellie's. "I can't believe this is you pulling these crazy stunts," he growled. "Do you realize you just held me hostage with a damn rifle? Your very own husband?"

"Seems I do recall it," Ellie said, her eyes gleaming mischievously. "Didn't think I had it in me, did you?"

"Hell, no," Howard said, taking the rifle from her. "Now let's get this straight. You think we can go back to that village and not get scalped? Surely you are jesting."

"Did I look like I was a minute ago?" Ellie said, placing her hands on her hips. "Now, when can we leave? After we eat? Or before?"

"You're serious," Howard said, kneading his brow. "You really mean to go."

"If you don't go with me, I'll go alone," Ellie said flatly. "I only realized how much I love Annamae since she's been gone. I feel horrible about how we forced her to do things she obviously didn't want to do."

She hung her head. "She felt the only way out was to leave us altogether," she murmured.

Then she pleaded with her eyes. "Howard, I know now that I love her like my own child, and I just can't sit by and do nothing to rescue her," she said. "Let's at least try."

"Even knowing the chances are slim that we'd even be allowed to get near that village without being killed?" Howard said gruffly.

"Again, Howard, let me say that I think my presence would make all the difference in the world," Ellie said. "I'm willing to chance everything to get her back with us."

"Ellie, I told you that she has feelings for that chief," Howard said. "So you see, you'd not only have the Indians to convince; you'd have to convince her, too. If she's fallen hard for that redskin, which I've heard happens when white women are taken hostage by savages, she won't come back home with us, no matter what you say."

"I've always been able to talk sense into her head," Ellie said, sighing. "I've got to at least try to make her see how wrong it is to want to be with a savage."

She visibly shuddered. "The mere thought of her being in bed with a redskin makes my skin crawl," she said tightly. "We've got to do this, Howard. We've got to. It's the only way to save Annamae from a life she will soon learn to deplore."

"It's quite a ways back to that village," Howard said, looking over his shoulder.

"But you weren't blindfolded, were you?" Ellie asked, searching his eyes as he gazed into hers. "You could find your way back there, couldn't you?"

"Ellie, I could, but it would go against everything I believe is right or safe," Howard replied. "Still, if you are this determined, I know there's nothing I can do to change your mind."

Ellie's eyes brightened. "Then you will go?" she asked, hearing gasps from those who were listening and watching.

"Yes, we'll go, but you'd better be praying every inch of the way that what we're doing doesn't land us in the grave."

"What about us?" Snake Man asked as he stepped up to Howard. "Are you just abandoning us? What about the carnival? You know we've wasted a lot of time already. There are people who are expecting our carnival show in their towns. What will they think? If we're so late in coming, they might not even welcome us."

"Our carnival acts are always welcomed, because the people who live in these small, dumpy towns are always looking for some fun and excitement," Howard said, gently patting Snake Man on the shoulder. "You sit tight. Take charge. Make sure everyone is fed and warm until we get back."

"But how will I know . . . if . . . you are coming back?" Snake Man gulped out. "What if they . . ."

He lowered his eyes and didn't finish what he was saying.

"If we don't make it back, you can have all rights to the carnival," Howard said, laying a heavy hand on Snake Man's shoulder. "Do you hear me, Earl? It will be rightly yours, because I am telling you it is so."

It had been years since Earl had heard his true name spoken, and he smiled broadly to hear it now. He was even more pleased to hear that he would be the sole owner of the carnival if Howard and Ellie did not return.

"Just see that everyone is treated right," Howard said, his voice breaking.

"I sure will," Earl promised. He flung himself into Howard's arms. "But I don't want to take over. I want you to come back to us. Please be safe."

"I'll do the best I can for me and Ellie . . . and Annamae," Howard said, easing himself from Earl's arms. "We'll be leaving now. Help rustle up some grub for everyone. Ellie and I'll eat after we're down the road a piece."

Ellie went to everyone, hugging each. She was beginning to wonder if the course of action she'd insisted on was foolishness, and felt the sting of tears in her eyes.

She brushed the tears away and hurried back to her wagon to begin gathering supplies for their journey to the Indian village.

After everything was chosen and the bag of provisions had been loaded on one of their horses, they waved good-bye and set out on a journey that they knew might be their last. Nonetheless, both held their chins high, knowing that Annamae's future lay in balance.

When they had taken her in after the massacre of her family, they had promised to care for her.

Somewhere along the line they had lost sight of that commitment and had forced things on her they now knew were wrong.

From now on, things would be different!

CHAPTER
THIRTY

After Cougar, Annamae, and Gray Stone had traveled a full day in search of the cub's original territory, where his brothers and sisters might still be roaming about, Cougar had suggested they stop for the night. They had not yet seen signs of bears anywhere.

Even now a small fire burned in the fire pit made of rocks placed in a tight circle where grass had been cleared for the campfire.

The sun was beginning to descend toward the horizon. The air was filled with the tantalizing smell of a rabbit that had been cooked over the fire.

Cougar and Annamae were stretched out on a blanket they had spread over a thick carpet of moss and pine needles near the fire. They were enjoying nature to the fullest before night fell.

"Gray Stone is already asleep," Annamae murmured as she glanced over at the child, who lay on his own blanket nearby.

It had been a long day of travel.

Neither Annamae nor Gray Stone was used to the grueling hours of such travel. Annamae worried that perhaps Gray Stone should not have come with them after having been so ill.

Today he had soon grown weary as he rode on his pony between Annamae and Cougar.

"We should have stopped earlier," Cougar said, leaning up and gazing at Gray Stone himself. "I believe now that we should not have brought him at all."

"But he would have been devastated if he were told to stay home while we left with the cub," Annamae murmured. "He wants as much time as he can get with the cub before turning him free."

"It's sad that we must do this at all," Annamae said, gazing at the cub, which was peacefully and trustingly snuggled in Gray Stone's arms. "And it seems so strange that we never named him."

"To have named him would have made giving him up even harder, for a name would make him truly a part of our lives," Cougar said thoughtfully. "It was best."

"The sweet thing, look how he is snuggled in Gray Stone's arms, as though he belongs there forever," Annamae said, tears filling her eyes. "He has no idea what is going on, that this might be our last night with him."

"When he finds himself with others of his kind, who will be as playful and loving with him as we have been, he will soon forget this part of his life and move forward into the existence he was born to live," Cougar said.

He turned his eyes away from the cub, for he felt it was best not to linger over watching him or talking about him. He knew how hard it was going to be on everyone to set him free.

"Look elsewhere, wife," Cougar encouraged, reaching over and taking one of her hands. "Fill your mind with other things. Look up into the sky. See how those ducks are flying just over the treetops, while far away you can hear the faint honking of migrating geese?"

"Migrating," Annamae murmured, doing as he suggested. She understood that he was trying to direct her thoughts away from what would soon be happening . . . saying good-bye to an animal that seemed to her almost human.

But she thought of the small child back at the village whose wounds were even now healing from the cub's claws.

Yes, she understood the need to take him back where he had come from. Still, it would be hard, especially for Gray Stone. The child would miss the cub terribly.

"Annamae?"

The sound of Cougar's voice made Annamae realize that her thoughts were still on the cub. She knew she must think of something else.

As soon as tomorrow she might be watching the cub romp away from them to join in play with others of its own kind, perhaps even his own brothers and sisters.

And it would be for the best. She did not believe it was wise for her to travel much longer now that she was almost certain she was with child. She wasn't sure how much activity a woman should engage in during her first months of pregnancy.

Could riding a horse long distances cause a miscarriage? That thought gave her a slight chill, for she had not yet even told her husband that he might be a father.

Soon.

Yes, as soon as they returned home, she would tell Cougar about the child. She would wait only until they were in the privacy of their lodge, where she had left the newly finished small moccasins.

It gave her a thrill to envision how it would

be when her husband knew the wondrous news. Soon they would share the ultimate joy of being husband and wife: they would share the love of a child.

Of course they already did that, for they both loved Gray Stone as if he were born of their own flesh.

She smiled when she thought of how Gray Stone would react when he first saw the baby. Surely he would be proud to be a big brother.

"Annamae, you are so filled with thoughts tonight," Cougar said. He reached over and took one of her hands. "And I understand. But we must do what we must. Setting the cub loose is the only way things can be."

"I know," Annamae said.

She wiped tears from her eyes with her free hand.

She longed to tell him that at that moment she wasn't thinking about the cub, but instead their child. But she would wait.

"Do you hear the geese?" Cougar said, looking in the direction of the continued honking.

"Yes, and I hate to see them migrating so soon," Annamae murmured. "That means we might be in for a cold, long winter."

"You will be kept warm enough in our lodge. I will see to it," Cougar said. He squeezed her hand reassuringly. "As for the geese, they are, indeed, endowed with great wisdom and foreknowledge of the weather. When they fly high, it is the sign of an early winter. This evening we cannot tell if they are flying high or low, since we cannot see them, but since they are migrating so early, I do believe that we will have a long winter."

"We had some terribly cold winters back home," Annamae murmured. "My papa somehow always knew whether or not it was going to be extra cold. When he expected it to be colder, he piled more firewood at our back door to keep the potbellied stove going. I don't ever remember having cold toes in our house.

"Oh, look over there," she went on, hurriedly sitting up and watching the flight of several short-eared owls that suddenly came into sight. "We had that kind of owl back home; they always fascinated me."

"Yes, I am familiar with this owl," Cougar said, watching the owls himself. "The flight of the short-eared owl is one of the most graceful of any owl, or, for that matter, of any bird."

"Yes, it's like that of a butterfly," Annamae said, nodding as she continued to watch them. "Always back home, the short-eared owls came out at sunset, not only for food, but to sky-dance."

She turned to Cougar. "The owls came out during the gloaming," she said.

"The gloaming?" he asked, raising an eyebrow.

"Yes, the gloaming," Annamae repeated, pleased that there was something she could teach him. Since they had met, he was always the one teaching her things. "It is that magic twilight time between day and night."

"I have never heard it called that," Cougar said.

"My mama told me that in myth, the gloaming is the place between the known and the unknown, the ordinary and the extraordinary," she murmured. "It is also the time when rarely seen creatures come out from the shadows. Mama said that the gloaming opens a portal to another world."

"Your mama?" Cougar asked, again arching an eyebrow.

"My mother," Annamae clarified. "I called my mother 'Mama' and my father 'Papa.' "

Cougar smiled and nodded.

"Back home, to the north, south, east, and west of our barn, dozens of short-eared owls emerged from their roosts in nearby hay bales, woodpiles, and trees," she said. "Like bats that flutter from caves at sundown, dozens of owls would suddenly take to the skies. Did you know that short-ears listen for their prey, which are small mammals like meadow voles and mice?"

She laughed softly. "Sometimes those owls festooned bare trees near our home like Christmas tree ornaments," she said.

"Christmas tree?" Cougar said curiously. "What is a Christmas tree?"

Realizing there was much Cougar did not know about her life and customs, Annamae told him about the meaning of Christmas, and how much she would enjoy having a tree with him this Christmas.

She laughed softly. "I realize there is no room in our home for a tree, but I can decorate one just outside the entranceway, if you don't mind," she suggested. "Could I?"

"You can do anything you wish," Cougar said, nodding. "It will intrigue my people, especially the children."

"I will show them how to make ornaments out of things I find in the forest," Annamae said, recalling those times she had wandered the forest with her mama, picking up pine-cones and nuts, which could be painted and hung on the tree they placed inside their home.

Oh, how she loved that smell of evergreen

in their house each year.

The sun had finally set, and the sky was quickly darkening. The owls took sudden flight and were soon lost from sight.

"Somewhere out there now, in the grasses, the owls are waiting for the next in-between time, the one that happens at dawn," Annamae murmured. She stretched out beside Cougar again, staring up at the starry heavens.

"And dawn brings the time when we must travel onward," Cougar said. "We will find a bear's den tomorrow. I feel it in my heart."

"I feel it, too," Annamae said, snuggling next to him. "But what if we don't? I don't think it's wise to travel much farther, with Gray Stone looking so tired. We still have to make the trip back to the village."

"If we don't find a den, we will have to set the cub free anyway," Cougar said. "He is born of the forest and has a built-in knowledge of where he belongs. He will sniff out a den that we cannot find."

"But will he let us leave him?" Annamae asked, turning to gaze at Cougar.

"We will leave him," Cougar said, his voice drawn. "Nature will take hold. I do believe that. The cub will feel comfortable enough to allow us humans to go to our own homes."

"I hope so," Annamae said, sighing.

"Do you miss your home?" Cougar asked, looking into her eyes. "I mean the carnival. You were a part of that life for so long. Do you ever think about it? Do you ever wish for it?"

"Never," Annamae said tightly. "I don't miss it at all. Not any of it. I always felt I was fooling people and I hated that."

"Do you miss those who rescued you and took you in as their own?" Cougar asked, searching her eyes.

"I must admit, I do think of them sometimes, especially Ellie, but not because I have a deep love for them," Annamae replied. "Especially Howard. He was despicable at times, so overbearing. When he chose to make me one of his carnival acts, I was horrified. I knew then that he had taken me in for only one purpose: to use me."

"And the woman — did she have a part in that, as well?" Cougar asked. "Or do you think she truly cared for you?"

"I believe that Ellie did have some deep feelings for me. You see, she never had children of her own," Annamae said.

"So you miss her?" Cougar asked.

"In a way," Annamae said, nodding.

"But mostly I'm just glad to be away from everything having to do with the carnival, even . . . Ellie," Annamae said softly. "I am so happy with you and your people. I hope one day to learn all I should know to be a true Blackfoot myself."

"You are an astute student," Cougar said, laughing softly. "You are both a good wife and a good student."

"And this wife and student is so tired," Annamae said, laying her head on his shoulder. "I need sleep badly, Cougar. I . . . don't remember being this tired for a long time."

"Sleep, my pretty, sweet wife," Cougar said, gently stroking her back through her dress. "I shall hold you as you rest."

"Then I shall have dreams of angels," Annamae said, laughing softly as she gazed into his midnight dark eyes.

"Dreams of angels?" he repeated.

"Happy dreams," Annamae said. "My mother called happy dreams 'dreams of angels.' "

"Then you have dreams of angels while I watch you sleep," Cougar said.

"But you need rest, too," Annamae said, searching his eyes.

"I, too, will sleep soon," Cougar said. "But first I want to watch you in your sleep."

She smiled and snuggled even closer to him, not conscious of the moment when she fell asleep, or when Cougar followed her into dreamland.

Nor did she or Cougar see the cub wake up and make its way off into the dark.

But soon Annamae awakened in a sweat.

She had not dreamed of angels at all.

She had had another horrible dream, in which Reuben was bending over her, leering at her as she slept.

She looked quickly around, as far as the fire's glow would allow.

When she saw nothing out of the ordinary, and no sign of that horrid man, she realized that she had just had another nightmare.

She looked over at Cougar, who slept so soundly and trustingly beside her, then snuggled once again against him.

No. She saw no need to awaken Cougar just to tell him that she had had another terrible dream.

Surely that sort of dream would end soon. The longer she went without seeing Reuben, the less she would dream such horrible things about him.

Within minutes she was fast asleep again, this time having sweet dreams of holding a newborn baby in her arms while her husband gazed down at them both with pride.

She smiled in her sleep.

Chapter
Thirty-One

The fire had turned to glowing embers as the sun painted early morning colors in the lightening heavens.

Reuben was startled awake by a sound behind him. It was a rustling of sorts, like someone walking across the leaves.

Before even looking to see who it might be, he sat up quickly and grabbed his rifle. He leaped to his feet then, and made a quick turn.

His heart was thumping wildly in his chest, and drool was streaming from the corners of his mouth as he searched the forest of aspen trees.

But fortunately he saw no one; nor did he hear anything other than the tiny owls that had just taken wing and were soaring high above him in the sky. Every once in a while, one would swoop lower and grab something in its talons, then fly away again after catching food for its breakfast.

Then he suddenly heard the same sort of rustling of leaves behind him again. He turned, wild-eyed, and looked once more for whatever might be causing it.

His eyebrows arched when he suddenly saw a small cub, and then two more, romping and playing in the shadows of the forest.

He recalled seeing a cub just a mite smaller than these. It had been caged alongside the Indian brave at the carnival. When the boy had come up missing, so had the cub.

"And so had Annamae," he growled to himself.

He lowered the rifle to his side, watched the cubs at play a moment longer, then settled down beside the fire, which had almost burned itself out.

He had gathered wood before settling into his blankets the night before. He shoved some of these branches into the hot coals, glad when the flames soon took hold.

His stomach growled loudly. He would catch something for his breakfast, and then he would make a retreat from this damn area. He had searched endlessly for the Blackfoot village, but something seemed to keep taking him away from it.

"Something mystical," he whispered to

himself, trembling at the thought of Indian spirits possibly being all around him, keeping him from finding their kin.

He had grown weary of the search, and frightened by feeling that he was never truly alone. Perhaps it was time to try to find his way back to civilization.

"And no more carnivals, or pretty women who interpret dreams," he growled out.

As he gazed into the flames of the fire, though, he could not help seeing Annamae's sweet, smiling face. He had wanted her so badly for a wife, but that desire had changed when he realized she had fallen in love with a savage.

Just the thought of Annamae making love with the Blackfoot chief made him feel as though he might puke. She was soiled now, and he did not even want to touch her, much less have her in bed with him each night.

Yes. His feelings for her had changed once he realized that she had allowed a savage to do more than touch her. He wanted to rid the earth of the likes of her, a white woman who actually cavorted with one of the savages' powerful chiefs.

"I would've liked to see the savage's face when I stuck my knife in Annamae's gut," Reuben said, chuckling. "That'd teach him a thing or two about who to take to bed with him."

But he didn't want to die, too, so he had to kill Annamae after stealing her away from the Blackfoot chief.

A loud growl sounded behind him, and then a rumbling sort of roar. It made the hairs on Reuben's arms stand straight up, he was so afraid. He had forgotten that where there were cubs, there was also a mother bear.

Here he was, thinking about searching for food, and instead he might be breakfast for the bears.

His pulse raced as he tried to think where he might be safe until the bears were gone again.

He looked at a tree that was close by, with limbs that could easily be climbed, then rose to his feet and scrambled to it.

Soon he was as high as possible, hoping the bears wouldn't sniff him out and try to climb the tree to get him.

He no longer saw the cubs. After the larger bears had made themselves known by their loud growls, the cubs had scampered away.

Perhaps the cubs had rejoined their parents and were even now moving on. At least he didn't hear the bears any longer.

But he wasn't ready to test his theory. He

would stay up in the tree for a while longer.

Able to relax somewhat as he rested against a thick limb of the tree, he began searching the forest around the spot where he had made camp. He was just enjoying nature this time, watching the owls as well as some eagles soaring high up in the sky.

But from this vantage point, he suddenly spotted something else.

"Smoke," he whispered, his eyebrows lifting.

He watched as a small spiral of smoke rose into the air through the trees some distance away. It was at least a half a mile off, far enough that he would not have smelled the smoke or heard the voices of those who were camped there.

"And so I have neighbors, do I?" he said. It was good to know that he was no longer truly alone with the spirits of dead Indians.

"I'll wait a mite longer, to be sure it is safe to walk through the forest. Then I'll pay a visit to my neighbors," he said.

But what if those who were camping close by were savages . . . ?

Yes, he must rethink how to approach the strangers. He must first determine whether they were even approachable!

Annamae was awakened by something tugging at her hair.

She screamed when she saw a tiny, fuzzy, potato-size animal scamper away, frightened off by her scream.

Her shout had also awakened Cougar and Gray Stone.

Cougar grabbed his rifle and stood up quickly to look around him. "What made you scream?" he asked Annamae without looking down at her.

"It was a tiny animal trying to get some of my hair," Annamae said.

She hurried to her feet, her eyes searching for the culprit.

"What did it look like?" Cougar asked, slowly lowering his rifle.

"It looked like a miniature rabbit, tiny, fuzzy, with a round body, prominent ears, and no visible tail," she said, trying to picture it again. "Although it frightened me awake, it was awfully cute."

"I know what it was," Cougar said. "From your description, I believe you were visited by a pika."

"A pika?" Annamae repeated.

"And what it was doing by tugging on your hair was gathering something warm for its bed," Cougar said, laughing softly. "It liked the look and feel of your hair."

"My word," Annamae said, reaching up

and running her fingers through the tangle of her hair where the small animal had been tugging.

"They are known to frantically gather soft materials for their hideaway beds. They also collect grasses and wildflowers for hay piles they place among rocks, storing the food for sustenance over the winter."

"I never heard of them, but I shall not forget the one that came to me, awakening me in such a funny way," she said, laughing.

"Your scream probably awakened the whole forest," Cougar said, laying his rifle aside and going to Annamae to draw her into his comforting embrace. "I'm glad it was only a pika that started you."

"Me too," Annamae said, then stepped quickly away from him when Gray Stone let out his own yelp.

She looked over at him and immediately saw why he'd cried out.

The cub was no longer with Gray Stone, or anywhere nearby.

"He left on his own," Cougar said. "Perhaps he caught the scent of his own kind and followed it."

"Then I won't ever see him again?" Gray Stone asked, trying not to cry at the thought of having lost the cub without even a good-bye or a last hug.

"Seems so," Annamae said, going to him and bending to her knees to gently hug him. "I think it's best that it happened this way. It means he knows what he's doing and is perhaps even now romping with cubs his own size."

"But what if it wasn't cubs, or even other bears, that lured him away?" Gray Stone said, slowly stepping away from Annamae. He looked into the dark depths of the forest. "What if some animal came and got him for its breakfast?"

"The horses would have alerted us to any predators," Cougar reassured him. "They would not have stood by without making a sound if a dangerous four-legged animal came close to where we were sleeping. My stallion has saved my life more than once by his alertness."

"Well, what do you know?" Reuben said, stepping up from behind them. "Annamae, I've finally caught up with you."

Annamae's heart seemed to drop to her toes when she recognized his voice and realized that he had been able not only to find her, but to catch her and Cougar off guard.

"Reuben . . ." She gasped, turning slowly and staring at him. She shuddered as she saw the drool roll in a slow stream from one corner of his mouth. "How did you find me?"

"Well, seems I'm a mite smarter than you thought, ain't I?" Reuben said, snickering. He gave Cougar a quick look. "Don't you get any ideas about grabbing for your rifle. You wouldn't live to even touch it, much less fire it at me."

Gray Stone stood closer to Reuben than Annamae or Cougar, but he knew that if he tried to grab the man's rifle, Reuben would kill him.

Then he caught sight of a movement behind Reuben. Gray Stone's heart pounded when he saw the cub creeping slowly up behind Reuben. Seeming to sense that he was an evil man, the cub pounced on his right leg, his claws sinking through the fabric of the man's breeches and into the flesh of his leg.

"Good Lord, oh, God a'mighty, what has hold of my leg?" Reuben cried, taking his eyes off Cougar long enough to see the cub now sinking his teeth into his leg.

"Help me!" Reuben cried, dropping his rifle in order to try to shove the cub away from him.

But no matter how hard he tried, the cub held on for dear life.

Even when Reuben shook his leg to loosen

the cub's grip on him, the tiny animal still held on.

Then one mighty blow from Reuben's hand on the cub's head caused the creature to let go. One of his paws reached up to the place that had just been hit.

Reuben started to grab for his rifle, but Cougar was too quick for him. He leaped on the man and wrestled him to the ground.

Reuben grabbed Cougar's knife from its sheath, causing both Annamae and Gray Stone to scream out a warning.

Cougar knocked the knife from Reuben's hand, then wrapped his right arm around the man's neck, holding him still on the ground.

Reuben suddenly thrust a knee up into Cougar's stomach, knocking the wind out of him.

Reuben took advantage of Cougar's momentary weakness, running into the forest. Cougar finally struggled to his feet and took off after him.

Annamae grabbed up the rifle and followed them, with Gray Stone and the cub on her heels.

When Reuben came to a steep drop-off, where the river ran wildly below, he stopped abruptly, panting. He stared down into the thrashing waters, then turned just as Cougar leaped on him and wrestled him to the ground once again.

They rolled over and over on the edge of the precipice.

Annamae grew pale and gasped when she saw just how dangerously close they were to the drop-off. She screamed out a warning for her husband.

Gray Stone was on his knees, the cub in his arms, as he, too, stared at what was happening. He saw that Annamae could not get off a clear shot at Reuben. First he was on top, but then just as quickly Cougar was there instead.

"Cougar, watch out or you will fall over the ledge!" she screamed, her heart pounding.

And then she heard a loud, shrill scream and saw that Cougar was lying alone, his eyes watching the quick descent of Reuben until he splashed hard into the water and was taken swiftly away by the current.

"Is he dead?" Annamae asked as she rushed to Cougar's side. She dropped her rifle and flung herself into his arms. "Oh, Cougar, it could've been you."

"Yes, he is dead. The spirits would not have allowed it to be me," Cougar said, holding Annamae in his arms as he rose to his feet.

"Spirits?" Annamae murmured, searching his eyes.

"They are everywhere," Cougar said mysteriously. "Everywhere."

Annamae swallowed hard, then shrank back when she heard a great roaring sound coming from the depths of the forest.

"A bear . . . oh, surely a grizzly . . ." she stammered, visibly trembling.

The cub leaped from Gray Stone's arms, gave him a lingering look, then ran into the forest.

It was obvious that he was following the sound of the great bear's roars. It was obvious that he had found his way back home!

There were no more sounds from the bears, only the roaring that came from far below as the water sped over the rocks and crashed along the embankments.

"It is all over," Cougar said, placing a hand at Annamae's chin and lifting it so that their eyes met. "Your nightmares about that man named Reuben should never trouble you again, for he is gone from your life now, forever and always."

"Yes, forever and always," Annamae murmured. "Thank you, my husband, for making sure he will never bother me again."

"He was a foolish man to come on the land of my ancestors to take my woman from me," Cougar said tightly.

"Yes, a very foolish man," Annamae said. Then she looked quickly at Gray Stone, who came and hugged both Annamae and Cougar at the same time. "And the cub is gone now forever, too, Gray Stone. Can you accept that?"

"I can now that I know he has found those who love him like we loved him," Gray Stone said, tears shining in his eyes. "Now I can concentrate on what I must do. I still have my vision quest to complete."

"Yes, your vision quest," Cougar said.

And Annamae had something of her own to do when they returned home.

Yes, she had a wonderful surprise to share with her husband. Afterward, she would bring Gray Stone in on the secret, too, since he was going to become a big brother in less than nine months.

She could hardly wait to share her news with the two men she loved!

Yes, she now labeled Gray Stone as a man, for he would be called that soon, once he finished his vision quest. She knew that this time nothing would lure him away.

Nothing!

CHAPTER
THIRTY-TWO

The morning sun was sifting through the trees overhead as Ellie awakened, but she found herself hardly able to move. She had never been on a horse for so long, for so many days. When she tried to stand this morning, her knees were rubbery and weak.

"Howard, I can't go any farther," Ellie said, awakening him. She looked over at him as he stirred from his deep sleep. "Howard, wake up. Listen to what I say. I . . . I . . . can't go any farther, and I don't even think I'll ever make it back to the others." Her voice broke with emotion. "This was a mistake. A horrible, horrible mistake."

Howard slowly sat up, stretched his arms over his head and yawned, then glared at Ellie. "You were the one who wanted to do this, so you'd better get yourself up this morning and get ready to move onward," he said in a low growl. "You should've thought of the discomfort of travel before heading out on your mission of mercy."

"I'm used to traveling, Howard," Ellie said, finally making it to a sitting position. She ran a hand down the wrinkled skirt of her dress, then through her tangled golden hair. "But not on a horse. I'm used to the comfort of our wagon, not a horse's rump."

"You'd better get used to it fast, because after we reach the Indian village, providing we live to see another day, we're gonna have a long trip back to the carnival wagons," Howard said, stretching again before slowly rising to his feet. "Sort through the food bag. Find us something to eat before we head out again. I know we're close. This landscape looks mighty familiar."

"We're almost out of food," Ellie said, groaning as she reached for the bag. "What then?"

"I'll shoot us a rabbit or two, that's what," Howard said. He crawled over to the fire pit and put more wood onto the embers. The wood caught hold, soon sending huge spirals of smoke heavenward.

Ellie watched the smoke, then shivered. "If the Indians see the smoke, which they will if we are as close to the village as you think we are, surely they will come and investigate," she said.

She pulled a package of what was left of

their bread from the bag, and then a jar of strawberry preserves that she had made herself after finding many ripe strawberry plants alongside a road they had once traveled.

She slowly opened the jar, and then took two pieces of bread from the package, along with a knife to spread the preserves on the bread.

"I'm tired of strawberry sandwiches," Howard grumbled, yet he took the one Ellie had made for him and gobbled it down before she even had two bites from her own.

"You should've thought of that when you made quick work of the cheese," Ellie said sourly.

When she heard the crackling sound of something breaking a twig behind her, she felt as if her heart stopped dead inside her chest.

She didn't have time to turn to see what had made the sound. Before she knew it, ten Blackfoot warriors had surrounded Ellie and Howard.

One warrior stepped closer to Howard, suddenly dropped his bow and arrow, then grabbed Howard by the hair and yanked hard on it, so that Howard was forced to look directly into his face.

"You were told never to come on Blackfoot land again, yet here you are," said the warrior called Two Moons as he glared into Howard's wide, fearful eyes. "And you even brought your woman with you? Did you fail to tell her the dangers of doing this? Did you tell her that you were forbidden to be here? That you were warned that if you came again, no mercy would be offered?"

"Please . . ." Howard begged, his heart thumping hard. "It wasn't my idea to come. It was all my wife's. I told her that I wasn't wanted anywhere near your people; yet . . . yet . . . she wanted to come. She is worried about Annamae."

"Annamae?" Two Moons said. "Did you tell her that Annamae is content among my people, that she is now my chief's woman?"

Ellie was frightened silent as she watched her husband forced to his knees, as though begging for his life.

"Please don't hurt my husband," Ellie found the courage to say. "He tells the truth. It was my idea to come. Annamae means a lot to me. I feel as though I am a mother to her, and she my daughter."

"She is more now to my chief than she ever was to you," Two Moons growled out as he looked over his shoulder at Ellie.

"What . . . do you mean?" Ellie asked.

"She is my chief's wife," Two Moons said,

a look of triumph in his eyes. He was so pleased to see the horror in the woman's eyes now that she knew the truth about this "daughter" she claimed to have such feelings for.

"She . . . married him?" Ellie said, paling at the thought. She took a shaky step away from the warrior. "Oh, surely she was forced into it."

"Ellie, I told you how Annamae feels about the chief. I know she wasn't forced into anything," Howard said, glaring at his wife. "I told you how foolish it was to come. Now you are seeing for yourself. Ellie, you'd better begin praying for our own welfare and forget Annamae's."

"You aren't going to hurt us, are you?" Ellie asked, begging with her eyes as she looked at from one warrior to the next. But each one looked as fierce and angry as the first.

"We come in peace," she blurted out. "As you can see, it's only the two of us. And it's my fault we're here, not Howard's. He told me you warned him not to come back, but I . . . I . . . talked him into returning. So please don't punish him for not obeying your commands."

"Ellie, shut up," Howard spit out. "Don't you see? You're just making matters worse."

"Howard, the truth will out," Ellie said, tears streaming from her eyes. "We're here only because we love Annamae, not for any other reason."

"Come with us," the warrior closest to Ellie said, taking his arrow from his bow and sliding it into the quiver at his back.

He slid his bow across an arm and anchored it on his shoulder, then grabbed Ellie and walked her toward the horses.

"Where are you taking me?" she cried out as the warrior forced her onto her horse, bareback. The saddle was still on the ground, resting against a tree.

She looked over her shoulder and saw Howard being forced onto his horse, as well.

"Ellie, just keep quiet," Howard shouted at her. "It's best that way. They have their minds made up. Nothing you say now will change anything."

Ellie trembled on the horse as a warrior kicked dirt on the fire, putting out the flames, while others collected blankets and provisions, as well as the two fancy saddles, and secured them on the backs of their steeds.

Then they all rode in the direction of the village. They arrived quickly, surprising both Ellie and Howard at how near they had been.

Everyone in the village stopped what they were doing and stared at the man they recognized very well, and the woman who was a stranger to them.

Ellie looked guardedly around her at the women, whose eyes were following her, and at the men, who were staring at Howard with a look of utter contempt and hate.

It was obvious that her husband was loathed by men, women, and children alike.

When she recalled how he had described his treatment the last time he was there, she wondered if she would be treated the same.

Would she be tied to a stake in the middle of the village for everyone to gawk at? Would they come up to her and spit on her, even hurt her?

She watched the Indians fearfully as she was taken just outside a tepee, where everyone drew rein. Howard was hauled from his horse and shoved inside the tepee.

She nervously bit her lower lip as she was taken from her horse, thank goodness much more gently than Howard had been treated.

She was walked into the tepee by a warrior who gently gripped her right arm.

She soon saw that it was a tepee where there were no belongings.

The fire pit held cold ashes within the rocks. There were no blankets or signs of comfort anywhere, except for bulrush mats spread across the floor of the lodge.

"You will stay here until my chief, his wife, and Gray Stone arrive home," Two Moons said flatly as he gazed from Ellie to Howard.

"Gray Stone . . . ?" Ellie gasped out.

She remembered the child so well, and how bad she had felt when Howard chose to place him in a cage.

"Gray Stone went with his chieftain uncle and our chief's wife to free the cub you captured. They are releasing the cub back into the wild," Two Moons said. "You sit. Wait. And do not try to leave. You will be well guarded. It will be up to my chief to decide both your fates."

Two Moons leaned into Howard's face. "Were it up to me, you would die even before my chief returned home," he growled out. "It is not good that you disobeyed his order and came back where you are not wanted."

"What do you think Chief Cougar is going to decide to do once he sees that I have disobeyed his orders?" Howard managed to say, searching the Indian's eyes. "I did not come with any men or guns. You know that the only reason I am here is because of Annamae."

"That you are here at all is enough," Two

Moons said flatly, then shoved the entrance flap aside and left.

"See what you have gotten us into?" Howard hissed at Ellie as she slowly sat on the bulrush mats spread across the floor of the tepee. "I don't believe we'll be alive very long once Chief Cougar comes back home."

"Annamae won't let him kill us," Ellie sobbed out. "She has to love us at least that much . . . to want to see that nothing happens to us."

"You and your wishful thinking," Howard spit out. He flopped on the floor beside Ellie. "I wonder how long we'll be made to wait? I wonder if they will give us food and water? Or fire? It's damn cold in here."

"Will you just for one minute quit thinking about yourself and think about Annamae? I can't believe that she is actually married to . . . to . . . a savage," Ellie said. "Surely he has brainwashed her into thinking she loves him. She just can't love a man with red skin. She just can't. It's taboo."

"Well, she does love him, so get used to it," Howard said, sighing heavily. "I saw her with him. I know it's real enough. That's why I knew how futile it was to come here. Yet . . . yet . . . you wouldn't take no for an answer, would you?"

"I'd have come without you, and you

know it," Ellie said. She lowered her eyes. "Well, I would have tried. I knew you had to come with me, though. I didn't know the way to the village. You did."

The rustling of the entrance flap as it opened made Ellie look quickly up, her pulse racing. She had no idea who might be coming, or why.

When she saw several lovely Indian maidens enter the tepee, each one carrying provisions that would make Ellie and Howard's stay there more comfortable, Ellie gasped with surprise.

One woman was carrying a tray of food, another was carrying an armful of blankets, and another one was carrying a jug of water.

The first maiden knelt beside Ellie. "My name is Blue Blossom. I know about you," she said as she placed the tray of food in front of her. "Annamae told me about you and how you so kindly took her in on the day her family was killed by renegades. She spoke kindly of you, so I am returning the kindness until she can come and be with you herself."

Ellie was at a loss for words. She was surprised by what the beautiful woman in the pretty white beaded dress had just told her. Annamae had actually spoken of her to this gentle-voiced woman, and spoken kindly. Annamae must love her, at least a little bit.

She started to say something, but stopped when a warrior came into the tepee, his arms loaded with firewood.

Soon a fire was burning in the fire pit, and Ellie and Howard were alone.

"Blue Blossom," Ellie murmured, no longer feeling endangered, but truly believing she and Howard would be allowed to leave once Annamae had arrived.

She glanced over at Howard.

She could tell by his ashen face, and the fear in his eyes, that he didn't have as much confidence as she.

"Things will be all right," she tried to reassure him.

But it seemed as though her words did not reach him, for he still gazed lifelessly into the fire.

"Howard, please don't give up," Ellie said, moving over to sit next to him.

When he still didn't respond to her, she knelt before him, blocking his view of the fire he was watching so determinedly.

"Howard, you must get hold of yourself," she pleaded. She placed a gentle hand on his cheek, glad when he finally gazed into her eyes. "I love you, Howard. I don't like a lot of your ways, but, honey, I do love you, and always will."

Tears filled Howard's eyes. He reached out for Ellie and yanked her close, hugging her so hard she could hardly breathe.

She realized that something unexpected had happened here today. She had reached inside her husband and found a place she always knew was there but that he had never revealed before. She had found a softness, a love for her, that he had always tried not to show. Perhaps he had thought it would make him look too weak.

Now, oh, Lord, now he had revealed to her how much he did love and need her.

"Things will be all right," she murmured as she clung to him. "You'll see. You'll see."

CHAPTER
THIRTY-THREE

The sound of horses arriving at the village awakened Ellie with a start, causing her to sit up quickly, her pulse racing. She was sure Annamae had just come back, for Ellie had not noticed any warriors leaving on horseback since she and Howard had arrived.

Hoping that Annamae would appear at the entranceway in the next moments, and that she would be able to clear up this misunderstanding, Ellie turned quickly to awaken Howard.

She glanced over to where Howard had fallen asleep. Her insides tightened when she found him gone.

"Howard?" she whispered anxiously as she looked quickly around inside the tepee. Moonlight cast its white light down through the smoke hole overhead, and the fire's glow lightened everything, so she could see clearly enough.

She gasped and felt the color rush from

her face when she saw a gaping, ragged slit at the back of the tepee.

To her horror, it was large enough for a body to fit through. Outside, the forest crept near the back of the lodge.

Trembling, Ellie scrambled to her feet and hurried to the opening.

She slowly reached a hand to the limp, ragged edges, then quickly held the buffalo fabric aside as far as she could get it.

"Oh, Howard, what have you done?" she said, realizing that he had fled into the night.

He had told her how he had opened the tepee covering that night when he had tried to talk Annamae into leaving with him.

But that night he had had a knife.

Tonight he had no weapons whatsoever. Everything had been taken by the Indians.

She looked around and spotted a sharp rock that he had managed to break from one of the stones encircling the fire pit.

Apparently it had been sharp enough to cut the buffalo hide covering. After he had managed that, he had left without another thought for his wife.

Her mind returned to that moment earlier in the evening, when Howard had embraced her so lovingly.

That hug had brought back to her the wonder of being in his arms and the love they had known when they first met and married. It had made her feel that perhaps this journey far from their carnival wagons was worth the danger they had found themselves in.

His love meant everything to her, and at that moment, she had truly thought that he did still love her!

Now she understood the real meaning behind that hug.

He must have known even then that he was planning to escape without her.

"Why, Howard?" she sobbed into her hands.

She turned her head quickly back toward the entrance flap when she heard horses stopping outside.

"Annamae," she whispered.

She wiped tears from her eyes. "Oh, surely that's Annamae," she said.

Two Moons stepped up to Cougar and Annamae as they sat on their steeds outside the lodge where the captives were being held.

"I have purposely led you to this lodge, telling you that we have hostages inside it, yet have not told you just who they are," he said solemnly.

Two Moons looked over at Annamae,

whose eyes were full of questions.

Annamae then turned her gaze to the tepee. She could see a shadow on the lodge covering, the shadow of someone standing very still.

"Who is it?" she blurted out, quickly dismounting.

She started to go ahead to the entranceway, but Cougar quickly slid off his horse, stopping her by gently taking her arm.

"Wait until we hear what prompted the captives to come into the village without being invited," Cougar said.

He turned to Two Moons. "Who is inside this lodge?"

"It is the man who was warned never to return, and the man's woman," Two Moons said stiffly. "We were led to their campsite by the smoke from their campfire. They were quickly surrounded by your warriors."

Annamae was astonished to hear that Howard had foolishly come back to the village after being led from it with harsh warnings never to return. And now he had even included Ellie in his foolishness!

What kind of a man would bring his own wife into the face of danger? Why would he come back at all, when she had made it clear that she wanted to stay, not leave!

She didn't wait for any more explanations.

She pulled herself away from Cougar's grip and rushed toward the entranceway of the tepee. No matter what Cougar thought about what she was doing, she had to see how Ellie was. Although Annamae had fled the carnival life, she had not been running from Ellie. Ellie had been good and kind to Annamae.

Even after Annamae had been forced into "performing" at the carnival, Ellie had been kind and reassuring to her.

She just could not let anything happen to Ellie.

To Annamae's knowledge, Ellie had not been on a horse for years. To have come this far on horseback, Ellie must have been truly concerned about her.

Annamae brushed the entrance flap aside, then stopped when she found Ellie alone, her eyes swollen from crying, her clothes wrinkled and soiled. Her hair was filled with what her mother had called witches' knots when Annamae had awakened in the mornings at home and her hair was all tangled.

"Annamae, oh, Annamae," Ellie sobbed as she rushed to Annamae and flung herself into her arms. "It's so good to see you, child. Oh, so good. When Howard told me you were going to marry a . . . a . . ."

"Indian?" Annamae blurted out, afraid

that Ellie was about to refer to Cougar as a savage.

"Yes, an Indian," Ellie said, stepping away from Annamae. Her eyes moved slowly over Annamae, taking in just how much she now looked like an Indian. She wore a bucksin dress, and her hair was arranged in one long braid down her back.

"You . . . look . . . like an Indian squaw," Ellie blurted out.

Then she gazed intently into Annamae's eyes. "Are you made to dress in buckskin and moccasins?" she asked. "Are you made to wear your hair in . . . such a way?"

"Ellie, where is Howard?" Annamae asked, suddenly aware that he was not there.

Until now, she had been so absorbed in her surprise that Ellie was actually there in the village, she had momentarily forgotten that Howard was supposed to be with her.

She covered a gasp behind her hand when she now saw the large, ragged slit at the back of the lodge.

"Oh, no," she said. "Did he leave through that . . . ?"

She hurried to the slit and ran her hand over the jagged buffalo skin, then held it open and looked outside.

The moon was bright enough for her to be able to see into the forest a little way.

When she saw no movement there, she turned back to Ellie, whose hands were nervously clasping and unclasping before her.

"He left me, Annamae," Ellie sobbed. "While I slept, he managed to find a rock sharp enough to slit the covering of the tepee. He actually . . . left me here, to face whatever fate the Indians were planning to deal us."

"He left you here alone?" Annamae gasped, stunned that Howard would be so heartless and so foolish.

Surely he knew that once the warriors discovered his escape, he would be tracked down and brought back?

Even she had no idea what to expect of her husband under these circumstances.

Suddenly the entrance flap was shoved aside and Cougar was there, his eyes quickly assessing the situation.

When he saw Annamae standing beside the gaping slit, his jaw tightened and he walked stiffly toward her.

"He's gone," Annamae said, her voice breaking. "He left his wife here alone, and is now out there somewhere, running, for he would not have had the chance to steal a horse."

"And so he left, did he?" Cougar said,

slowly running his hand down the ragged edges of the opening.

"Yes, while I slept," Ellie offered. "When I awakened . . . he was gone."

"How long ago would you say that he did this?" Cougar asked, going over to stand before Ellie.

"I don't know," Ellie said, her voice trembling with fear at being so close to a man she knew was a powerful Blackfoot chief.

"I was asleep," Ellie rushed out. "I am a sound sleeper. I never hear anything once I am asleep."

"The fact of the matter is that he is gone," Annamae said, gazing into her husband's eyes when he turned toward her. "Are you going to send warriors out to find him?"

Cougar thought for a moment, weighing the pros and cons inside his mind and heart, then shrugged.

"No, I will not waste my warriors' time going after the foolish man," he said. "He has left what he thought was a bear's den to venture out into something much worse. He has no weapon. He has no horse. Just how far do you think he will get . . . and remain alive?"

Ellie gasped. Tears flooded her eyes again. "You believe that he will die, don't you?"

she asked, sobbing.

"He will die," Cougar said, flat and matter-of-fact.

Ellie let out a strangled gasp.

Annamae saw Ellie's reaction and understood it. Even though Howard had proven himself a faithless coward tonight, they had had many years together as man and wife.

She knew that Ellie still loved him, although he did not deserve it.

She went to Ellie and embraced her. "When you feel sad about him, always remember how he left you tonight, without any thought of what might happen to you," she murmured. "Also, think about those times when he was cruel to you. You know what I mean, Ellie."

"I know, but we've been together for so long," Ellie cried. "We put together the carnival and ran it together. What will become of those who are even now waiting for our return?"

"Surely someone was left in charge," Annamae said, reaching up and gently wiping tears from Ellie's cheeks.

"Yes, Earl is in charge," Ellie said, her voice breaking. "He is the most dependable of all the men."

"Yes, Earl the snake man," Annamae said, nodding. "He is a dependable man, and when you start worrying about things, just think about how proud Earl must be to have been given charge of the carnival."

"Yes, I know," Ellie murmured.

She looked past Annamae at Cougar, then turned back to Annamae. "What's to become of me?" she asked, her voice breaking. "What is the chief, your husband, going to do with me? It was my idea to come for you. Not Howard's."

"It was?" Annamae asked. "You knew the dangers, yet . . . you came . . . ?"

"Annamae, you know how much I care for you," Ellie sobbed out. "I will never forget that day when I first saw you. You were so tiny and helpless. It didn't take much thought before I knew what we must do. We took you in, darling. And you were happy enough until Howard forced the dream interpretations on you. I'm sorry about that, honey. Damn sorry."

Cougar was taking this all in as he listened to the two women talk, realizing just how much each thought of the other.

"I don't want to be involved with the carnival any longer," Ellie went on. "Not even if Howard manages to get back to those who are waiting for him. He wronged me tonight terribly. He revealed to me just how little he cares for me. I . . . I . . . have wasted the better years of my life being a wife to that . . . that . . . heartless man. I don't ever want to see him again . . . if he does make it out of this alive."

"Are you saying you would like to stay here, with me?" Annamae asked. She knew how Ellie felt about Indians. She had seen what the renegades had done to Annamae's family and had despised all Indians ever since.

But surely Ellie saw just how much Annamae loved Cougar. Surely Ellie understood that it wasn't this clan of Blackfoot that had had a role in the murders. It wasn't a clan at all, but instead ruthless, bloodthirsty renegades.

"I have nowhere to go, no family anywhere that I know of," Ellie blurted out. "When I left home, oh, so long ago, I was a mere child myself. I traveled with Howard, eventually marrying him. I left everyone who meant anything to me. I . . . I . . . haven't kept in touch. I just got caught up in the excitement of carnival life and being married to Howard. That was all I cared about. So . . . even if my family is still alive out there somewhere, they wouldn't want to see me. I truly have nowhere to go, except . . ."

"Except?" Annamae said, gently placing

her hands on Ellie's shoulders. "Except what, Ellie?"

"Can I stay with you?" Ellie blurted out. "You are all the family I truly have, Annamae. I . . . see you as that daughter I could never have."

"Ellie, life as an Indian is very different from the way white people live," Annamae softly explained.

"Annamae, I've lived out of wagons and tents the better part of my life, traveling and never settling down in any one place. Being with you and living in a tepee in one place would be a welcome change."

She eased away from Annamae's arms. She stepped closer to Cougar. "Chief, may . . . I . . . stay?" she asked softly. "May I be a part of Annamae's life with you? Or has what Howard has done made you see only bad in me?"

Annamae scarcely breathed as she awaited his response, yet she knew deep down what it would be. He was a man of heart, and before him stood a woman whose life had been torn apart.

Yes, surely he would agree to let her stay.

And Annamae was truly happy that Ellie had made this choice. Ellie was getting older, and each year, as she traveled from town to town by wagon, she seemed to be aging more quickly than normal.

Just as Annamae had craved a different life, surely deep down inside, Ellie craved the same.

"You can stay," Cougar said, his voice filled with compassion. "If this is what my wife wants, so shall it be."

Ellie turned quickly and faced Annamae. "Is it what you want?" she asked, searching Annamae's eyes. "Do you care enough for me to allow me to have a role in your life now?"

Annamae suddenly thought of the surprise that awaited her husband once they arrived at their lodge, where she had hidden the tiny pair of baby moccasins.

She realized only now how much it would mean to her to have Ellie be a part of her baby's life. Surely Ellie would regard Annamae's baby as her very own grandchild!

It was hard not to blurt out the news about the baby right away, but Annamae had to wait a while longer. Her husband would be the first to know.

Annamae hurried into Ellie's arms. "Yes, I care enough," she murmured, hugging her. "I truly do care. It will be so wonderful to share things with you, as I did when I was a child. Ellie, yes, please stay and put down roots here, as I have done."

"Thank you," Ellie murmured. "Oh, thank you."

Even though Annamae was so happy about this turn of events, she could not put Howard from her mind.

Yes, he was out there, somewhere.

Would he once again try to interfere in her life? Would he try to contact Ellie?

Would he think about how he had discarded his wife as though she were no more than a puppet whose strings he had controlled for so long?

Yes, Annamae would always wonder about the man, but she did not care what happened to him now, as heartless as that might seem.

Tonight he had proven himself unworthy of her concern.

CHAPTER
THIRTY-FOUR

All was quiet at the village as Annamae and Cougar settled in for the night in their tepee.

Gray Stone was staying the night at a friend's home with some of the other young braves. They were all glad that he was home safe from his journey.

Gray Stone was spending this special night with his friends because tomorrow he was to leave again to seek the vision that would make him a man. He would then hold the title of warrior instead of brave.

He had assured Cougar and Annamae that this time nothing would interfere in his quest for a vision. He had promised to stay in one place until he received his vision, and with it the blessing of the Great Mystery.

Annamae and Cougar believed his promise, already seeing in Gray Stone the man he would soon become.

They were, indeed, proud of him already.

Their love for him would grow and grow, just as Gray Stone would grow into a magificient speciman of a man one day. The girls would flock around him, hoping he would choose one of them to be his bride.

The shadow of the fire's glow was softly playing over the inside fabric of the buffalo hide lodge covering. Annamae had purposely waited for all to be still outside the lodge before giving her husband the good news about their child.

They had spent more time with Ellie than she'd expected, reassuring her that she was welcome to stay in the village.

"I always thought that Howard loved Ellie, even though at times he was cruel to her, both verbally and physically," Annamae murmured as she sat snuggled against Cougar as they enjoyed the warmth of the evening fire.

Empty dishes sat beside the entrance flap. They had eaten a delicious meal that Blue Blossom had prepared for them, a dish of tongue and greens.

The first time Annamae had been offered tongue after she had arrived at the village, she had immediately shoved it away, refusing to eat any.

But when she saw that there would be no substitute brought to her, she ate it, mainly to keep her strength up for whatever she had to face later.

Now she knew that it was a delicacy among the Blackfoot tribe. She had expected it to taste horrible, but it did not.

After deciding that she was going to stay in the Blackfoot village as Cougar's wife, Annamae had adjusted to many things unfamiliar to white people, among them the food.

She smiled at the thought of how Ellie must have reacted when the meal of tongue had been taken to her earlier in the evening.

"And what about Howard?" Annamae asked. "What would you do if he does return? Would you . . ."

She could not say the words. She didn't really want to know whether her husband would kill Howard for having interfered once again in the Blackfoot's lives.

She could not help thinking he deserved whatever happened to him, whether it was at the Indian village or in the forest.

"Oh, Lord, what if he comes across that huge grizzly we saw?" Annamae blurted out. "He —"

"Whatever happens to him has been brought on by his own actions," Cougar said sternly. "And you do not have to wonder any longer about what I might do to him if he returns, for, my wife, he will not ever show his face among my people again. He would not dare test my patience further."

"I still can't believe that Ellie had the courage to come all this way with only Howard as her protector," Annamae said, turning her eyes back to the fire and watching it wrap its orange flames around the logs in gentle caresses. "She does care for me . . . she truly cares for me. I never imagined she would stay here and not return to the life of a white woman."

"I am certain that, like you, she will adapt quickly to her new home, since it was her choice to stay," Cougar said.

He smiled into Annamae's eyes and took one of her hands. "Tomorrow Gray Stone leaves again for his vision quest," he said. "I am so proud of him."

"I am proud, too," Annamae murmured. She frowned as a disturbing thought came to her. "Howard. Oh, Lord, what if he sees Gray Stone while he is alone on his vision quest?"

"Gray Stone will be in a remote, safe place, far from the path Howard will travel to return to where his people await him," Cougar said reassuringly. "And this time Gray Stone will remain alert. He understands the importance of not allowing anything to interfere with his goal."

"He'll be gone for four days and nights?" Annamae asked softly.

Cougar nodded. "Yes, four days and nights," he confirmed.

He could tell by the look in her eyes that she was still concerned.

"My wife, nothing will happen to Gray Stone," he said, drawing her close and embracing her warmly. "Nothing except for what should happen."

Annamae knew that the time had finally arrived for her to tell her husband her special news.

"I have something to show you," she said, easing herself out of his arms. "I'll get it."

"And what is it that takes you from my arms when I wish to hold you?" he teased, watching her go to the back of the tepee, where she picked up a small buckskin bag.

"You will be pleased with what I have to show you," Annamae said, smiling.

She felt the heat of a blush flood her cheeks as excitement built within her. She had been forced to wait to tell her husband the good news, first until she was absolutely certain she was with child, then until they were finally alone together.

She took the small bag back with her and sat down beside Cougar again.

She saw the puzzlement in his eyes as he stared first at the bag, and then at the heightened color of her cheeks, which he knew from experience was caused by excitement.

"What have you brought to me that makes you look so radiantly happy?" he asked.

"What is inside this bag is something that will fill you with much joy," Annamae murmured.

She slowly opened the drawstring on the bag, but still hesitated before reaching inside. This was the moment she had waited for.

"You fill me with much joy, only you," Cougar said, placing a gentle hand on her flushed cheek. "What else could there be that could give me the same sort of joy?"

Then his eyes widened, and he drew his hand back from her when a thought came to him that would bring him even more joy.

Could his wife be with child?

Oh, surely so, for he only now realized that she had not had a blood flow since they'd made love that first time.

She must be with child!

And did she not have the same glow that most women had when they were carrying a child?

Yes, it was so!

But he didn't let her know his suspicions. He knew that she had gone to certain lengths in order to make this a special moment between them.

He waited impassively as she pulled out a very small pair of beaded moccasins, the sort only a baby could wear on its tiny feet.

When Annamae saw his mouth drop open and his eyes widen as he took the moccasins and held them in the palm of his right hand, as though nestling a tiny, precious bird there, she knew that she had been right about what his reaction would be.

He was as happy, as joyous, as she had been the moment she suspected she was with child. For this was not just any child.

It was a child born of their wondrous love!

"I hope the first child is a boy," she murmured, watching how he gazed in awe at the moccasins as he held them. "My darling, I want our firstborn to be in your exact image. Only a son could assure that."

Joyous and proud, Cougar held the moccasins in his left hand, while with his right he drew her toward him.

"You make me so proud . . . so happy . . . I feel blessed," he whispered against her lips, then gave her the sweetest kiss she'd ever known.

She would cherish this precious kiss during her waking hours and while she slept, guaranteeing that she would never have a nightmare again for the rest of her life!

CHAPTER
THIRTY-FIVE

The tiny moccasins rested nearby on a blanket as Cougar and Annamae slowly undressed, smiling into each other's eyes. Once their clothes were tossed aside, they knelt facing each other, nude.

Annamae noticed how Cougar's eyes shifted to her stomach. She thrilled inside when he ever so gently, so lovingly, splayed his hands across her belly. Then he moved them as he lowered his lips to where his hands had just been.

Tears of joy came into Annamae's eyes when she saw Cougar behaving so tenderly toward a child that had not yet even been born. She was beginning to realize just how devoted and loving a father he would be.

She wove her fingers through his thick black hair and threw her head back in ecstasy as his lips traveled slowly upward, making a path of kisses from her stomach and stopping at one of her breasts.

She sighed and closed her eyes as his tongue swept around her nipple, and then went to the other breast and did the same.

His eyes flared with hungry intent as he gazed into her eyes, which were open now, watching him. He cradled her within his powerful, muscled arms and led her down onto her back on the plush pelts and blankets.

His lips were on hers as he gave her a meltingly hot kiss, while one hand reached between them and traveled slowly down her body until he found the soft of hair at the juncture of her thighs.

She writhed in ecstasy as his fingers swept over the place where her heartbeat seemed to be centered.

She drew a ragged breath when she then felt something else where his fingers had been. His manhood had found her hot, moist place.

With one insistent thrust he was inside her, plunging into her, withdrawing and plunging again. She twined her arms around his neck and clung to him.

With a knee, he ever so gently eased her legs farther apart, giving him easier access to her. His body moved rhythmically as he made love with her.

He lowered his lips to a breast again, his

tongue rolling the nipple.

Waves of liquid heat seemed to be pulsing through Cougar's body as his lean, sinewy buttocks continued to move.

He paused momentarily and gazed at her. Her face was such a vision of loveliness, and she was his wife!

"I love you so," Annamae murmured, seeing how intently he was gazing at her. "I love being your wife. I . . . will . . . love being a mother to your children."

"Our children," he said huskily, brushing soft kisses across her brow.

Then he brought his lips to hers again, kissing her this time with an easy sureness that made her grow weak all over. She felt such passion, she let out a cry of pleasure against his lips.

She was truly flooded with emotions she had never thought possible, and knew it was only her husband who could bring out such feelings from deep within her.

She clung to him as he buried his face next to her neck, his heated breath tickling her ear.

Then his tongue brushed her lips lightly.

She was wonderfully bubbly inside, ready to burst, it seemed, into a million points of sunlight. The warmth of love was sweet throughout her body.

"I want you . . . all of you . . ." Cougar whispered huskily into her ear. He rested his body for a moment as he gazed down at her with passion-filled eyes, readying himself for the ultimate pleasure with his wife.

"And I am yours . . . all of me," Annamae whispered back to him. "I want all of you . . . I want you now."

Smiling almost wickedly down at her, their bodies straining together, Cougar made another wild plunge inside her, filling her with his heat over and over again.

Then, as though a bolt of lightning flashed between them, they found that ecstasy they were both seeking.

They quivered and clung and then lay quietly in each other's arms.

"It is a wonderful thing how a man and a woman can bring such pleasure to each other," Annamae murmured, still reveling in the remembrance of those sharp contractions of pleasure that had just knifed through her.

"Looking at you, loving you, making love to you, makes me a complete man," Cougar said thickly. "Until I met you, I did not know the true meaning of love. Now I do, and I embrace it with such passion, my love. These moments with you are like the days of spring, when everything is new, warm, and beautiful."

"I cherish everything about you," she murmured. "I treasure being your wife and being able to give to you what only a woman can give a man."

"Not any woman," Cougar said, smiling into her eyes. "Only you."

"And soon your people will see that I am bringing a child into their chief's life," Annamae said as he rolled away from her and lay on his side, facing her.

She ran a hand across her tummy. "Yes, soon I shall be showing," she murmured. "Will your people accept a white child, if that is what I give birth to?"

"The color of the child's skin will not matter, just as it does not matter to my people that my wife's skin is white," Cougar said, placing a hand on her stomach and slowly caressing it.

"Are you certain I am completely accepted by your people, or are they forced to pretend because you are their chief?" Annamae asked, searching his eyes. "I don't feel resentment when I walk among your people, but are there some who do resent me because of the color of my skin?"

"There will always be those few who cannot forget what the white government has taken from them," Cougar said. "But although they despise those who wronged them, they know you are different, because they see and feel your goodness."

"I hope never to disappoint you, or them," Annamae said, her voice breaking. "I am not proud of what my people have done to the red men and women of our country. It has never made any sense to me how or why the white people in Washington, especially our president, can condone what has happened too often to the red man."

Cougar sat up and reached a hand out for Annamae.

She sat up and drew close to him as he placed a blanket around them, their shoulders touching.

"Tonight is not the time to think about the wrongs that have been brought upon the Blackfoot people by white eyes," Cougar said quietly. "Tonight is the time to celebrate our love and the child that will be born of such love."

Annamae gazed into his eyes. "I have dreamed of our child," she said softly. "Even before I realized that I was with child, I dreamed of holding a baby as you sat beside me."

"Tell me about the dream," Cougar said, placing a gentle hand on her cheek. "Was it a boy child, or girl?"

"It was a son," Annamae said, smiling.

"A son," Cougar said, beaming. "And so our first child will be a son."

"And I even dreamed of the name we would give him," Annamae blurted out.

"And that is?" Cougar asked. "Tell me. What name did you dream of giving our son?"

"Golden Wing," Annamae said cautiously as she gazed into his eyes to see if he approved or disapproved.

"If you give birth to a son, his name will, indeed, be Golden Wing," Cougar said, nodding his approval. "That is a good, strong name."

"I like it, too," Annamae murmured, leaning closely against him. This moment in time with him was so perfect.

But even now, her thoughts went to Howard. She wondered if he would live or die after leaving the Blackfoot village without a horse, food, or anything else that could help him survive.

And Ellie.

She found it hard to believe that Ellie would so quickly accept life among the Blackfoot people. At times she had shivered at the very thought of being near an Indian village while putting up the carnival tents.

But Annamae brushed such thoughts from

384

her mind, for tonight was special, and she did not want to ruin it by thinking of anything but this moment, and the love she shared with her husband.

She reached over for the tiny pair of moccasins that she had made and held them in the palm of her hand.

"One day our child will actually wear these," she murmured.

"It is a good night tonight," Cougar said, gently taking the moccasins from Annamae. "And it be a wonderful day when our child comes into the world. My wife, the moccasins are beautiful."

Annamae giggled. "Not truly," she murmured. "Before Blue Blossom showed me how to make these moccasins, I had never sewn much. Mama never had the time to teach me what I needed to know to become as skilled a seamstress as I would like to be."

"Blue Blossom is a good teacher," Cougar said.

"Yes," Annamae said softly. "She had a lot of patience while teaching me how to make these moccasins."

"I have said it — you are an astute student," Cougar replied, setting the moccasins aside.

He drew her into his embrace and gently

urged her to lie on her back again, the blanket falling away from both of them as he stretched himself out atop her.

Their bodies quickly strained together as once again they made tender love.

Outside owls hooted among the trees, and somewhere along the river loons sang to one another.

But neither Annamae nor Cougar was aware of any outdoor noises, not even of someone stealing away into the night with two of Cougar's most prized steeds.

CHAPTER
THIRTY-SIX

Five Years Later

The ride on the horse had been long, but now Annamae was resting in a canoe as her husband and others swept their paddles through the emerald green water. They were on their way to where they would have council and feast with another band of Blackfoot, the Fox Clan. It was the time for midsummer festivities. Annamae and Cougar had already participated in those festivities at their own village, but were now on their way to join others.

They had ridden for some time after leaving their village, and had had one night beneath the stars before traveling onward.

On the second day, they had met up with several warriors of the Fox Clan, who had brought canoes for the rest of their trip to the Fox Clan's village. Some of those warriors stood guard over the horses even now, while others went in the canoes with Cougar and his wife, and those warriors who had been chosen to join this merry adventure.

Annamae was the only woman present, for she was the chief's wife.

Annamae looked ahead, where Gray Stone sat just behind Cougar. His muscles flexed as he drew his paddle through the water.

Annamae felt such pride in that young man. He had successfully achieved his vision quest years ago, when Annamae's tummy was not yet showing that she was with child.

When he had returned after his fourth day of being away, a wide smile on his face, Annamae knew that this time nothing had disturbed his prayers on the butte overlooking the lovely valley below.

Yes, she was very proud of Gray Stone. She could not be any more proud were he her own son.

The thought of her son, who awaited her return after this festival, made Annamae feel warm and wonderful. Golden Wing was five now, and already showed all the qualities that proved he would be a great warrior in his father's image one day. But he would not be chief. Gray Stone had already been promised that he would take over the duties of chief when Cougar reached the age when he chose to step down and spend more time with his family.

Annamae slid a hand to her belly. She stroked it through her doeskin dress, so happy that finally she was with child again. She had begun to think that she would never again know the thrill of holding a newborn, born of the love she and Cougar shared.

But now it was so!

And she did hope for a daughter this time.

She had dreamed of her name already: Pretty Willow. She had told her husband of that dreamed name, and he had approved the moment it had slid across her lips.

But now she just wanted to enjoy these special days with her husband, her Blackfoot people, and Gray Stone.

Yes, their time with the Fox Clan of Blackfoot would be one of rejoicing. They had much to celebrate. Their villages had not been disturbed by whites. And soon, a new child would be born into the Turtle Clan.

Hers and Cougar's.

As for Golden Wing, he was staying with Blue Blossom during his parents' and big brother's absence. She was a second mother to both of Chief Cougar and Annamae's sons.

Annamae gazed over at an island as they

slid through the water past it. It reminded her of another island that was not far from their village. It was called Dream Island. Cougar had taken her there one day, also at midsummer, the time when the ducks and geese dropped their feathers.

While on Dream Island, she and Cougar had gathered the feathers the birds had dropped, to be used for Cougar's new arrows.

She was drawn from her thoughts when the canoes began moving toward shore, where she saw horses waiting with warriors holding their reins. She knew that from there on they would ride again until they reached the village.

Once they were on shore, Cougar came to Annamae and drew her into his gentle embrace. "How are you?" he asked, gazing into her eyes. "Should you have come? You look tired."

"I am, but not too tired to enjoy this special outing with you and Gray Stone," she murmured. "It will be so nice to dance and sing with the Fox Clan."

"Among them are many of the friends with whom I once hunted," Cougar said. He smiled. "But, wife, that was before our time. Since I brought you into my heart and home, I do not venture as far to get food and lodge coverings for my family. I would rather spend the extra days that would be taken up traveling to and from the Fox Clan's village with you, our son, and Gray Stone. He must observe everything I do as chief, since he will one day be chief himself."

Gray Stone came up to them, tall and slim, yet very muscular. Like Cougar, he wore only a breechclout and moccasins, his sleek black hair hanging in one long braid down his perfectly straight back. On his waist was a sheathed knife, and in one hand he carried a rifle. "Are we almost there?" he asked, smiling at Cougar and then at Annamae.

"I see more anxiousness in you today than yesterday," Cougar said, his eyes looking teasingly into Gray Stone's. "I believe you are more eager to look at the pretty girls than to eat or compete with the other warriors."

A blush rose to Gray Stone's cheeks. "I have heard there are many pretty girls there, so, yes, I am eager to see them," he said, looking over at Annamae, who was smiling mischievously back at him. "But none could be prettier than you, Mother."

Every time he called her "Mother," Annamae felt proud. Of course, he would never forget his true mother, but she was happy that he regarded her as a second mother.

She stepped away and drew him into her arms. "You make me so proud," she murmured. "You look at as many pretty girls as you want. One day soon you will be wanting to find that special one."

"I am now a warrior, so, yes, one day I will be doing more than watching; I will be taking and loving," Gray Stone said.

He stepped quickly away from her at the sound of a loud shout.

Cougar broke away from Annamae and Gray Stone and ran to a bluff that overlooked a vast stretch of land down below.

What he saw disturbed him deeply.

He slowly looked over his shoulder at Annamae. He knew that she would be more alarmed than he. A carnival was camped on the plain below, the tents planted everywhere, their colorful flags blowing in the wind.

Annamae saw a look on Cougar's face that alarmed her. She wondered what he had seen that could cause such anger in him.

A fort.

Yes, perhaps a fort had been established close by the village of the Fox Clan of Blackfoot.

If so, was their future as a clan numbered? Thus far, the white man had built no forts near their homes.

She hurried to Cougar's side.

When she gazed down and saw what he had just seen, her insides grew cold with alarm.

"Do you think they — Howard and Ellie — are among those who came with the carnival?" Annamae asked, her voice catching. "Since Ellie fled in the middle of the night with two of your most prized steeds, we have not seen her or Howard. Do you think she found him that night and they then both rode to safety? Do you think they returned to the carnival?"

Two Moons brought Cougar a pair of binoculars that he carried with him. He handed them to his chief.

Cougar raised them to his eyes and scanned the land down below him until he came to the carnival.

He gazed intently at the people milling about outside those tents. He recognized many of those he had seen that day he had first set eyes on Annamae.

He saw the man with the tattoos on his body, and the man with the forked tongue who was called the snake man.

And then he felt an anger deep inside his soul as he found himself looking directly on the face of none other than Howard Becker.

A moment later, Ellie came into view. She went up to Howard and embraced him. Apparently she had forgiven him for leaving her that day.

Everything she had said about wanting to stay with the Blackfoot had been a lie, told in order to gain Cougar's trust so that he would not order a guard to watch her that night.

He had thought she was there to stay.

"Is it them?" Annamae asked tightly. "Do you see Howard? Do you see Ellie?"

Cougar gave the binoculars to Annamae and let her see for herself.

When she saw Ellie and Howard embracing, hurt filled her heart. She was recalling how Ellie had lied as she told Annamae just how much she loved her. She had said she wanted to stay with Annamae and the Blackfoot people. She had even said that she despised Howard.

All along she was planning her escape after Annamae and Cougar trustingly left her alone in a warm tepee, beside a fire.

"Do not let the sight of them alarm you too much," Cougar finally said. "As you know, we are far now from our home. They are doing as they were told, staying away from us."

"But they are close to other Blackfoot

homes," Annamae said worriedly.

"They might not know they are," Cougar pointed out. "The large river separates them from the land of the Blackfoot."

She looked farther and saw a neat little town not far from where the carnival was established.

"Yes, perhaps you are right," she murmured. "Surely we have nothing to fear. It would be hard for them to cross the river. It is too wide, and in some places dangerous."

"Then let us move onward and not think any more about them," Cougar encouraged. "A good time awaits us. Let us go and enjoy it."

"Yes, let's," Annamae said, her chin lifted stubbornly as she gave Two Moons the binoculars.

And she did find that it was easy to forget her momentary fears of what she had seen. It had been five long years since she had last been with Ellie, and she had not heard from her since.

Yes, she believed she was free of them finally, forever. If they had any intention of trying to see her again, they would have already done it.

She put them from her mind and mounted the horse assigned her, enjoying the beautiful landscape around her.

She adored the prairie dropseed plants. They were two feet high, with cascading emerald green foliage that turned a pumpkin orange by autumn.

She watched butterflies flit around, and then gazed heavenward when she saw the great shadow of an eagle fall across the ground before her.

Cougar sidled his horse closer to hers. "It is a good life, is it not?" he said, pride in his voice.

"The best," Annamae murmured. "My darling husband, I could never be happier. Thank you for finding me and Gray Stone that day when he was so ill from the bee stings. Thank you for taking me in to live one with you and your people."

She laughed softly. "But, of course, it took a few days for you to trust me enough to relax around me," she said. "Are you glad you did decide to trust me?"

His eyes gleamed with happiness. "Trust is earned," he said. "You did so."

Annamae laughed softly and rode onward, marveling, at the happiness she had found with this powerful Blackfoot chief. Those days of being a dream interpreter were in her past — forever.

And her dreams now were only of wondrous things . . . of her husband, her family, her beloved Blackfoot people.

No, her life could not be any better than this. She would never think of Howard and Ellie Becker again, for she knew now that they cared nothing for her.

"I see the village up ahead," Cougar said. "I hear laughter and music. It is going to be a good feast, my wife. I can hardly wait to show you off to friends whom I have not seen for far too long now."

"I look forward to everything, my husband, as long as I am with you," she said, kicking her horse with the heels of her moccasins and riding off at a gallop alongside her husband, her long, black hair flying in the wind behind her, her cheeks flushed with the warmth of happiness.

Dear Reader,
I hope you enjoyed reading *Savage Quest*. The next book in my *Savage* series, which I am writing exclusively for Leisure Books, is *Savage Intrigue,* about the proud Dakota Indians. The book is filled with much romance, authentic history of the Dakota, and a few surprises.

Those of you who are collecting my Indian romance novels and want to hear more about the series and my entire backlist of Indian books can send for my latest newsletter, autographed bookmark, and fan club information, by writing to:

Cassie Edwards
6709 North Country Club Road
Mattoon, IL 61938

For an assured response, please include a stamped, self-addressed, legal-sized envelope with your letter. And you can visit my Web site at www.cassieedwards.com.

Thank you for your support of my Indian series. I love researching and writing about our nation's beloved Native Americans, our country's true first people.

Always,
Cassie Edwards

ABOUT THE AUTHOR

Having always loved history, **Cassie Edwards** immediately became hooked on reading the historical romances friends lent her, which one day led her to write her own. Cassie can now say she has written one hundred books, most of which are Indian romances. They have appeared on bestseller lists all across the country, including the *New York Times* list. She has also won the *Romantic Times* Lifetime Achievement Award.

Cassie lives in Mattoon, Illinois, in a lovely plantation home, with her husband, Charlie. They have two grown sons, Charles and Brian, and three adorable grandchildren.

We hope you have enjoyed this Large Print book. Other Thorndike, Wheeler, and Chivers Press Large Print books are available at your library or directly from the publishers.

For information about current and upcoming titles, please call or write, without obligation, to:

Publisher
Thorndike Press
295 Kennedy Memorial Drive
Waterville, ME 04901
Tel. (800) 223-1244

or visit our Web site at:

www.gale.com/thorndike
www.gale.com/wheeler

OR

Chivers Large Print
published by BBC Audiobooks Ltd
St James House, The Square
Lower Bristol Road
Bath BA2 3SB
England
Tel. +44(0) 800 136919
email: bbcaudiobooks@bbc.co.uk
www.bbcaudiobooks.co.uk

All our Large Print titles are designed for easy reading, and all our books are made to last.